PIECES of CAMDEN

YESSI SMITH

ISBN-13: 978-0-9971199-2-3

This book is dedicated to Jill Sava and Madelyn Valle.
I couldn't do this without either of you.

To Lee Casey, who was the first to love Camden and always pushes me to be better.

And Mary, who never fails to show her endless love and support.
Our friendship means the world to me.

I'm not afraid
to carry some of my past
on this skin.
the dirt is as real
as the beauty,
and I have trouble
separating
which nights
had one,
the other,
or both
now
anyways.

—J.R. ROGUE

PROLOGUE

No one hears a child's cry. The sounds of screaming and breaking glass in a sorrow-filled house go unnoticed by neighbors too preoccupied with their own lives. The silent fear is all-consuming until even leaving your room brings on a terror that makes the boogeyman look friendly.

They hear the laughter though, the lies that fall so easily from my lips. Feigned feelings are far more welcome than the emptiness that embodies me.

You don't know my name, but you've heard my story countless times before. That of an abused child. An unloved little boy. Ignored by society.

I am more than my story though. More than the doubt, the guilt, the hurt.

Because of her. She saved me, so I did the only thing I could do when my dad called Yanelys a whore. I fought back, wanting to right all the wrongs of today. Wanting to wash away her sorrow and cleanse myself of her shame filled eyes.

Screams bar the walls of my bedroom. They're mine, my mom's and every other child who has fallen victim to their parent's hot anger.

My dad pounds his fists into my face, my stomach, my back. Blood spills, pain spreads. I crouch into a cocoon, the hatred of my dad pouring over my beaten body like hot lava.

"So, you're a man now, huh!" my dad shouts. "Twelve years old and you have a girl between your legs!"

"It's not like that," I whimper, because it wasn't.

Everyone thought it was, and I let them, not wanting any of our classmates or teachers to see where my dad had stabbed me this morning. Yanelys had simply been trying to clean up his mess when our PE coach walked in on us in the bathroom. Yanelys went along with the assumptions because that's what she does. She looks out for me. She protects me and I let her because I'm a coward. A stupid, selfish, coward.

But today, I stood up to my dad and while I don't regret it, I wish I'd had one last chance to tell Yanelys how much I love her.

"Where's your little whore of a friend?" my dad barks.

From the floor, I push at him, wanting him to take back the ugly words he said about my best friend. Vicious laughter falls from his lips and he kicks me repeatedly. My gut, my head, my legs. Everywhere, all at once.

I breathe in the slow burn of my dad's increasing anger and bursts of violence. Dizzy, my mind grows foggy and I follow the delirium until I no longer feel my dad's fists raining over my body. My eyes roll to the back of my head and I picture Yanelys's smiling face. I reach for her hand, knowing she'll always hold on.

ONE

CAMDEN

Worn shoes and tattered clothes are a direct contradiction to how I carry myself. Even when the smell rolling off my body turns my empty stomach, I keep my shoulders square and my head held high. Not that it matters. No one looks directly at me anyway.

I see myself though—the vision of broken glass bleeding on humanity — but I won't succumb to the hunched figure of a tired man. Society doesn't see the fragility of my grief or my desperation for help.

No, what they see is the reality I've painted for them. A cold thin figure with sunburned skin and the pitiless smile I grant them if they look in my direction. Wincing, they turn away to look at anything but me.

I'm worse than invisible. At least the invisible can't be seen.

Me? I'm an outcast. Deplorable by definition. Unworthy. Unapproachable.

Twenty-four years old and completely alone.

My only human contact comes from rushed figures pushing past me as I walk on the sidewalk to make my way home from work.

Home. The word itself is laughable. As if I have a home.

I have a place where I stay. A couch I sleep on. But no actual home to speak of.

There are days though, days like today, when I don't want the company of my old pastor. When I don't want a couch or a bed or even a corner to sleep in.

I just want myself. My eternal silence where all there is to hear is the crushing of every broken dream I've had since youth.

The North Carolina rain complements my damp mood, so it's only fitting for me to be outdoors for a while. Unemployed from a job I never really needed. A martyr made to survive off scraps because of a dignity I can't be stripped of. It's all I have because *they* took away everything else. I don't know what I did to piss Karma off, but she's an unforgiving bitch. Relentless in delivering her punishments to me.

In my worn shoes and tattered clothes, I lie down on the concrete ground outside of an abandoned building and let the sky's tears fall on my face. The cold rain makes my teeth chatter as lightning flashes above me.

A lifetime ago, I felt the gentle caress of a palm on my cheek. And, damn it to hell, I want it back. I want *her* back. The familiarity of her touch. The lull of her voice. Her eyes that could see past every mask I wore, as well as the answers to questions she never asked. All of the broken promises I uttered in desperation, fully aware I could never keep them.

Her warmth soothed me, made me whole.

Yanelys.

I met Yanelys when we were eight years old. She was my beginning, the reason I started living, and I always thought she'd be there until the end.

From the moment I met her, her brown eyes became my constant. When my parents fought, I'd quietly creep out of my bedroom window and into her bedroom, knowing she'd keep her window unlocked in case I needed her. When the police arrested my parents and took me away, her parents gave me a home after my social worker had deemed them fit as my guardians. And when we were teenagers living under the same roof, I'd sneak into her room and crawl into her bed, needing her strength to hold me together.

The only time we were away from each other was when I'd lived in a group home. This happened before we lived together, before I knew what it meant to have a family, when my heart still teetered on the edges of dejection. My life at the group home wasn't optimal, but it was safe, which somehow made everything worse.

I was twelve years old and away from my best friend, my safety blanket, who knew all my secrets and kept her promise to never expose them—until she felt she no longer had a choice.

I never held that betrayal against her. Even on the longest nights on a hard, lumpy bed, I'd count my blessings with every inhale and exhale. I was alive because of her. My dad would have beaten me to death if she hadn't told someone.

The day she'd told her parents, her dad had shown up at my house and held my parents at gunpoint while Yanelys and her mom broke into my bedroom through the window. They stayed with me until the police and ambulance arrived. That night, I thought God had finally seen me. I was safe.

But then the police took me away. Sure, no one hurt me while I was at the group home, and Yanelys and her parents would come visit me, but it wasn't the same. Split-second decisions to seek out Yanelys's comfort when I couldn't cope were a thing of the past.

And there was so much I couldn't cope with back then.

There's still so much I can't cope with.

Starting with Yanelys's tears.

She was the one who pieced me together when I was nothing more than a jigsaw puzzle with missing pieces.

And I was the one who tore us apart, ripping my heart straight out of my chest in the process.

It's okay though. Without her, I have no use for a heart anyway.

Forced or not, it was my decision, my doing.

My consequences.

There was never any coming back from that decision. I knew it the minute I walked away from her. I felt the ache in my bones with the emptiness she left behind.

With my back arched, I can reach into the back pocket of my jeans and take out my wallet, knowing exactly where I'll find Yanelys's old high school picture.

It's worn, far worse than my clothes, with the edges wrinkled and torn. My callous fingers touch her face, tracing her full lips with my finger. Her light-brown eyes look back at me, reminding me of the carefree young woman I fell in love with. Her smile isn't just permanently fixed in the picture but inside of my soul as well.

The memory of her smile dulls the ache in my chest, a poor substitute for the relief her presence used to bring me. The passion we shared made me feel like I could conquer everything, including myself. It was the same passion, the same irrepressible demons within me, that made me leave. Every time she smiled at me, touched me, breathed the same air as me, my heart would threaten to break through its cage to not just love her but to let her know of that love.

But I wasn't a fairy tale. And, news flash, the beast never turns into a prince.

My scars run deeper than mere flesh wounds. They're a part of my soul, having seared themselves into the fiber of who and what I am.

When the rain stops, I put away Yanelys's picture, touching the outline of her dirty-blonde hair, and I stand up from the hard floor to make my way inside the vacant building. Shoulders hunched to keep me warm, I am now the vision of the tired, lonely man I've become. After I find a room and huddle in the corner, I close my eyes and allow the loud thunder to lull me to sleep.

I don't think of Yanelys or the job that I lost. I don't think about where my tomorrows will lead me. I only think of the rain hitting the rooftop like a million heartbeats.

Searing heat. The crackle of wood splintering and collapsing. The heaviness of the air choking my lungs. I wake up to a nightmare.

An all-encompassing fire flares and leaps in all directions. Orange embers twirl in a fiery dance while clouds of dark smoke wind itself around the room I'm staying in, making it difficult for me to see, let alone breathe.

I hack out a cough, waving my hand in front of my face in a futile attempt to identify what's ahead of me.

Smoke. Fire. Hell. That's all there is.

From a distance, sirens grow louder as the firefighters race toward me and the burning building, but the idea of them entering the building is ludicrous. An abandoned building where only squatters stay. No one worth risking a life for. No one worth saving.

With my shirt clamped over my mouth and nose, I run, not knowing if I'm running toward safety or more danger. But running's better than sitting and waiting for death.

A wall of heat meets my desperate escape, threatening to burn my lungs before the fire even touches my skin.

Falling to my knees, saliva drips from my mouth onto the floor. My body weeps at the blazing storm nearing me, the weight of the smoke settling in the silent corners of defeat. My frantic heart roars, refusing to give up, as darkness clings to me, threatening me with the truth.

The fire's too big, too wild. And I know…the fire will devour me, and all they'll find of me will be ashes.

Finally, I'll be set free.

TWO

YANELYS

NINE YEARS OLD

Yanelys Sanchez + Camden Riley = 4-ever

I scribble that all over the outside of my journal until every inch is covered in our names. When Camden walks into my room, I show him my work, and he nods, a stray strand of his dark hair falling over his forehead and into one of his bright blue eyes.

Camden isn't just my best friend. He's also the boy I'm going to marry. My parents think I'm silly for thinking these thoughts, but my heart knows. And Camden...well, he doesn't like the idea of getting married—to anyone, not just me. He thinks people come to hate each other when they get married, but I know that's not how it works. I *promise* him, that's not how it works.

His parents hate each other because they're hateful people. They probably hate the sun for shining too brightly or the night sky for being too dark.

Hateful, mean, horrible people.

Not at all like Camden, who lets happiness in, even when he's in his darkest place.

I hate his parents. More, I hate that I can't protect him and that he won't let me. I know his secrets. Sharing them and his pain is one of the things that brought us close to each other. It also made us grow up faster than the other nine-year-olds we know.

No matter how old we are right now, I know my feelings are real and that we'll always be together.

"Do you ever think about running away?" I ask him. My attention goes to the inside of my journal that details my everyday life, mostly with Camden.

"I used to."

I don't look up, but I feel him shrug his shoulders.

"Why'd you stop?"

"I met you." His voice is calm, confident, but he shuffles his feet, his uncertainty bouncing between us.

"I'd run away with you." I look up from my journal into his unsmiling face and wring my hands together on my lap, anticipating his reply.

"Your parents would find you." Camden's matter-of-fact tone makes my heart hurt.

"We could go somewhere they'd never find me."

"Your parents love you." He flinches on the word *love*, as if it were a bad word that left a sour taste in his mouth. "They'll always find you."

"That's true." It's my turn to shrug my shoulders.

I want him to believe me, to know I'd do anything for him, but the words stick in my throat. Instead, I lean my body over my desk to scribble on my journal, but my eyes stay trained on Camden.

"I love you, Cam, which means I'll always find you, too."

Camden exhales a loud breath, his nose whistling in the process. "One day, I'll leave, Yan," he says, his eyes looking away from me and toward a future I can't see. A future he doesn't want me to see. "When I do, no one will find me."

"I will." Turning, I cup his chin with my hand, making him look at me, but after a short second, his eyes dart to the corner of my room.

"I'll make it so that even I can't find me." Defiantly, he folds his arms over his chest and continues to look away from me.

"*I'll* always find you."

He opens his mouth to answer, probably another smart retort, but stops when his cell phone chirps. The angry ring drains him of the will to speak. I know that look, and I know what it means.

"Will you come over tonight?" I ask him, knowing I'll leave the window to my bedroom open regardless of his answer.

"Yeah," he breathes.

He's still not looking at me, but I see the dread building behind his eyes, and just once, I wish I could save him.

"You really think we could do it?" he asks.

Immediately knowing what he's talking about, my heart fills with fear. Not for myself or for Camden. But for my parents and the idea of them waking up one morning to find me missing. I'd do it for Camden though. To keep him safe. To keep him with me.

"Sure." I smile.

"Then, you're stupider than me." He walks out of my room without even looking at me or acknowledging the tears suddenly falling down my face.

I'm not stupid, I think, balling my hands into tight fists. *I'm just a girl desperately in love with a boy who's hurting more than I can bear.*

After dinner, I take a quick shower and brush my teeth. I do it all without argument because I'm ready to go to bed. I'm ready to wait for Camden to sneak into my bedroom and lie with me in bed.

What I'm not ready for is the bruise beneath his left eye. No matter how angry his parents get, they never mark him somewhere others can see. Never. It's like some unspoken law between them.

Brushing the covers to the side, I swing my legs over the bed. With two long steps, I'm by my window, lightly touching Camden's face, while he looks at anything but me. My thumb runs over the blue bruise that can no longer hide the hurt. The filthy stain of his parents' hatred runs across his face.

Camden stands there, motionless, aside from the rise and fall of his chest.

I've never kissed him before, but he looks so lost, so sad, so alone. With my heart thundering in my ears, I place my lips on his cheek, and I'm surprised when he puts his arms around me. I hug him back, wanting to take away the hurt and the fear, but he winces when I hold on to him too tightly.

"I'm okay," he reassures me.

But I know better. He'll never be okay as long as he lives with his mom and dad.

"What did he do?" I ask, referring to his dad.

His mom's just as awful as his dad, but it's usually his dad who delivers the beatings while his mom watches with a glass of wine in her hand.

"Can we just lie down?" Camden looks at my bed with longing, his eyes unblinking, as he shrinks away from his reality.

I already know I could never say no to him. No matter what he wants, my answer will always be yes.

Take his hand in mine, I lead us to my bed where I climb in first and then scoot to the other side so that Camden has room to lie down. With slow movements, Camden gets into bed with me and lowers himself, hissing in pain as he lies flat on his back. My hand reaches for his again, and our fingers lock onto one another. My chest aches as I listen to Camden's silent pleas, calling me, pulling me to him.

"Tonight, can we play pretend?" he asks me.

I nod even though I want to ask him about what hurt when I hugged him and again when he lay down.

"What are we pretending?"

"Tonight, I want to be a white knight in shining armor."

Sadness hits me. My amazing Camden—who's already my white knight, braver than any other knight out there because he fights dragons every day—has no idea who he is.

Playing along with him, I ask, "What's your horse's name?"

His body shifts slightly, and pain temporarily crosses his face as he tries to readjust himself into a more comfortable position.

"All knights have horses," I explain. "So, what's your horse's name?"

He thinks about it for a long time, and when he comes up with a name, a beautiful big smile spreads across his face, his eyes lighting with joy.

"Stark," he replies.

I roll my eyes. "You can't name your horse after Tony Stark."

"I just did."

"Whatever." My eyes roll back again, but I lean my body closer to his so that my breath lands on his bruised cheek. "Do you and Stark save princesses?"

"No." He shakes his head once, disgust crossing his face before he faces me. "Saving people is stupid."

"What kind of knight doesn't save people?" My brows furrow in question.

Camden sighs and turns his attention to my ceiling. "Yan, in the real world, the knight doesn't become a knight to save anyone but himself. No one cares about him or sees him until he becomes a knight."

Emotion crosses over his face, pain darkening his eyes. My face drains as I take in and absorb his words.

"That's not true, Cam." I give his fingers, still interlaced with mine, a quick squeeze to make sure I have his attention. "I see him. I care."

Camden squeezes my fingers in return and then turns his whole body so that he's lying on his side. His chest heaves from the pain and exertion, but the only way Camden can fall asleep is on his side. Our faces are close enough to each other that our noses touch, and our breaths unite us.

When Camden closes his eyes, I reach over to him, and my fingers comb through his medium-length hair.

"I care, Cam," I repeat to him. "Don't you ever forget it."

He opens his eyes and stares at me for a long time before he shuts them again. On a whisper, he says, "I care, too, Yan."

10

THREE

CAMDEN

Walls and smoke surround me. The smoke has hands that lash out and grip me, throw me, hit me. Rather than choke me, they beat me, blaming me for living. The smoke then turns into *them*, and his hatred consumes me while her screams make me cower.

I am nothing.

Nothing but a worthless burden.

A scream echoes in the distance, and I hear a boy crying into the night, begging for help. His pain, his loneliness, and fear are mine so I follow it through the thickening cloud of smoke until I'm kneeling in front of a little boy. Dark curls cover his bruised cheek while tear-filled, bloodshot eyes look up at me.

"You're not alone," I tell him. "You still have her."

You're not alone *yet*. You still have her. But, one day, you won't. Only then will you truly know what loneliness feels like.

Although I keep those words to myself, the boy hears them anyway. It's too much for him to carry, and he cups his hands over his ears and screams while the smoke strikes at both of us, whipping us, leaving marks on our backs and chests.

I pick him up and run, but I can't save us. Men and boys like us can't be saved.

"I'm not here to save you."

A light reaches toward us, and when it morphs into delicate long fingers and touches my cheek, I lean into it, needing her. Shivers ripple down my spine as my heart focuses on her.

"I just want to make it hurt less."

The boy climbs out of my arms and into hers, and she carries him away, leaving me alone, the same way I once left her. My heart rips from my chest and crashes onto the floor into a million pieces of agony.

With too much clarity, the veil lifts from my dream, and I repel against it, desperate to go back to Yanelys, wanting her to lessen the hurt the way she always did.

But my subconscious fights back until I'm lying on my back on a soft surface, staring at a white ceiling.

I blink several times and take a quick survey of my surroundings as I try to orient myself, but I can't make out where I am—until I move my hands to sit up and find them bandaged with an IV sticking out of one arm.

Disbelief washes over me.

It wasn't a dream. At least not all of it.

I cough to test my lungs and immediately wince in pain.

"Finally awake," a man says. He stands from his chair on the other side of the room. When he crosses to my side, his wide frame looms over my bed, his familiar eyes brimming with the same love he unconditionally gave me as a child.

My eyes narrow in speculation, and when his pensive eyes meet mine, I drop my gaze as shame washes over me.

After a strangled moment, I say his name, "Santiago." My voice is slightly above a strained whisper, so I cough again to clear my throat.

"Stop coughing," he instructs. "You're only making it worse."

"I was in a fire?" I ask.

He nods.

"And now?" Tension eases into my shoulders, my heart slamming a thunderous beat in my chest.

Santiago smirks and lays a gentle hand on my left shoulder. His hand stays there, barely touching the fabric of my hospital gown that hides even more bandages.

"You're in the hospital, Cam." His grim eyes meet mine. "You're not dead—at least, not yet. When Yan sees you, she might fix that for you."

His words fill me with panic, but the bastard just winks at me.

"Yan can't see me. Santiago, please," I plead with him, rubbing my bandaged hands over my face. Even with the dressing on my hands, I can feel more bandages on my face.

The fire, the flames that licked and taunted me, was bad. I should feel pain.

12

The blissful numbness will eventually subside, and I know I'll feel more than the emotional pain that grips my chest whenever I think of Yanelys. Agitated, I hit the button to my morphine drip, desperate to evade the unwanted agony.

It won't be enough. It never is.

"That girl has worried about you every day since the day you disappeared. We all have," he emphasizes and I shy away from him and his disappointed face. "If she knew I had seen you and didn't say anything…" He shakes his head. "I couldn't do that to her. Yan is my number one concern, Camden. There was a time when you topped that list too, but…"

"But now?" I ask, needing him to finish although fear of his oncoming words makes me quake.

"You left us," he says simply. "You're back now, not because you want to be but because fate brought you back to us. I still love you." His jaw ticks as his brown eyes bore into me. "That'll never change. Neither will the part where you turned away and never once called or reached out to us."

"Santiago," I start but don't bother finishing. There are a thousand excuses I can give him, a million reasons, but right now they all seem insufficient. I clear my throat before I say, "Yan's coming then?" My eyes dance around the room and I try to come up with a plan to escape.

"Not yet. I left her a voice mail to call me, but she hasn't called me back. I told Carmen, though. I imagine they're both on their way." His strong fingers grip around my wrist and squeeze hard enough to get my attention. "Stop trying to get away, Cam. You're not going anywhere."

Hoping it'll lighten the intensity in the room, I mutter, "Ballbuster," under my breath.

Loud and unrestrained, his laughter radiates off the walls and crashes into me, the sadness in my soul growing with the sound.

"That would imply you had balls to bust, boy." He laughs harder until his laughter turns into the small wheezes I've missed since I left. "Pretty sure you lost those when you walked out on your family and the girl who's loved you since you two were just kids. She hasn't stopped, ya know."

In spite of myself, I find myself grinning at Santiago's admission. He's the closest thing I've ever had to a father figure. There was a time when I didn't just wish he were my dad, but I also secretly referred to him as that.

I take him in, fully assessing him for seven years' worth of changes. The wrinkles on his face have deepened, and the gray hairs have become more pronounced, but he's still Santiago. Physically fit, mentally aware, and with a smile spread across his face, as if he was always only seconds away from cracking his favorite joke.

It's not until I see black residue beneath his normally clean fingernails that I finally ask him what he's doing here.

"I was one of the guys called to the building you were in when it caught fire."

"And you went in?" I want to yell at him, but my voice is still too hoarse to carry any strength. "By the time I woke up, it was an inferno. You can't go into fires like that, Santiago. You have a family. Think about Yan and Carmen. What would they do if something happened to you?" My chest heaves while the words bleed out of my mouth in a frenzy of guilt and fear.

My heart slams against my ribs, and I press the button to release more morphine into my system, but nothing happens. Desperate, I press it again. When nothing drips down, Santiago takes the button away from me and gives me two Tylenols from the front pocket of his jeans.

They won't help.

But I take them anyway.

"It's my job, Cam," he says, repeating the same words he once told me when I was a teenager, warning him not to go into burning houses.

I didn't understand it back then, but after what I've experienced these past few years, I get it.

Santiago was born to make a difference. It doesn't matter that he comes from a wealthy family or that he doesn't have to work. It's in his blood, the core of who he is—a good man with strong morals and a desire to help.

"I get that; I do." With careful motion, my body leans forward and tries to sit up, but when I see the bed's remote, I use it to prop me up. "But there was a lot of smoke. It would've been too dangerous. You swore, you never went into buildings that were too dangerous."

Santiago rubs his hands over his face—a gesture I picked up from him and use often—and sits on my bed, resting his hand on my left foot.

"I don't." He squeezes my foot and looks at me before he shakes his head. "The fire was huge. It was out of our control. None of us were gonna go in until it'd died down, but, hell, Cam, I heard my baby girl scream." His lips turn into a scowl, and he rubs his hands over his face once again. "I heard Yan screaming, and I didn't have a choice."

My eyes widen at his declaration, and fear burns into my lungs until I can't breathe.

"Yan?" I whisper.

"She's fine," he reassures me, squeezing my foot again. "She left me a voice mail, telling me good night, while I was in the building, looking for her."

"It wasn't her then." I breathe out a sigh of relief.

"It was her all right." Creases spread at the corners of Santiago's mouth, and he laughs.

Confused, I wait for him to continue.

"Yan wasn't in the building with you, but you tell me, has she ever really left you?"

"No," I whisper.

He shrugs, a simple lift and drop of his shoulders. "Somehow, she knew you were in there. Her spirit called to me because she wanted to make sure you got out safe."

FOUR

YANELYS

ELEVEN YEARS OLD

"My mom would kill me if she knew we were eating this," Camden whispers into my ear. He motions toward the pizza and soda my parents bought us.

"Then, we'll make sure she doesn't find out," I whisper back.

A beautiful smile stretches across his face, his eyes dancing with anticipation.

My mom groans and leans back into her chair, rubbing her full stomach. "I think maybe we should have eaten after racing."

My stomach lurches in response, but I don't say anything. There's no way I'd let a full or upset stomach stop me from going on the karts. It's all Camden's been talking about since my parents mentioned taking us kart racing for his birthday.

I wish that were all we were doing for his birthday. After I told my mom I wanted to make his birthday special because his parents usually forgot about it, she called his mom, Maureen, and planned a surprise party for him. With my help, she called his friends from school, bought burgers and hot dogs for his parents to barbeque, and ordered his cake. We picked up his cake this morning, and while I distracted Camden, my mom brought it into his house where Maureen hid it somewhere in the kitchen.

For Camden, I hope his parents won't mess up his birthday. Just this once. My mom did so much to prepare for it, and I want him to have one birthday with nothing but good memories.

We're off to a good start.

While we wait for my parents to throw away our trash, Camden picks out the kart he wants to drive—a black one that he says reminds him of the Death Star. I pick a blue one because it reminds me of Camden's eyes.

"You're obsessed with that color," he jokes, pushing me to the side with his shoulder.

"It's a good color." I beam at his smiling face, not wanting the happiness of the day to ever leave him.

"All right, kids"—my dad rests one hand on my shoulder and the other on Camden's—"who's ready?"

My stomach tightens in both fear and excitement. I mean, I've never driven before, and now, I'm going to race. And the karts go really fast.

But my fear immediately vanishes, as if it never existed, when Camden shouts, "I am!"

"Cam wants the black kart, Dad."

"Then, we'll make sure he gets the black kart." My dad winks at me and then ushers us forward with minimal pressure on our shoulders.

"Don't be nervous." Camden separates the hands I've subconsciously been wringing together and squeezes my fingers with his while we wait for our turn.

"I'm not nervous," The lie falls easily from my lips and Camden narrows his eyes at me.

"Liar," he says. "I'll make sure you're buckled in good, Yan. You'll be okay."

"It's okay to be nervous," my dad tells us. "Just never let it stop you from trying new things."

"I'm not nervous," I counter again.

My dad laughs. "Why would you be? You have Cam to take care of you."

Camden's eyes, blue and brilliant, level on me, and he puffs his chest out just a bit. I lean into him and rest my head on his shoulder, happy we're the same height so that the motion isn't awkward.

Ever since the night I kissed Camden's cheek in my bedroom, we've been more affectionate with each other. When we were younger, it was always in secret. But then it was obvious his parents never showed him what it meant to be loved, so I started holding his hand in front of my parents one day. My mom suspiciously looked at me, and I knew she didn't like it, but I held on to him tighter while his eyes nervously skated over the floor. My dad's laughter broke the silence, and when he winked at us, I knew he'd talk to my mom. Like me, he saw Camden's sadness, and he knew Camden needed someone to hold on to him, to ground him.

"We take care of each other," I whisper.

He hugs me closer to his side.

As we wait our turn, Camden and I watch the karts drive by. My dad pretends to watch them as well, but he keeps glancing at us with a small smile on his face. My mom calls him an old romantic, and I know he's picturing us walking down an aisle one day. I'm pretty sure he knows I dream about the same thing.

When we reach the front of the line, we give the attendant our tickets, and he points at a red kart for Camden to drive, but with a soft hand on his shoulder, my dad stops Camden from moving to it.

"It's my boy's birthday today," my dad announces to the attendant.

Camden visibly stiffens at my dad's words, but when I look at his face, all I see is surprise and wonder.

"He wants to drive the black kart." My dad winks at Camden, who looks up at my dad in awe.

My heart swells with love and pride for my dad. No one remembers Camden or what he wants. That's my job. It makes me happy to know that my parents love him as much as I do. Now, he knows it, too.

"Can Yan have the blue kart?" Camden asks the attendant, shuffling his feet.

"Sure, bud," the attendant agrees.

"I'll buckle you in," Camden informs me. "Then, I'll get in mine."

My dad leaves us to get in his own kart. His watchful eyes track us as we make our way to my kart. Camden helps me in, and when I'm sitting down, he fastens my belt and tugs on it twice to make sure it'll stay safely in place.

"Be careful, Yan." His voice is serious while his eyes mirror the fear I had earlier.

"I'm fine, Cam."

"You're important." He looks away from me after he utters those words, but our eyes meet before he speaks again, "Just be careful."

Surprised, my mouth opens, but no words come out. Before I have time to fully process what he said, my dad's excited voice booms in the arena, and my focus returns to my kart. I gently push the gas pedal and lurch forward with a giggle escaping my throat.

"Hit the pedal softer!" Camden shouts at me, his voice encouraging me to try again.

I do. After a couple of more false starts, I finally feel comfortable in my kart and push my foot down a bit harder, driving by Camden where I hear his laughter dancing in the air.

Halfway through my second lap, Camden flies by me, his obvious joy stays with me long after he rounds the corner and I no longer see him. I hit the accelerator harder, urging my kart forward, so I can see him and my dad battle out the last two laps.

My mom cheers us on from the sideline, and I imagine her alternating between her phone and a camera to take pictures of us.

On the final lap, my dad's laugh mixes with Camden's, their karts neck and neck. My dad leads, but Camden's gaining, and I shout my encouragement at them. They battle for first position as they round out the last three turns, and a few feet before they cross the finish line, my dad's kart visibly slows down, allowing Camden to take the win.

After parking, Camden jumps out of his kart and throws himself into my dad's arms while my dad praises him for winning. Once I park and get out of my kart, I see Camden's embarrassed shuffle, but my dad ignores it and tussles Camden's curly dark hair, teasing him about cheating.

"Don't be a sour loser, Santiago," my mom chastises, putting an arm around Camden when we reach her. "I saw it, and Cam won."

My dad leans in and presses a soft kiss on my mom's lips.

Then, he puts his arm around Camden's shoulders. "Next time, I'll beat you. You just gotta tell me your secret about driving into the turns."

"I don't have a secret," Camden answers, his smile never wavering.

"Fine, keep your secret to yourself," my dad jokes, making Camden's expression grow somber.

"Honest, Santiago, I don't have a secret."

My dad brings Camden closer to him and barks out a loud laugh. "Guess you're just naturally good at racing then."

The drive to Camden's house is short. Too short.

Knowing what awaits us makes me feel like a terrible friend for not warning Camden in advance. But I promised my mom I wouldn't, and I didn't want to go back on my word. My dad continues to rave about Camden's racing skills, so I look at the window and tune him out.

I only look at Camden when he takes my hand in his and squeezes. His brows crease together, and I smile at him, squeezing his hand back in reassurance. It's our way of letting the other know we're okay, but he continues to look at me to make sure I'm not lying, so I lean my head on his shoulder until the intensity leaves him.

"Yan?" Camden says my name under his breath when we arrive at his house where a little over a dozen cars line his driveway.

My mom looks back at us from the front seat and smiles. "Let's see what all the fuss is about."

Camden doesn't move from his seat. When my parents close their doors, I tell him about his surprise party.

"My parents remembered?" His brows furrow together again.

Before I have time to reply, a heartbreakingly beautiful smile spreads across his face, and I don't have the heart to confess the truth.

Music thunders loudly from speakers when we step out of my parents' car, and Camden walks quickly to his front door, passing my parents in the process. I follow him, clutching his present to my chest. He pauses before opening the door, and although no one bothers to shout, *Surprise*, the smile never leaves his face. He walks through his large house, passing his parents' friends who clap his back as he walks by them, looking for his parents.

I follow closely, just in case he needs me.

When he reaches his dad, he interrupts with a quiet, "Sir?"

Herb, his dad, takes a long drink from his whiskey. "The man of the hour!" he calls out, lifting his glass before taking another drink with his friends, and turns his back to his son.

But, again, Camden's smile never leaves his face.

He walks to his mom, who we find sitting at their outdoor bar, and she puts on a show of hugging him and kissing him when she sees him. Maureen's words are slurred, and her eyes are bloodshot, but either Camden doesn't realize it, or he's grown too accustomed to it to see it.

When he turns around, his body crashes into mine, and we both giggle as we try to gain our balance.

"They remembered, Yan," he repeats.

My heart breaks for my best friend.

"Let's go swimming," he says.

While Camden runs to his bedroom to change, I put my present for him on the living room couch where only three other presents await him. I leave the room, careful not to disrupt any of their expensive furniture, and when I find my mom, I put my arms around her waist. Looking up at her, I thank her for making Camden's birthday special.

"I didn't do anything," she says, playing down her role, as she swats me on the butt. She then hands me a bag with my bathing suit and a towel.

After I finish changing, I go outside to find my mom putting sunblock on Camden, and I wait for my turn.

"Hey, Cam!" one of Camden's friends, Sean, shouts from the pool. He tosses him a football.

"You mind if I play with the guys?" Camden asks me.

And my mom chuckles.

"No," I reply, curiously eyeing my mom.

"You two are too much," she says, smiling at us with an amused lift of her lips.

After my mom finishes torturing me with the cold spray sunblock on my back, I walk into the pool and stay by the shallow end with my friend Marissa.

She and I welcome the cool water surrounding us. After a short underwater acrobatic competition that neither of us wins, we take turns talking to each other underwater.

"Did you ask if I like Hawaiian pizza?" Marissa asks and I pull a face, making us both burst into laughter. "Try again."

Underwater, I slowly shout, "I want to pet a starfish!"

When we come up for air, my attention is drawn to the end of the pool where the guys were playing football. A small circle surrounds the deep part of the pool with kids and adults shouting, and it only takes me a couple of seconds, two short breaths, to realize that Camden is the cause of all the commotion.

My dad jumps into the pool, fully clothed, along with another adult. He grabs Camden by the waist while the other adult does the same to the boy Camden was punching. Rage fuels him forward though, drowning out my dad and whatever he's telling Camden. He fights against my dad to hit his bleeding friend.

Unfazed, my dad swims with Camden tucked in his arm to the steps I'm sitting on, and I tightly brace my arms around myself as they get closer to me. When they are within an arm's length of me, I reach out to touch Camden and get his attention, but my mom joins me on the steps and pulls me close to her.

Camden's eyes, crazed and wild, finally start to clear when he sees me. Shame washes over him, and his body goes limp in my dad's arms as he looks down to my knees.

"He said you were ugly," he whispers. He stares at me, a sickening look washing over his face.

Panic blazes within me, burning me from the inside. I shrug out of my mom's arms and go to him.

"He said you were ugly," he repeats, his eyes meeting mine. "He called you fat."

The other boy—I think his name is Danny—walks up the steps with his dad beside him and glares at us before muttering, "Freak," under his breath and going inside.

At that moment, I'm glad Camden busted Danny's lip open. I'm glad he's bleeding and in pain. Not because he said I was ugly, but because he was ugly to Camden.

My mom hands my dad a towel and another to me. She then wraps the last towel in her hands around Camden's shoulder, guiding him out of the pool in the process.

"What that boy said about Yanelys was mean, Camden, but you can't go hitting your friends because of it," my mom says.

Her lips pull into a thin line while Camden looks at her through fear-filled eyes.

"Ah, Carmen." My dad puts his arm around my mom and kisses her forehead. "How many boys have I gotten into fights with for the same reason?"

My mom's lips twitch in response, and Camden's shoulders release the tension they were holding.

"Still," she says through a smile. "There are better ways to handle things."

"Yeah, Cam." My dad's face grows serious, making Camden look at his feet as guilt takes over the expression on his face again.

I open my mouth to defend him, but my dad interrupts with a quiet chuckle.

"Next time, just call him a shit. That'll teach him not to disrespect girls," he teases, sending my mom a sly smile.

My mom playfully slaps my dad on the chest and then leans into him as she erupts in laughter. "Not helping, Santiago."

As my parents continue to talk to Camden and me, the partygoers start to go back to their groups and talk among themselves.

Maureen walks out of the kitchen through the open glass doors, slurring the words to the "Happy Birthday" song and carrying the cake my mom ordered in her arms.

My heart thunders in my ears. I look from my parents to Camden's mom. Her eyes are red-rimmed, and she's swaying on her feet. I see her fall before she actually trips, a premonition of how this day could get worse. Camden's face contorts, but he inches his body in front of mine when his father roars out in anger, but Herb doesn't see me. I don't think he even sees his wife or the mess on the floor.

All he sees is Camden, his personal punching bag. Although Camden's terrified of his dad, he puts his body in front of mine, shielding me from his living nightmare.

"I knew it!" his dad bellows, grabbing Camden by the shoulders and pulling him away from me. "We wasted a day on you!" His face turns red, and it'd be almost comical if the fury behind it wasn't so frightening. "A waste is what you are," Herb spits into Camden's face.

Camden stares beyond his dad, beyond us.

"Herb," my dad interrupts but puts his hands up when Herb turns on him. "Let's just go inside," he speaks calmly, as if he were pacifying a child rather than an adult.

My eyes lock with my dad's and silently pray he doesn't let Herb have any more drinks. While my mom kneels down in front of Maureen, helping her pick up the ruined cake, I tug on Camden's arm, wanting to go to his room, but he won't budge.

He's stuck, unable to move. I'm not really sure he's even breathing, so I move closer to him until our bodies are touching. I tug on his hand harder until he looks at me. His eyes move from my face to our joined hands and then back to my face.

"I'd never hurt you. You know that, right?" he asks.

I nod my head, confused as to why he'd even bring that up.

"What you saw"—his voice grows small—"that wasn't me. That was my dad."

His eyes peer into me, searching. Squeezing the hand I'm still holding, I give him my best smile.

"That wasn't your dad either," I reassure him.

A long breath whooshes out his mouth and into my face, sending the tendrils of my hair flying.

"I'd never be scared of you. I know you wouldn't hurt me."

Dread tugs at us while my blood pumps loud and hot.

"I wouldn't," he promises, sucking in a calming breath.

FIVE

YANELYS

ELEVEN YEARS OLD

When I hear grown-ups talk about abuse, they always refer to the abused as victims, but Camden isn't a victim. He's a fighter.

Every day, he fights. To be here. To stand and not flee. To be remembered.

Every day, he fights. And, every day, he wins.

But one day…I'm afraid, one day, he won't win.

My eyes close tightly at the thought, and I force air into my lungs, making my chest hurt worse.

On light feet, I walk to the kitchen for a glass of water, but I stop when I hear my parents arguing in hushed tones. They rarely ever fight—at least, not that I've heard—but here they are, fighting over Camden.

"The way he looks at her," my mom pleads for understanding, "it's not right, Santiago. They're too young." She sighs, her voice wobbling. "He's too intense."

"Carmencita," my dad starts. I imagine him wrapping her into his arms. "Love has no age."

"You're an old romantic," she scoffs and they both laugh. "But you know what I mean. You saw him today. The way he hit that boy." There's a long pause before my mom speaks again, "He lost control. He wouldn't have stopped if you hadn't interfered."

"He's a good boy," my dad says.

In silent agreement, I nod my head.

"He is. I know that." She pauses again. "But something's wrong with him."

My dad curses loudly, and I hear him pace the floor. I lean my body closer to the wall, molding myself against it, as I try to swallow my own emotions.

"His parents are what's wrong!" he shouts and I startle. "Drunks! Where were they—"

"I know," she interrupts him, her voice sounding sad. "I know, but what can we do?"

"If they ever touch him…" My dad pauses and pounds his fist against our kitchen counter, making me jump.

My parents stop talking after that. On light feet, I tiptoe back to my room, so they don't hear me and feel like they need to tuck me in again. Ever since the fight, my parents have been checking on me to make sure I'm okay.

I am okay. Of course I am.

It was just one fight. One little fight.

Where Camden completely lost it. He blanked out, his eyes losing their focus by the time my dad brought him to the steps where I waited.

It was crazy. But it was also Camden.

After crawling into bed, I hug a pillow longer than my body and bury my head into it when I hear Camden coming through my window. Once I feel my bed give a little at the weight of his body sitting on it, I peer up at him and try to smile.

"I'd never hurt you," he says, reading my watery smile wrong.

"I know." I sit up, putting my pillow on my lap.

He sighs. "I'm tired, Yan." With a frown, his gaze falls to my bed, and he brushes his hands over my sheets, his finger following the pattern stitched on my comforter.

"Come lie down then." I take his cold hands into mine and try to warm them on my lap.

"No, you don't get it." His voice cracks as he looks away from me, not wanting to make eye contact. "I'm really tired."

I push the pillow on my lap to the side and get off the bed without saying a word. Camden's eyes follow me as I make my way to the other side of my room. Trying to make as little noise as possible, I go to my dresser where I put Camden's present after I had taken it back from his house, knowing no one would open it if I'd left it there. I hand the box wrapped in Star Wars paper to him. My heart drums loudly in my chest as he flips it from side to side.

"Just open it," I say, my heart stammering with impatience.

A ghost of a smile appears on his face before he tears into it.

Suddenly shy, I stand in front of him, my feet shuffling, as I look at anything but Camden. He opens the cardboard box holding his presents and pulls out a picture of the two of us enclosed in a frame that says, *Yan + Cam = 4-ever.*

Behind long eyelashes, I peek up at him when he carefully puts it on my bed with a smile on his face, and then he reaches in for the fake plane tickets I made us.

"Warderick Wells?" he asks, reading the destination on the plane tickets.

"I looked it up," I state, my eyes glinting to his. "It's a park in Exuma, which means it's far away from everyone, but the best part is the Visitor Center. It's on an island all by itself, and only the park ranger is allowed to live there. On the beach there's a skeleton of a huge whale that I guess washed ashore and a trail that leads to Boo Boo Hill, which is supposedly haunted."

"By the whale?"

"No." I roll my eyes but giggle.

"You wanna move to Warderick Wells then?"

"Yep," I answer, nodding my head. "There are other islands close by, like Hog Cay, which I kinda hope means they have wild pigs."

Camden's laughter bounces off the walls, so I cover his mouth with my hand and shush him.

"What would you do with wild pigs?" He wants to know.

"Visit them," I explain, excited that he hasn't told me my present is dumb. "Maybe we can even have picnics with them."

"Ham sandwiches?" He laughs at his own joke.

"No," I let out a horrified whisper. "Don't say bacon either!"

"It sounds like a horrible picnic." His lips twist into a beautiful smile while his eyes gleam at me.

"Whatever."

Camden reaches over, takes the picture of us in his hand, and his fingers trail over our faces. Over and over, he outlines us and the inscription on the frame.

"This is us," he says without looking up at me. "And we're moving to Warderick Wells."

SIX

CAMDEN

The quiet in the air hangs over us and pulses through my veins, but I recognize the pattern of Santiago's silence. His silence beckons me to talk, to bare myself the way I once did years ago. To explain how I wound up in an abandoned building. I don't need his words to hear his plea. The tone of his concern is deafening.

But I like the quiet, like the quiet padded room where I've locked away all my thoughts.

Just as I told Yanelys years before, one day, I'd disappear, and no one would ever find me. Not even myself.

"I lost my job." I avert my eyes because that's not the reason I'm homeless.

The truth is, I can afford to stay anywhere I want to. I can also buy the abandoned building that was just recently brought to ashes, tear it down, build a new building, refurnish every apartment, and then live in a different apartment without any other occupants for the rest of my life.

The truth is, I don't have to work or go without.

But I do it anyway.

Because I'd rather have an infinite amount of days of strenuous labor, followed by sleepless nights on hard concrete floors, than take the money my father left for me when he died. I'd rather live my life as a recluse and an outcast than see my mom's bloodshot eyes threatening me and demanding me to give her that money.

As it is, I see her too often.

Her breath, immersed with the smell of alcohol, curls in the air, polluting everything around her. Including me.

There are days though, when she'll pass me on the street, too lost in her drunken stupor to see me or recognize me. Those are the days I crave. The days I'm not her son. The days I don't have to see myself in her.

It isn't until the words are out that I realize I've even spoken of my mom out loud. I backtrack, trying to remember if I've made any mention of the money my father left me, but Santiago only looks back at me through his concerned eyes. He doesn't know about the money. If he knew about the money, there'd be confusion entwined in there as well.

"How can you see yourself in a woman who is nothing like you?" he asks, his voice laced with the harshness he reserves only for when he speaks about my parents.

"We're related." I shrug, not able to meet his eyes.

He doesn't know just how alike she and I really are. I hope he never does.

"Her blood and my blood—it's all the same," I continue.

"You share nothing with that woman!" He hits his thigh with his fist.

I fight back a smile. There's a reason I always wanted to call this man my dad, and it isn't simply because he took me in when it felt like the whole world had turned its back on me. He's always seen the good in me, even when the good isn't much of anything.

"Right." I rub my bandaged hands over my face again. When the bandage moves, revealing the burn marks on my hand, I pull back the dressing even more and flinch in pain when I touch the area just before the real damage.

My hand's swollen and black.

Angry and ugly. Permanently scarred.

Need chokes me, numbing me from the effects of living and feeling.

"Considering the size of the fire, you got lucky," Santiago reveals.

Not wanting to assess the damage any further, I close my eyes.

Too much. The emotions of the past seven years build up inside me, suffocating me with the tendrils of memories I can't wish away.

"Actually, you got off real lucky. You have some minor burns. You will have to take pain medicine for a bit and keep it clean, but overall, you're a lucky man."

Santiago glares at me, his eyes daring me to counter him, but I can't. I can't fathom the idea of disappointing him again, so I silently agree with him, and he pats my ankle in approval. The boy in me who still worships him smiles up at him, and I begin to unload everything.

I leave out the nights before I left when Yanelys and I slept together, our bodies entangled. For three nights, I defied the one rule Santiago and Carmen had set, and I showed Yanelys how much I loved her. Those nights, she claimed me, making my soul forever hers.

The first night, Yanelys's doe eyes met mine, and without me uttering a word, she knew. When I leaned over her on the bed we shared, her eyes grew with wonder and anticipation. She brushed a finger over my mouth and then replaced it with her lips, kissing me so softly that all I felt was her breath dancing over my mouth, but the intensity grew with my desperation. Simultaneously, she eased the agony raging inside me while she fed my scalding need for her. I bathed in her, our love moving down my spine, and for a moment, she removed the hatred my heart had latched on to.

Our tongues swirled together in an exotic dance, and when I placed my palm against her breast, Yanelys quivered beneath me as she threaded her fingers through my hair.

"So beautiful," I murmured, coming up for air.

I bent down and kissed her neck, my lips trailing down her sleek flesh. I licked and tasted while she panted my name. Her body shook when I traced two fingers around her swollen clitoris, making me throb painfully as I hardened. When she arched her back, I experimented with my tongue, savoring her. When she moaned, my length pulsed, and I pulled away, knowing I'd orgasm before I could have my fill.

Her eyes were bright, her face glistening from raw passion. She was mine, if only for that night. So, I took what she offered without remorse.

I kissed her slowly, and my heart raced. I brought my hips down to her, and she pressed against me. Sighing softly into her mouth, I moved inside her.

"Cam," she whispered, raking her hands over my back.

Needing to make sure she wanted to do this, I pulled back but her grip on me hardened, bringing me back, and I chuckled lightly into her neck. I kissed her as I slowly move inside her and then kissed her again. Our bodies connected, we continued to kiss, feverish in our ecstasy. Her rapid hot breaths urged me, and I pulled her closer. With each push, she moaned louder, freeing us both. When she locked her lips once again with mine, chills ran down my spine when I thrust a final time inside her.

Sated, she caressed my nose with a lazy finger, and through the pale moonlight, I saw her smile.

Sleep came quickly after that. Her hand found mine, and our fingers stayed interlaced as we slept, bringing me comfort, showing me she found me worthy of love. I was afraid of all the tomorrows before me, but her simple touch gave me the safety I sought. She was beautiful and pure.

I would survive without her because of the quiet moments we shared as well as the passion we experienced while wrapped around each other.

My cheeks heat up as I lie in front of her dad, remembering our night.

Knowing he doesn't need to hear any of that, I cough into the uncomfortable silence, making my chest and throat hurt. I press on and tell him how I left Yanelys at the door to her first period class and walked away, my heart deadening with every step I took away from her.

My heart stutters in despair when I realize I want to tell him why. Without thinking it through, I grasp on to my bed's handrail and stare at the peach-colored walls while I speak for the first time about what happened when I was seventeen years old and decided to run away from the only family I'd ever had.

My father visited me a couple of days before I left Yanelys so I could dredge through this world alone, and while we stood outside the restroom of the local mall, he told me he was dying. I wanted to celebrate his words and hoped my smile would bring him to his knees. Instead, he smiled back with the same ruthless smile he'd give me before he hit me. I braced myself, and as usual, he brought me to my own knees.

"I'm leaving you all my money," he told me.

I shook my head at him, not wanting any part of him. "I don't want your money."

Of all the things I'd wanted from my parents, money was never one of them. Of course, money was the only issue they never had.

My father's smile grew sad. "Camden"—he inched forward, and when I stepped away from him, he threw his hands up in a sign of retreat—"you have a lot to hate me for, but your mom…" His eyes met mine, and I tightened my hands into fists. "She wasn't always like this. The woman I'd married was happy and loving. I'm the reason she turned bad."

"Leave her the money then." The plea in my voice was transparent and I hated myself for showing a sign of weakness.

"I can't." His voice came out rough and raw. "She's doing heroin. If I leave her the money, she'll kill herself with it."

"If you leave me the money, she'll find me," I said, each word searing itself like a brand on my heart. "I just want peace from both of you."

"Camden—"

I grabbed him by the collar and threw him against the wall. Through clenched teeth, I repeated, "I don't want your money."

"You'll kill her then."

My grip on him loosened. While I hated my parents, wanted them dead, the reality of what he'd said still hurt.

"Save her," he pleaded.

Confused, angry, disappointed, I reared back and punched him in the face, making him go down hard. Blood fell from his nose while he looked back at me, stunned. I'd only fought back once, and I had nearly died when he retaliated.

"Fuck you," I spit at him.

He scrambled to his feet, wiping the blood with the back of his long-sleeved shirt. His hands gripped my wrist and he pulled me to him. I felt him slip something in my jacket pocket as I turned away from him. Once I turned the corner, my hand slipped into my pocket where I found a piece of paper.

I didn't pull it out to see what it was. I already knew whatever it was would change me. At that moment, I knew I had to leave. Four years of peace, that's what they'd given me. Foolishly, I'd actually thought I could start anew, that I could bury my parents before their deaths.

But life had never been easy for me.

My mom would come for the money. Her poison would spread, suffocating and destroying me as her venom seeped inside me. Like a spreading disease, it would affect Yanelys, and she would suffer right along with me.

Not this time though.

Her heart was already too scarred because of me, because of the suffering I'd put her through every time I crawled through her window with yet another bruise.

I'd hurt her when I left, but the pain would be manageable.

It had to be better than the alternative. Watching me die on the inside as my mother inevitably clawed her way back into my life…that would be far worse.

Santiago's warm hand clasps on to mine while I struggle for my next breath. I never cried about my decision. I know I did the right thing.

But, right now, with Santiago sitting on my bed, it's all too real.

My past and my decisions—they're too much.

I close my tired eyes and tell Santiago about the purpose that once filled me. I'd wake up, knowing the truth—I mattered. I'd hold on to that tiny shred of realization, not wanting the moment to slip away to the real truth. The ugly truth that still leaves me clasping for nothing but air. The truth that screams at me, telling me no one cares about me.

There's nothing I can really do to make the world better. God is indifferent, a faraway fairy tale.

"I don't know your story," Pastor Floyd told me seven years ago after my third day of sleeping in his church.

With a plateful of spaghetti and meatballs, he sat down next to me and offered me his plate, his weathered hands steady as I took it from him.

Three days had passed since I saw Yanelys. Since I saw Santiago and Carmen. Since I left my family.

In doing so, I'd left a gaping hole in my heart. That stupid little bleeding thing that belonged to Yanelys, with Yanelys.

"But your story isn't over yet," Pastor Floyd continued.

I took my first bite into the spaghetti he'd offered. Red sauce dripped down my chin, and I quickly wiped it with the back of my hand.

He then told me about a trip to Haiti that his church was organizing, and he asked if I'd want to join. I originally scoffed at the idea, but his words rooted itself into my rotting heart, and hope began to bloom.

I'd have a purpose, a life worth living. Maybe, just maybe, I'd make Santiago proud of me. He'd always seen more in me than I would ever be able to accomplish, and this was the only way I had to prove him right.

Knowing I'd have to be over eighteen years old, I contacted the son of one of my parents' friends and had him make me a fake ID and passport. The following two months, I learned Creole and immersed myself in their culture, needing to be an actual asset on the trip.

Haiti wasn't what I'd expected. I knew of hunger pains but not of famine. I knew nothing of poverty, growing up a slave to wealth. I knew of family, of love, of hate and aguish. But nothing could have prepared me for Haiti.

I lived in Haiti for seven months, most of which I spent at an orphanage, giving babies and kids love that I never knew to dream about. Within the first few months, I fell irrevocably in love with a little girl named Jocelyn Marie and her older brother, Yvon. And while I knew I was too young to adopt them, they became my purpose. They became my truth that kept all the other truths at bay.

When I turned eighteen, I would claim my inheritance and give them a better life. I'd do for them what Santiago and Carmen had done for me. I'd give them a family.

I spoke to Pastor Floyd, who already knew I had lied about my name and age but decided to take me on anyway, and he agreed to help me adopt Jocelyn Marie and Yvon.

My story with Yanelys had ended, but I wasn't over. Suddenly, that realization filled me. I had a new beginning, a new story.

Then, the earthquake hit. And total devastation came upon us.

It measured a magnitude 7.1 on the Richter scale with fifty-two aftershocks recorded. Hundreds of thousands of lives were lost. Houses and schools were destroyed. Families disappeared while even more fell ill to cholera.

Death surrounded us. Choked us.

I should have died in the orphanage.

The last bit of me died that day, and I should have died with it.

But I didn't. Instead, I woke up in a hospital room, much like this one. No longer in Haiti, I learned I had been unconscious for three months.

Pastor Floyd visited me hours after I'd awoken, and I hated him for being there with me instead of Jocelyn Marie and Yvon. And the other kids.

When he told me they were gone, my hatred spread and imprinted itself within me.

The boys and girls I loved as my own, including Jocelyn Marie and Yvon, were gone.

Not confirmed deaths. Simply missing.

I held on to hope that we'd find them though, and as soon as I was released from the hospital, I spent Pastor Floyd's money and went back to Haiti. They were my purpose. But with each day that passed, my faith faltered. Still, I spent five years searching orphanages around the country to find Jocelyn Marie and Yvon.

Five years of my life.

Until the last bit of my meandering faith disappeared.

There was no purpose. There was no reason. There was no lesson.

The ugly truths had stolen the last bit of my humanity, and I knew no one cared. I didn't matter.

A small sniffle comes from the door of my hospital room, and I see her—Yanelys. Her name coils itself around my heart like a boa, leaving me barely any room to breathe or for my heart to beat. She's standing by the door, her once dirty blonde hair now a dark chestnut, cascades around the beautiful face that is never too far from my dreams. Eyes, dark and gleaming with tears, take me in as I try to remember how to breathe. When her bottom lip trembles, my heart slices open with feelings I long ago suppressed.

Her small frame takes over the room, consuming me, and I can't look away.

"I cared." She braces her thin arms around her chest. "You always mattered to me."

SEVEN

YANELYS

TWELVE YEARS OLD

Anxiety grows each time I look at the clock on the classroom wall. It's almost noon, and Camden still hasn't come to school. I tap my foot on the floor, eager for the bell to ring, letting us know that class is over. Then, I can leave school. It'll be my first time skipping class, but I have to know if Camden's all right.

The beatings started getting worse a month ago. Every day now, he's hiding a new injury, and my dad has begun questioning us. I want to tell my parents the truth, but I made a promise to my best friend.

He lives in a world where broken promises are his norm, and I don't want to add to his ever-growing pile of shit.

His reality is a nightmare. What's hardest to swallow, it's one he can escape from, but he's worried. If he reports the abuse and the police take him away, then they'll also be taking him away from me. He's told me countless times that he'd rather go through the beatings than not have me at the end of the day.

But even in his sleep, he's afraid now. Even in sleep, when the body should be at rest, he moans, and if I try to soothe him, he flinches in response. As he dreams, tears pool down his face and soak into my pillow. So, I stay awake while he sleeps, making sure every one of his tears is accounted for.

My worst fears are his reality, and every day, his parents' hatred consumes us.

A lump forms in my throat when Camden finally walks through the doors, and I swallow hard. He has a slight limp, but our teacher's too preoccupied with his tardiness to realize he's hurt. I notice it though, and my foot stops tapping on the floor when he walks past me without looking in my direction. But my gaze stays on him anyway, and my body cringes with his as he eases himself onto his seat.

Not caring if I get caught, I scribble a note onto my notebook paper with the words *How bad?* scrawled quickly across it. I pass it to him, but he refuses to take it. Frustrated because I've been worried about him and he doesn't seem to care, I slam the note on his desk. He stares across the room while the girl sitting behind us giggles, and our teacher coughs to get our attention.

Without looking at me, Camden takes the note, crumples it into a small ball, and then throws it into his book bag. I glare at him, but then I feel my own lips twitch when I see him bite back a smile.

After the bell rings, Camden snatches his bag, but he can't move quickly, which makes it easy for me to follow him. I grab his arm and don't pull away until he stops and faces me.

"Lift your shirt," I demand, using my best no-nonsense voice.

"You wanna see me naked, huh?" His voice is laced with malice, but his eyes track my face for understanding.

I've come to learn that he's only mean when things are bad, so I keep my mouth shut and don't reply.

Taking his hand in mine, I lead us to the gymnasium. After I make sure no one is around, I lift his shirt and shudder. A quiet cry echoes in my chest when I see the fresh bruises already forming along his stomach and ribs.

Angry, I ball my hands into fists but force them open so I can continue to inspect him for further injuries.

"I'm fine, Yan." He lowers his shirt before I do something stupid, like kiss his bruises.

"You're not." Tears well in the back of my eyes so I blink them back. When I'm certain I won't cry, I meet his gaze. "What's wrong with your leg?"

"Not a damn thing." He moves away from me, trying to put distance between us, but I hold on to his hand because someone has to hold on for both of us. "Mind your business."

"You are my business." I keep my voice low but firm, and his eyes soften. "Should we put ice on it?" I ask.

He shrugs and his eyes dart across the room before they lock back on mine, and he nervously licks his lips.

"My thigh," he admits. "I didn't get a chance to clean it."

Holding his hand again, I guide us to the girls' locker room, understanding what he hasn't spoken. He's bleeding, and he must have bandaged it up without cleaning it, because he wouldn't want to miss any more school.

Most kids pretend to be sick, so they don't have to *go* to school. Camden pretends everything's okay, so he doesn't have to *miss*.

"How bad is it?" I ask, pursing my lips together into a thin line. The idea of seeing blood hazes my vision, and I hope I won't get sick and vomit.

"I got it, Yan. I'll clean it."

"I'll do it."

I bite my inner cheek as our eyes meet again, and he nods his head once before looking back at the floor.

"He stabbed my thigh. I was using a cutting knife to butter my toast, and he got pissed because I should've been using a butter knife. I didn't get a chance to clean the cut, but I covered it up so I could come to school."

"Nerd," I joke.

He laughs. "If I hadn't come to school, I'd have had to wait until tonight to see you. I'd have probably bled to death, waiting for you."

"Don't say that," I whisper, my heart dropping at his stupid joke. "Besides, I was going to leave after class to check on you."

"Don't ever do that." He brings his eyes back to me. "Don't skip school or do anything that could ruin your life because of me."

I roll my eyes at him, but my mom's words about his intensity creep into my mind, and I shudder.

"Whatever, Cam. Just drop your pants so I can clean your wound."

My cheeks flush at the same time that Camden's cheeks turn a crimson red and we look away from each other as he brings his pants down to his ankles. I take the paper towels from the dispenser and soak them with warm water and soap. We both inhale sharply as I remove his bandage and press the paper towel to his open wound.

It's bad. As in he should probably go to the hospital.

"We have to tell someone, Cam," I say, already knowing his response.

"No." He shakes his head, his eyes narrowing. "I told you, they'll take me away. I can live with this. But living without you..." The desperation in his voice cuts me, and I bleed right along with him.

"You can move in with us."

He laughs, the sound chilling me.

"Cam, my parents—"

"Stop!" he shouts, making me jump. "We've talked about this too many times. Don't you ever get tired? I told you, no. I'm staying with my parents, and you're keeping your mouth shut."

Frustrated, I turn away from him to get more paper towels, and I bat my eyes several times to keep the tears away. I bend down, making it easier for me to have access to his cut and press the towels against his thigh. After a hesitant glance in his direction, I bandage it up again. I'm about to suggest we go to the hospital when our PE coach walks in and starts yelling at us. She advances toward us and separates us, giving Camden just enough time to pull up his pants before she can see his stab wound.

"What were you thinking?" My mom's disappointment is reflected in my dad's eyes.

"I wasn't," I reply, my stomach dropping as a blush creeps up my neck.

Unable to tell anyone what really happened, I let my parents think the worst. My PE coach caught me between Camden's legs while he stood there with his pants down. My parents think what everyone else thought when the rumors ran wild throughout the school.

Two weeks of suspension isn't that bad though. Neither is being grounded for three months. What's bad is that my parents no longer trust Camden or me, which means I can't see him anymore—except at night when he climbs through my window and into my room.

I crawl into bed with the memory of Camden and I being ushered into the principal's office while the girls in the school laughed and called me names, and the boys cheered and congratulated Camden with slaps on his back. Thankfully, our coach had a firm grip on his shoulder, so he couldn't attack any of those boys. I should've let Camden hold my hand when he went to grab it, but shame washed over me in that moment, and I moved away.

It was the only time I'd ever moved away from him, and I know it's changed us forever. He wouldn't even look at me after that.

I lie in bed, awake, until two a.m., when I realize Camden's not coming. He's never *not* come, no matter what.

Fear grips me, threatening to choke the breath out of my lungs, and I finally run into my parents' room and wake them. Through tear-stained cheeks, I tell them everything.

I share Camden's story. Our story.

Neither of my parents says anything, but just as I'm finishing, my dad stops pacing the room and goes to his closet where he comes back with a gun in his hand. I step away from him and run into my mom.

"Stay here," my dad orders.

But my mom and I follow him.

Not able to match his speed, my mom and I run a few feet behind my dad. I don't see my dad go to their front door because my focus is on Camden's bedroom window. When I get to it, I push it upward, but it doesn't budge. My fists bang on his window in desperation, and I call out his name. My mom moves me aside as my dad shouts obscenities at Camden's dad. With my heart in my throat, I watch my mom hit Camden's window with her elbow. She then reaches into the room through the small shattered hole, unlocks the window, and pushes it up.

My mom helps me climb into the still room, and I hear her call 911 as I go to Camden's bed where I find his lifeless bloody body. I brush his hair back and hear him groan, so I carefully ease myself into his bed and lie down next to him. Without opening his eyes, he reaches for me and tries to move his body closer to mine.

"You're gonna be okay, Cam," I whisper repeatedly to him while I continue to comb my fingers through his hair.

His labored breaths fall on my cheek, but I to try to soothe him, even after I hear the sirens approaching.

EIGHT

YANELYS

TWELVE YEARS OLD

My mom and I rode with Camden in the ambulance, but the EMTs made me sit in the front seat while my mom sat with him in the back. My heart, already broken, broke a little more when the doctors and nurses wheeled him away from me and led my mom and me to a waiting room where we've been sitting for close to an hour.

I wish my dad were here. He's good at making me feel better. Not that my mom isn't, but my dad's better. And since he's a firefighter and works with paramedics, he knows a lot of the people in the emergency room, and he'd have had answers by now. But he had to stay at Camden's house to talk to the police.

I let the tears fall down my face, hoping Camden can feel them and know I haven't left him. My mom takes me in her arms, and I crawl into her lap, needing to feel like her little girl, being comforted and taken care of.

In my mom's arms, I close my eyes and reach for the quietest corner of my mind. I think about Camden, needing to believe that the harder I think about him, the more likely he'll be okay. Images of his bruised body torture me. I hate leaving Camden in the hands of fate. I mean, it's not like fate has been good to him so far.

"He's in God's hands," my mom says, correcting my thoughts.

Her words sooth me like a balm to my soul and I feel better knowing that because God doesn't let bad things happen. People do that all on their own, but God fixes things. He fixes people. He brings them together, like He did with Camden and me.

"Let's pray," she says.

With my head tucked under her chin, she begins to say "The Lord's Prayer" in Spanish.

With each word whispered from my mom's lips, my stomach muscles begin to loosen, and my tears stop. Just as she is halfway through the prayer, my dad opens the door to the waiting room with a doctor and two nurses behind him. I move my bottom, trying to get off my mom, but she holds me tighter. My dad stops at the door and bows his head while my mom finishes her prayer.

"Dad?" I whisper when I hear the word *Amen*.

His head snaps to me. He runs his hands over his face and rubs his tired eyes with the heels of his hands. After a long sigh, he walks over and sits down next to us while the doctor and nurses talk among themselves by the doorway.

"Yanelys," he says softly.

I look down while my heart thunders in my chest. My parents only use my full name when they're upset.

"If you had told us before…" He trails off and looks at my mom.

My throat closes when he doesn't continue talking. "Please, Daddy. Please tell me Cam's not dead." With my words hanging in the air, I can't control the flow of tears or the hiccups choking me with every second that ticks by.

"He's gonna be okay." From his chair, my dad takes my hand and brings me to him for a tight hug.

I bury my face into his neck, but when he pulls me away, I look him in the eyes, giving him my full attention.

"But, baby girl, you can't keep these types of things from us. He could have died."

"Santiago," my mom warns.

My dad doesn't look at her. "You know that, right?"

"Yes." I nod my head as fresh tears start to roll down my face even faster. "But I promised…" I look from my dad to my mom, not wanting them to be angry with me. "He said if I told, the police would take him away."

"They won't." My dad looks at my mom. "Cam is going to come live with us."

"Santiago," my mom says again, her voice dripping with uncertainty.

Her concern barely registers as I reach around my dad's neck for another hug.

"After everything he's lived through, Carmen"—my dad shakes his head—"he can't live with strangers." His voice is sad without even a hint of the strength I normally hear behind it.

44

"Of course not," my mom agrees, which only makes me sob even more.

In all the things Camden has been wrong about, this is the worst. My not telling almost cost him his life. And in the end, he was wrong. The police won't be taking him away. He'll be coming home where he belongs.

"How bad is he?" My mom wants to know.

I step away from my dad's embrace, so I can pay better attention.

My dad sighs again and looks at the doctor he came in with, who's now standing by the door by himself.

"I'm Dr. Mursuli." The doctor extends his hand toward my mom.

She stands up to shake it. He then does the same to me, and after a moment's hesitation, I also shake his hand.

"Per Santiago's request, I'll be treating Camden during his stay at the hospital. The majority of his assault took place on his face and chest, which resulted in a dislocated jaw and a broken nose. His eyes are swollen and bruised, but he'll be okay. Those are just the minor injuries."

My mom takes in a sharp breath. "There are worse ones?"

Dr. Mursuli nods his head and looks at the clipboard in his hand. "He's suffered a concussion, and he has been in and out of consciousness since he arrived. He also has three broken ribs, a punctured lung, and some internal bleeding."

The doctor looks at all of us to make sure we understand, but I can't listen anymore. I move away from them and stare at the vending machine, not wanting anything from there but needing some space.

What's happened has changed Camden and me. Another scar on top of all the others scars we've received every time Camden's parents hit him. It'll be up to me to help us move past it. I just hope I'm strong enough for him. For both of us, really.

Lost in thought, I startle when my mom puts her hand on my shoulder, but I smile when she finally utters the words I've been waiting for. We can go see Camden. He's still asleep, or unconscious, but relief fills me, knowing I get to see him.

When we get to Camden's room, the police stop my dad to ask him more questions—something about holding Camden's parents at gunpoint—but my thoughts only circle around Camden, and although I hope my dad isn't in trouble, I leave him to defend himself.

On weighted legs, I walk slowly into Camden's room. I go to his bed and sit on the chair next to it. Ignoring a beeping machine next to us, I take his hand in mine and swallow hard when I see him on oxygen. I squeeze my hand around his once to let him know I'm there, and then I take in his bruised face. Beneath the swelling and angry bruises, there's a cut that goes through his top lip to his bottom lip. The gauze over his nose doesn't hide the swelling, and there's still dried blood under his bottom lip.

Too scared to brush away the hair from over his eyes, I squeeze his hand again and quietly cry while my mom stands beside me with her hand on my shoulder.

My mom and I stay in Camden's room as day breaks while my dad stays in the waiting room after seeing Camden for a few minutes. A nurse tried to argue that I should leave, too, but my parents argued right back until she gave up. It's not like I would have left anyway.

I'm right where I need to be.

I know that to be truer than anything else when, just after ten a.m., Camden finally opens his eyes and sees me. Sunlight shines through the open blinds, slivers of rays dancing on Camden's bed.

"Yan," he whispers, squeezing my hand that's still holding his. His beautiful face softens beneath the ugly scars.

He looks down when I try to meet his eyes, so I do the only thing I know that will make him feel better. While my parents nap on the bed the nurse brought my mom a few hours ago, I crawl into Camden's bed, careful not to touch his chest or any of the IV lines. Once I settle beside him, he inches closer to me and turns to face me, wincing as the pain radiates throughout his body.

"I knew you'd save me," he whispers, his breath falling on my cheek.

For the first three days in the hospital, Camden and I are questioned by the police and the hospital social workers. They separate us, asking both of us about details neither of us wants to answer. When we are separated, my dad stays with Camden, and my mom takes me to the cafeteria. From the look on my mom's face, I know she isn't happy. When she starts to voice her concerns about Camden moving in with us, shock makes me clench my hands into fists.

I get that we're young, and I know most kids our age don't act like us. Boys want to hang out with other boys while girls want to play with other girls. But that's not us. Whether we like it or not, Camden's parents made us who we are. His parents brought us together and made us grow up faster than any of the other kids we know. I'm the one Camden reaches for, so I reach back as often as possible because I know how alone he always feels, how unwanted he thinks he is.

I explain that to my mom, but her deep sigh and wrinkled forehead let me know that she doesn't understand.

On the fourteenth day, my parents and I arrive at the hospital just after nine a.m., only to find Camden's room empty.

In that moment, despair conquers all of my thoughts, grasping on to me so that I can't move. My dad lied to me. He said they wouldn't take Camden away, and they did. Even though my mom reassures me that he's okay, I can't be sure until I see him. We haven't even met the social worker who was assigned to him and took him to the group home, even after my parents had told everyone—the police, doctors, hospital social workers—they wanted to be his guardian.

Camden's right. People go about their business, unaffected by your wants. They only do as much as they have to, nothing more.

And no one had to make sure Camden came home with us. They didn't care about what he wanted.

He's nothing more than another job. Another voiceless face.

Walking into the group home fills me with dread. Dread of the sad stories that fill the place. Dread of the bland walls waiting for me inside. Dread for the boy I love who now has to live within these walls, full of secrets and shame no one wants revealed.

After meeting Camden's social worker, I follow her instructions to get to Camden's room while my parents go with her to meet with the woman who runs the home. I hesitate by his door, but then I remind myself that it's Camden.

Life around us might change. But we'll always be us.

I walk through his open door with a big smile on my face, and I find him lying on his bed, staring at the ceiling.

"What's so interesting up there?" I ask.

He looks at me for the briefest of seconds before he returns his gaze to the ceiling.

Not knowing what else to say, I sit on his bed and look at anything but him. Like I suspected, the walls are bland. The furniture is worn. And the tiles are chipped.

A doctor's office is more welcoming than this place. At least they fill the walls with happy pictures and uplifting posters about cats and hanging on.

"He called you a whore." Camden clears his throat, his eyes still fixated on the same spot on the ceiling while mine double in size. "So, I fought back." He clenches and unclenches his fists while his chest heaves up and down. Breathless, he finally looks at me.

Guilt washes over me. Camden fought back for me, and his dad nearly killed him in the process.

Unable to meet his eyes, I fidget with a thread hanging from my jeans. "You shouldn't have."

"Don't say that to me, Yan." His tone stings me, and I wrap my arms around my stomach, finally finding the courage to look at him. "You protect me. I protect you. That's what we do. Don't take that away from me. It's all I have."

"Okay." I nod. "Cam…" My eyes skirt away from him, but when I look back at him, I find him watching me with his lips pulled into a frown. I miss his smile and the way it lights up his eyes, but I know it'll take time for him to get that back. "I'm sorry," I say, letting the words rush out of my mouth on an exhale. "I shouldn't have moved my hand away from you when we were going to the principal's office."

Camden's eyes cloud over, but he doesn't cry. "I'm always gonna reach for you even if you don't want to hold my hand in return."

"I'll never stop holding your hand."

To prove my point, I lean over and take his hand in mine. Silently, I sit with our hands connected while Camden stares at the ceiling until my parents come to get me.

Two and a half months pass before my parents get custody of Camden. Every day during that time, he becomes more withdrawn.

Shut down, shut in, shut off.

I can't reach him, so when we spend our time together it's in silence, holding hands.

When my mom finds out Camden is coming home, she wants to throw him a party. Thankfully, my dad convinces her that pizza and some balloons will be more than enough.

While my dad and I pick Camden up, my mom stays home to set up the balloons and order the pizza.

As we approach our entryway, my dad smiles at me, and I hope my mom hasn't gone over the top. My dad opens the door, and I hang back as he and Camden walk through it. When Camden stops and takes a step back, a short gasp catches in my throat while my heart beats violently. I look over his shoulder and then step beside him when I see a *Welcome Home* banner hanging on the wall with balloons decorated beside it.

After my mom hugs us, I take his hand, and together, we follow my parents into the dining room where we find enough pizza and cupcakes to feed us for a week. Camden furrows his forehead as he takes it all in, and just as I'm about to get angry with my mom for going overboard, he smiles. It's the first smile I've seen on his face since the day at school when our lives went to hell.

"Let's eat in the living room," my mom says, surprising me.

We always eat at the dining room table. It's like a set law. My eyes meet hers, but she shrugs her shoulders, a nonchalant lift and drop, so we start to serve ourselves. When we walk into the living room, we find more balloons, and the TV screen is paused on the opening scene of *Iron Man*.

Camden's smile reaches his eyes, the sea of blue growing in intensity, and I smile back at my mom.

"This is a one-time deal," my mom informs Camden. He nods. "After tonight, we eat only in the dining room."

"Yes, Mom," I say, my tone full of humor and wonder, and she smacks my bottom lightly as I walk past her.

My dad hands the remote to Camden, and when he takes it, my dad keeps hold of it until Camden's eyes meet his. "This is your home." My dad points to himself, my mom, and me. "Wherever we are, wherever you are, the four of us are a family. We're your home."

Camden nods, and when my dad lets go of the remote, Camden places it on his lap without saying a word or turning on the movie. We begin to eat our food in silence, and just as I'm about to eat my second slice, Camden turns to my dad.

"This has always been my home." He looks at my mom and me. "Thanks for letting me live here."

Camden turns his attention to the remote control in his hand and presses play, letting his words hang in the air and fill us.

My splintered heart breaks even further for Camden but not for his hurt or his losses. My heart hurts for those things, but what kills me, what shatters me, is his love.

Life has lashed out at him, has beaten him, leaving behind nothing more than a prisoner of life. But no matter what his past has taught him, he still reaches for love. To love and be loved.

NINE

CAMDEN

Piercing brown eyes stare at me, taking me in, and I wonder what they see. *Does she see me as the boy I used to be or simply the pieces of me left behind?*

Because I'm no longer whole. Or maybe I never was, and Yanelys only made me feel like I was.

Disjointed, muddled pieces. The remnants of a life wasted. Young and broken and tired. So damn tired.

It's been years since I felt my father's belt against my skin, but the memory lives in every cell, awakening at the slightest touch. My mom's words and insults assault my brain, always reminding me of who I am. And whom I belong to.

My dad died almost seven years ago, and my mom's addiction holds her in the poisonous prison cell of her mind. Somehow they still own me. My mind and body have never really belonged to me but to them. Everything is theirs.

Even though I ache for Yanelys's warm touch, I'll push her away just as quickly. Even a simple touch will trigger memories—both good and bad. Like a sad movie playing on the screen of my mind.

I turn away from Yanelys, not wanting her to see the pieces she has never been able to put together. An unfinished puzzle with broken chunks and missing bits. Marred and scarred and unable to be redesigned so that I could portray a better picture.

I am my past. Ugly and polluted. Breathing but barely alive.

My breath counts the seconds as the silence in the room thickens. I feel Yanelys's stare burn into my flesh, but I can't bear to meet her gaze again. When

I finally find the courage to look at her, I open my mouth to apologize for being here, for leaving in the first place, for existing, but a large sob escapes her lips, and she backs away until she's out the door.

"Yan," I whisper her name when the door closes behind her. I let out a huff of air and wait for her to come back.

Seconds turn into minutes, and slowly, the numbness I was once granted lifts, and my body feels as if it has been buried under a sea of agony. My skin burns, my bones ache, my limbs and organs radiate a pain I'm not sure I can survive.

"You hurt her," Carmen says, approaching my bed from the door. She leans over me to place a gentle kiss on my forehead. "You hurt all of us."

"I didn't mean to." I look into her sad eyes, and pain shoots throughout my body when I rub my hands over my face. "I was trying to make it easier for you."

That's the honest-to-God truth.

Yanelys, Carmen, and Santiago were my family, my everything, and with my father's pending death and the money I was destined to inherit, I'd have wound up dragging them through a hell none of them should have to go through. That was my burden, not theirs. They'd carried enough of my load. And for what? To carry more? It had to end. At some point, it had to come to an end.

So, at seventeen years old, I made the hardest decision of my life. The night before I left, I crept into Yanelys's room and watched her sleep as I lay next to her. The rise and fall of her chest, her eyelashes fluttering as she slept, her lips turning to a small smile. I traced my fingers over her cheek and ran them through her hair. I memorized the feel of her skin and the smell of her hair, knowing I'd need it in the future.

The following morning, I walked her to the door of her first period class and stared at her one last time. She blushed under the intensity of my eyes, but still, I held her gaze and again tried to memorize every angle of her face, every eyelash, and every strand of hair on her head. I folded my fingers between hers, and when the bell rang, I kissed her, our final kiss. When I walked away from her, I silently prayed for forgiveness.

I stayed away from them not because I wanted to, but because if I saw them for even a moment, my resolve would crumble, and I'd beg them to take me back.

Even now, I know they're better off without me, without the demons I've taken on. I've done my best to pretend they don't exist, that my time with them didn't affect me.

"You made it harder," Carmen replies.

"So, how do I make it right?" The words spill out of my mouth before I can stop them, and I'm surprised to find that I don't want to continue running.

I want to make things right. Selfishly, I want Yanelys to piece me together until I'm no longer my grim past but something, someone, with a future.

I want to be saved—not just from the things I've experienced, but from myself as well. Mainly from myself.

"I tickle Carmen's feet when she's mad at me," Santiago jokes and I surprise myself even further when I laugh.

"You want me to tickle Carmen's feet?" I joke back.

"If you touch Carmen's feet, you and I will have some words," Santiago warns, making Carmen laugh.

After lightly slapping Santiago on the shoulder, Carmen sits on my bed and takes my hand. "You made a mistake, Cam, and it cost you the only girl you've ever loved." Her sad eyes turn to Santiago, who nods his head. "You can't undo a mistake, but you can fix it."

"What are you going to do to win her back?" Santiago asks with a smirk. "I love my daughter, but she's as stubborn as her mom. She'll fight you and push you away, so make sure you push back even harder."

"And don't give up, Cam. Beg if you have to. But, for both of your sakes, don't give up," Carmen adds.

Pain throbs where the fire licked my skin, but worse than that is the pain in my chest. Every agonizing beat of my heart reminds me of one thing. I've lost Yanelys.

I smile at Santiago and Carmen, but the attempt makes my lips tremble. Unable to flee from the memories, I turn my face away from them.

Away from her memory.

The girl who believed in Karma and hoped for better days. The girl who never gave up on me and spent her days laughing and nights crying with me. The girl who made me strong and loved me until my weaknesses didn't exist. The girl who picked me up every time I had fallen.

TEN

YANELYS

FIFTEEN YEARS OLD

After a full day at Disney World, Camden and I go down to the hotel's arcade room while my parents eat dinner. Being the only ones in there, we run around, screaming and knocking into games. We giggle and play-tackle one another while we dash across the arcade floor.

This is our life, the one we were re-gifted. It was a steep climb, but we got through the pain and anguish. The constant drain of the fear-filled years is gone. It's only a memory away, so we cherish and nurture the good to keep away the bad.

When Camden takes my hand in his and pulls me to the water-gun game—the one where you shoot a target and whoever fills up the target with water the fastest wins—I follow. After Camden puts in our tokens, I take my place behind the water gun and squint my eyes, so I can better see my target.

As soon as the light turns green, indicating we can shoot, I press the trigger. With all of my concentration on the task at hand, I startle easily when water hits the side of my face and makes its way down to my ear. I jump up from my seat, screaming, as I bat my ear with my hand, only to hear Camden howling with laughter.

While he rocks back and forth on his seat, I take my gun, point it at him, and shoot. Laughter stops. And when he opens his mouth at me, I aim for it.

His eyes narrow, and he reaches for me in retaliation, and I do what any sane girl would do. I run. But he's faster than me, and he quickly has me by my waist and is pulling me toward him. Sitting me on his lap, he turns the gun around so that it's pointing at me. He shoots, and I laugh while trying to block the water with my free hand.

When our time is up and we both lose with the sudden stop of the water flow, I lean back into his chest, breathless from all the laughter. Camden moves his hands from my waist to my neck, moving my hair to one side. My breathing stops altogether when he presses his warm lips against my neck.

I slightly turn my head to face him and find his eyes looking back at me with both fear and desire. I try on my best sexy smile—you know, the one I've practiced in the mirror but haven't perfected yet—and he traces his thumb over my bottom lip, making them part at his tender touch.

His bright blue eyes wash over me, taking in my face, as if it were the first time he's seeing me. I blush at the intensity of his stare, but when I bow my head, he slightly touches my chin, and I look back at him.

Licking his lips, he looks down at mine and leans into me. Raw instincts take over, and I curve into him until our lips meet. The bells from the games around us melt away, and all I hear is Camden's heavy breathing.

The time for pretend has come to an abrupt end, and I open my heart to love. The tender moment is driven by a fire that has been burning inside of us since we were kids.

Camden opens his mouth, and I feel his tongue touch my lips, so I part them for him. Time stands still. The hands of time have forgotten to move as Camden explores my soul. Soft and slow, our kiss deepens, but out of breath, I eventually pull away.

"Should I apologize?" Camden asks so low that I barely hear him.

My head snaps back at him in surprise. "Are you sorry you kissed me?"

Hurt and embarrassment cloak over me, and I get up from his lap while he thinks over my question.

"No. I mean…" Camden runs his hands through his long hair and sighs in frustration. "I don't know what I'm doing here."

He stands up and paces, his legs pounding on the floor. When he stops and looks at me, I see the uncertainty in his eyes, so I walk to him and put my arms around his waist while he rests his chin on the top of my head.

"You kissed me," I murmur into his chest.

"I kissed you," he breathes.

Wanting him to see me when I speak, I pull away from our embrace. "It wasn't my lips you kissed though, Cam, but my heart."

His lips spread into a smile before he leans down and kisses me again. My heart stammers and then picks up pace when I look into his adoring eyes.

"Let's go outside," he says, taking my hand.

When the doors slide open for us, the hot, humid air hits us. I lift my hair up and put it in a tight bun, hoping that small act will prevent it from frizzing. As soon as I finish, Camden takes my hand again, his large hand immediately swallowing my small one. My eyes follow the length of our arms to where our fingers touch, connecting us, and when I look back at Camden, I find him smiling at me.

"Like a puzzle piece"—he holds up our hands—"we fit."

My cheeks brighten under his gaze, but when I try to turn away, he tips my chin toward him and kisses my forehead.

"You heal my brokenness. Only you, Yan."

Once we get to the pool, we take off our flip-flops and ease our feet into the water as the silence of the night surrounds us. I don't know what to say, so I find my voice in the stars and look up at them with newfound love blooming in my heart.

"What are you thinking about?" Camden asks me.

"I'm not," I answer honestly. "I'm just looking at the stars and enjoying what we have. You?"

"I'm thinking about"—he leans in and kisses my cheek—"how I haven't thought about running away in three years."

"Good." I nod and then lean my head against his broad shoulder. "Because this is your home. I'm your home," I clarify as I look away, embarrassed by my confession.

He cups my chin in his hand and forces me to look back at him. "You've always been my home, Yan."

His lips take mine, but this time, it's with a ferocity that wasn't there before. I moan against his kiss as I pull his head closer to me. His hands reach beneath my shirt, and his long fingers trace lazy circles on the small of my back.

I swear when my phone chirps, alerting me of a text, and Camden and I both pull away from each other with our breathing coming in fast and labored.

"It's my mom." I show him the text and wrinkle my nose, making him laugh.

"We can't keep Mom waiting."

Camden takes my hand in his, and we walk back to our hotel room where my parents await us in the three-bedroom suite they rented. When we walk in, my parents greet us from the sofa, and when Camden drops my hand and steps away from me, my mom and I both curiously look at him. My mom arches an eyebrow at me in question, and I shrug my shoulders.

Since we were kids, we've always held hands. Us kissing shouldn't change anything.

After we say good night, we go to our separate rooms, and although Camden only sneaks into my bedroom at home when he's had a nightmare, I still expect him to come to me tonight.

I mean, things between us have changed. Now more than ever, we should want to sleep together.

My cheeks heat at the thought and I fan my face to cool it down while a sudden pulsing between my legs picks up in pace.

Just sleep, right?

Frustrated, I leave my room and go to the kitchen, loudly opening and closing cabinets, unsure of what I'm looking for. Unless, of course, the answer is Camden, and I already know where to find him.

I glare at the door to his room, and when I salute it with my middle finger, Camden opens the door and walks out. I try to play it off, but his grin lets me know he saw me throwing a temper tantrum.

"What are you doing awake?" I accuse.

"You were making enough noise to wake up the dead."

He puts his hand on my shoulder, and I curl into him in an awkward embrace that ends with him stepping away from me. His eyes, wide and shocked, dart to my parents' door and then to me.

"I thought you'd come to my room tonight." My bottom lip trembles, and I bite it, so it doesn't give me away.

"Oh, Yan," he sighs my name as he pulls me into his arms. "I wanted to, but—Yan, I love you."

My heart leaps out of my chest, and I smile up at his beautiful face. I press my lips against his square jaw. "I love you, too."

"You're my best friend. And, now, you're my girl?" It comes out sounding like a question, so I nod. "I also love your parents. What they've done for me…" he trails off. "I respect them, and I respect you. If I were to go to your bed right now…" He stares back at me without finishing his sentence, and I feel myself blush. "Yeah." He laughs, blowing air on my face.

"What if I want that, too?" I ask once I'm able to speak again.

Camden lets out another long whoosh of air on my face. "I want you, Yan. I want you so bad." He manages to hug me closer to him. "But not now." His voice pleads for me to understand. "When we're older and not living with your parents."

I pull back and pout, pulling my bottom lip into my mouth. "That's a long time from now."

"You're killing me." He laughs, his intensity softening. "I've had a lot of wrongs in my life. You're my only right, and I want to do right by you."

My heart swells while my body tingles at his words.

"Can we at least watch TV, or is that wrong, too?" The tease falls from my lips and he narrows his eyes at me. "I can't sleep." I shrug and sway my hips as I walk to the couch.

My eyes flutter open when the sound of my dad slamming a cabinet door shut wakes me from my sleep. I sit up straight so that I'm no longer leaning on Camden's shoulder. He's still asleep, and I kick his foot. When his eyes pop open, I massage the base of my neck.

I can't believe we fell asleep like that. I thought I'd be able to coax him into my bed, but he proved to be as stubborn as me, so we eventually passed out on the couch.

I guess that means I won. Kind of.

Without saying a word, Camden and I pour cereal into our bowls and then join my parents at the kitchen table. Before taking my first bite, I feel Camden's eyes on me. I glance up and when he looks away, I smile.

My mom coughs loudly, and we all turn our attention to her.

"I think we should set some ground rules." She looks at my dad, who looks back at her, confused. "Cam, you live with us. You are as much a part of this family as the rest of us."

Camden looks down to his bowl on the table and plays with the spoon.

"Son," she says firmly. She stays quiet until his eyes meet hers. "We love you. We trust you. But you two can't date—at least, not until you're older."

My mouth hangs open, and for the first time in my life, words seem alien to me.

"You're dating?" my dad asks, his voice mirroring the shock on his face.

"No," Camden says too quickly. He looks at me with a guilt-ridden expression on his face. "I mean, I like Yan. No, I love Yan." He clears his throat while his eyes nervously roam over the table. "But nothing happened."

My dad slams his hand on the table, and we all jump. Camden's face loses color, but his eyes steady, staring holes into the kitchen table.

"Cam wouldn't let anything happen because he loves you guys," I say, trying to help the situation. I put my hand on my dad's arm and watch his eyes soften.

"Cam," my dad says and Camden finally looks up at him. "There's no one else Carmen and I would trust with our daughter but you. If ever there were two people meant for each other, it's you two." He meets Camden's eyes until understanding flashes across his face, and Camden nods. "But you're still young."

"This is what I was afraid of when you moved in with us," my mom whispers. "You two are too close. I told you this would happen, Santiago." My mom turns her narrowed eyes toward my dad, who smiles sheepishly back at her.

"Carmencita, have you forgotten how we were when we were their age?" my dad asks. "I knew you were the one when we were just ten, remember? I bought you a ring and asked you to marry me."

My mom blushes, spinning her cup of coffee on the table. "It was different." Her voice is stern, but her eyes are already losing their anger. "We didn't live together."

My dad reaches over the table and traces my mom's knuckles with a single finger. His eyes seek out Camden's, and he doesn't speak until they're staring at each other.

"If you want to date other people, you can," my dad says, making me pale.

"I don't," Camden answers quickly.

"Neither do I," I say.

My dad knowingly smiles back at us.

"No more touching"—my dad leans forward, putting his elbows on the table—"holding hands, or hugging. When you watch TV, you can't sit close to each other. Once you graduate high school, you can start dating. We're trusting you, okay?"

I want to argue with him, to tell him how unfair he's being, but I bite my tongue. Saying anything to oppose them right now would only make things worse, so I let Camden speak for both of us.

Camden holds my dad's gaze but looks away to include my mom. "When I'm older, I'm going to ask you for your permission to marry Yan."

I inhale loudly and cover my mouth as I feel my eyes water.

"Until then, I won't do wrong by her or by you. I swear it."

"Our answer is yes," my dad says. He looks at my mom for confirmation. "When you ask, our answer will be yes."

ELEVEN

CAMDEN

A hopeless fraud. An undercover mess.

Pastor Floyd walked into my hospital room only five minutes ago, and already, I can hear his accusations. I flinch inwardly while I do my best to keep an outward appearance of normalcy in front of Santiago and Carmen.

They don't see me, how I'm sewn together with lies and disappointment. But Pastor Floyd does.

He was there the day God cursed me.

God had saved me from my parents. He'd saved me from the earthquake. Not because He'd had some divine plan for me but simply because He could.

I'm a puppet, and He's my puppeteer.

I was in a coma for three months after the earthquake, being fed painkillers the entire time. When I awoke to find I'd lost everything once again, there wasn't an opiate out there that could diminish the pain. Sleep left me while anxiety racked my body.

My doctors did their best to help but refused to do the one thing I'd begged for—to put me in a medically induced coma until I died. I'd asked, even offered them my inheritance.

Fucking doctors with their stupid morals.

Pastor Floyd was determined to help me though, and that was how he became my drug dealer.

Painkillers. Anti-anxiety pills.

He got them all for me, on top of what I was already being prescribed. It held me over while I searched for Jocelyn Marie and Yvon for five years in Haiti.

But then I came back, empty-handed. I added alcohol to the mix and made myself a concoction that finally took away the pain.

At least for a short while.

Pills gave me a light, showed me a destination I hadn't yet traveled. For many years, my soul had been burdened by pain. And anger. Too much anger. Pills numbed me to those emotions and became my best friend, reliable and always by my side.

But pills bestowed other gifts on me as well. Shakes, nightmares, cold sweats, and visions I never want to see again even if it means giving up my eyes.

They controlled me, ravished me, and possessed me.

They lied and manipulated me, telling me things would get better but they never did.

The anger built until my limbs trembled from it. So, I drank and took more pills—my faithful friends that would follow me past the grave. Self-respect and dignity were long forgotten. I'd been stripped bare without any morality left by my side.

I tried to put up some sort of resistance to the pills, but my will slipped away, destroying me as easily as the emotions I'd worked so hard to hide from.

I'm a failure at life—not because I try to be, but because that's where my talents lie. In failure and mistakes. I carry out my own punishment, making my body toxic to myself. Life has beaten me, cutting a wider gash into my already torn heart and delivering the slowest kind of death.

I can't go back and undo what's already been done. But I want to move forward, so I can have Yanelys. So the lonely planet of my heart can find its way back home. So the screaming in my head quiets down. I'm tired of drifting, of standing still, of stepping over landmines, secretly hoping one detonates.

I want to be saved.

And she's the only one who can save me from myself. Her tenderness is irresistible and healing. She's the only one.

Will she see me? Can she look past my abandonment and deception, past the rough exterior, and peer inside me? Layer by layer, strip me of my defenses until all that's left is me.

Will she find anything worth saving?

"This is your family then?" Pastor Floyd asks, ruthlessly snapping me back to the reality of my hospital room.

Pastor Floyd stands at the foot of my bed while Santiago and Carmen sit by my bedside. Pastor Floyd's presence overpowers the whole room, and I shrink away from the smile on his face.

"Yes," Santiago beams, his eyes dancing with pride.

I squirm away from the undeserved pride. Carmen, who always sees too much, curiously eyes me. She exhales a small sigh when my eyes dart away from hers.

With his hand outstretched for a shake, Santiago takes two long strides toward Pastor Floyd, and a moment of silent understanding passes through them when contact is made.

Both men care for me, probably see themselves as father figures of sorts. But both care in different ways.

Santiago would never have permitted me to take painkillers after my injuries had healed. And I would have listened to him.

Pastor Floyd, with his tender heart, only wanted to help, and I let him, knowing full well where the path would lead. My mom, being an addict, had strengthened my resolve and fueled my fate. When Pastor Floyd tried to reason with me, to get me to stop, I didn't listen. Instead, I pressured him, manipulated him, until he caved and got me more drugs.

"I've heard a lot about you," Pastor Floyd tells Santiago and Carmen.

Carmen rests her hand on my shoulder. "You're the pastor who's taken care of our boy?"

Pastor Floyd nods.

"Thank you," she says.

There are a lot of things I could say. They hover on the tip of my tongue but remain unsaid, withering in the stagnant air. My tortured soul hears through the silence though, and the hands from my punishment strangle me.

Santiago's phone chirps a nineties pop song from the Spice Girls, and I chuckle at his embarrassment when he scurries away with the phone.

"Yan," Carmen explains and I jerk away from the sound of Yanelys's name.

My face begins to tingle, the first sign of an upcoming migraine, and I push the button for morphine. Pastor Floyd shakes his head, disappointment dripping from his eyes, but I ignore him when I see a small drip fall.

Migraines have become a side effect to living, and since the earthquake in Haiti, I've been graced with them on a regular basis.

"Say that again!" Santiago barks into the phone.

Everyone in the room turns their attention to him.

Santiago raises a finger at us, his way of letting us know he's too busy to speak to us. After a lot of head-shaking and grunting, he finally says, "I'm on my way."

Carmen crosses the room and places a delicate hand on his arm, and he turns to her.

Santiago rubs his hands across his face and grunts. "Yanelys is in jail."

TWELVE

YANELYS

Camden had pushed us away, yet life or fate or God heaved him back toward us. I should have seen it coming, but I was blinded by the comfortable ease of my life.

His world isn't for me. His rejection can't hurt me anymore. I've covered those wounds with gritty sand and pretty lies. But that doesn't mean I don't still care. That I don't still see what even he can't.

His mom did this. Maybe it's intuition or simply because I know Camden and the life he led better than anyone else, but I'm certain of it.

Fueled by assumptions, I leave the hospital. I go to the building Camden had been found in and search alleyways and other abandoned buildings nearby until I find her sleeping under a bridge by a small river.

She's covered in dirt, her thinning hair matted. Her presence slithers over my skin like a disease. Much smaller than I remember, she doesn't intimidate me anymore.

When I awake her, somber silence passes between us, but then her vacant eyes recognize me. She stands and her lips turn into a malicious smile, her eyes calculating me through the haze of sleep and drugs.

"He's just like me." His mom laughs.

Spite and conceit clamp their claws into me, wrapping me tightly.

"He's everything you hate." A scornful smile twists her lips, her self-righteousness lacing through her words.

"You set the building he was in on fire," I accuse, my rattled nerves colliding against one another in my chest.

"He prefers pills over any other drug." She scratches a scab on her chin, and the grime under her once manicured fingernails repulses me.

"You tried to kill your own son!" I stalk toward her and shove her hard, making her stumble to the ground. My breaths heave in and out of my chest, but I stand firm, looking down at her.

"Camden's nothing to me!" She pushes herself off the concrete floor but loses her balance and falls. Her eyes narrow, pinning me with a purposeful stare. "He's nothing to you either. He's better off dead before he spends all of *my* money on *his* addiction."

Anger rolls off of me in waves, leaving my limbs shaking in its wake. My heart trembles with sore emotions. I leap on top of her, pinning her body to the ground, while my hands wrap around her neck, and my fingers squeeze. Blinded by the sight of the malice that continues to pass over her face, I screech.

Lost in the past and the evil that Camden endured by her hands, I never see the person who slams into my body and throws me off of Camden's mom.

I quickly stand up, ready to pounce on her and her protector, until I see the man in blue standing before me.

A police officer. Not just any officer, but my dad's oldest friend. Of course.

"Henry," I huff in greeting.

Brushing dirt from my knees, I take my time before I meet his gaze. My dad will hear of this, and while he'll understand why I came here, he'll also reprimand me. Twenty-four years old or fourteen years old—it doesn't matter—I'm still Daddy's girl, and I hate upsetting him.

My white Converse are slightly torn, so I fixate on the tear rather than the pair of eyes watching me, questioning me.

Henry's laughter breaks my concentration. Finally discovering the courage to look up at him, I find him holding Maureen by her shoulder. She squirms under the weight of his hands without any real will to fight him off.

When our eyes meet, he arches a brow in question. I explain myself and tell him about Camden and my confirmed suspicion that Camden's mom was the one who set last night's fire. She doesn't deny it or reply when he questions her.

"Police are here for a reason." Henry's voice is stern, his eyes strict and lined with wrinkles on the sides.

Squinting back at him, I tip my chin upward. "You gonna arrest me, Henry?"

"Yep"—his brow straightens—"that'll make for a fun Thanksgiving dinner."

My lips twitch. Thanksgiving is only two weeks away and always the spectacle with Henry and my family getting more than our fill of food and drinks.

"My mom would poison your food." I smile while Maureen tries to shrug out of Henry's firm grasp.

"She'd give me the runs for days," he agrees, "and probably hold back on her famous *cafecito*."

"She'll probably do that anyway because you knocked over her little girl."

"Don't tell your parents." Henry coughs, narrowing his eyes at me. "I'll never be invited to Thanksgiving dinner again." His voice, etched with worry, makes me giggle.

"I'll make sure to let my parents know you only want them for their turkey."

"You're the devil," he says behind a smile. "What happened to the sweet girl I knew?"

What happened? Maureen did. Her husband did.

Even when Camden no longer lived with his parents, they always stood between us. Until they drove him away.

Maureen breaks up our banter with a hacking cough that I hope she chokes on.

"Maureen," Henry addresses Camden's mom with a tired sigh as he slips handcuffs over her wrists.

"I didn't do anything, Henry," she whines.

"I'm sure you heard Yanelys. Your son was involved in an accident last night. Our lead detective has been investigating the case, and all the evidence points toward foul play. You're our prime suspect."

When Henry looks over at me, I shrink away from his knowing glance. Of course they are investigating the fire. My dad wouldn't be happy until they found the person responsible.

"I'm sorry for coming down here." The tip of my right shoe pushes the gravel as shame washes over me. "I hope I didn't cause any trouble."

"Oh, Yan." Henry ruffles my hair, instantly making me feel better. "Follow me to the station and you can give your statement on what Maureen told you."

"You locked my daughter up?" My dad's voice booms over the noise in the jail and I can hear him clearly from my prison cell.

After I spoke with the Chief of Police, Camden's mom confessed to starting the fire in the building where Camden was squatting. Only she didn't stop there. Because she's a ruthless bitch, she went one step further and told Henry and everyone who could hear her that she wanted to press charges against me.

I assaulted her. It's true. I could've denied it, or better yet, I should've told them it was self-defense, but the truth is, I'd kill her without immediate cause. After speaking with the Chief, I was put me in a solitary prison cell while Henry called my dad.

Hence all the screaming.

Flushed, my dad charges into the room I'm being held in and growls when he sees me behind bars. My mom chuckles, shaking her head in bewilderment at my predicament.

"Hey, Dad." I wave and smile at my mom, who winks at me.

"Henry," my dad warns as he points at me.

Henry lifts his arms in a sign of retreat and sighs. "My hands are tied, Santiago. The only way Maureen will drop the charges against Yanelys is if we drop the arson charges."

"No!" I shout. On weak knees, I run to the bars, bracing myself against them. "You can't do that, Henry," I plead with him. "She can't get away with this."

"And what should we tell your daughter, Yanelys?" My dad turns his angry eyes on me.

My heart pounds behind the thin fabric of my shirt and I cower.

I hadn't thought of Olivia.

THIRTEEN

YANELYS

Muffled footsteps jolt me awake but disappear into the ensuing darkness. With my surroundings too quiet, I burrow myself deeper under my covers, bringing my knees closer to my chest. Movement from the corner of my cell catches my attention, but when my eyes scan in its direction, I find the space empty. The vision of ghosts rack my brain, so I shut my eyes and hide my face under the covers.

Thanks to Henry putting me in a solitary cell, I don't have to worry about inmates, but fear still drapes over me, making me shudder. Unreasonable or not, I hate ghosts, and damn Henry to hell and back for sharing so many ghost stories with me throughout the years.

I'm not the first person to spend a night or two in jail. There have been millions before me. In this very prison, there have been hundreds of habitants. While I can't see them, I take solace in believing that, just like me, they spent their first night just as scared.

The food Henry brought me for dinner was awful, and I'm pretty sure he took great delight in seeing me struggle through a few bites before I put it to the side. This is one big funny joke to him, which makes it seem at least a little funny to me. My parents, on the other hand, are furious. I'm pretty sure my mom is, at this very moment, planning the perfect punishment for me rather than drifting off to sleep.

But it's worth it, knowing Maureen will pay for what she did to Camden. I'd spend a month in here if I had to. I hope I don't though.

My daughter needs her mother, and I need her. She's the source of everything that's good in my life. She's my laughter, my joy, the very heart that beats in my chest.

While she's too young to understand, I want her to know, to take pride in knowing, that I'd do just about anything for what's right. And me sleeping in this cold cell is right.

It's the only way I know I can ensure life is, for once, giving Maureen the hand she deserves. Just once, I want her to pay for the pain she's caused Camden.

Just once. I don't think that's too much to ask.

But fate has never been on Camden's side. His parents got away with years of abuse and neglect. Not once did they ever think about Camden. About the little boy they tormented. About the man she tried to *kill*.

Herb died, never knowing the backhand of Karma. Maureen has existed without ever showing the tiniest bit of remorse. I know because, in all the years I searched for Camden, I kept coming across Maureen. Her addiction has taken over every aspect of who she is that she's barely recognizable anymore. The refined, bitter woman of my youth has been replaced with sunken, tired eyes and a worn body.

Today, I made a decision and went against my parents. I stood up for Camden, for the boy who had left me, and the man who couldn't look away from me when I walked into his hospital room.

Familiar anger grounded me, but eventually, the pain bled through and made room for the love Camden and I have always shared. The bond we share is insane, incomprehensible. I should hate him. Hell, it'd be easier if I did.

Instead, now that he's back, my emotions run rampant in all different directions, including hate, but mostly love and gratitude. I've missed him. I've worried about him. I've prayed for his return while wishing he'd never entered my life.

Sweat builds at the base of my neck, saliva thickening, as these controversial feelings continue to swim and swirl and torment me. Abruptly, I push the sheets away from me and stand up on weak knees that carry me to a nearby trash bin. Tears cloud my vision, bile rising inch by intolerable inch, and I empty the anxiety thrashing in my stomach into the trash. My limbs shake, and I crouch down onto the cold floor, my fingers grasping the sides of the bin. I wait for the nausea to subside, but instead, I dry-heave into the dense air. More unwelcome tears fall, and my knuckles turn white as my grip tightens.

And I know, I know, *I know* I can't do this. I can't see Camden when I get out of here, although he'll want to see me. I can't face him, knowing he abandoned me. Knowing he'll look at my daughter and wonder. Knowing he'll flee again and break me even further.

Because, even though I can't do this again, I know I will, just on the off chance that he'll stay.

Camden is my weakness. My kryptonite of sorts. And no matter how angry and hurt and scared of him I am, I can't turn away. I just hope my parents buy me some time before they bring him to my house. Not that it'd matter because I'd never be ready to see him again, to let him back into my life.

Wiping my mouth with the back of my trembling hand, I stand up and shuffle my tired feet to the hard bed where I lie down and send out a silent prayer for an impenetrable heart.

FOURTEEN

CAMDEN

Each day, I've put on my masks and played my role in the dramatic piece that is my life. I've smiled on cue, laughed and eaten when I was supposed to. The only time I've been true to myself has been when I helped Pastor Floyd with the church. I cleaned the floors and painted the exterior of the run-down trailers that house his church as well as the office that has been my home for years. I mowed the lawn and pulled out weeds. I made sure the volunteers ate and had plenty of coffee to fuel them. I felt useful during those times.

But night inevitably creeps in and morning follows. And those periods in between morning and night, my sins become more obvious. The masks melt away as unsealed wounds continue to tear open, hatred and anger heating through my veins.

In front of my bed, the clock hanging on the dull wall ticks loudly, each second hitting my wasted heart like a hammer. My fingers twitch by my sides, and when the pulsing in my head magnifies, I reach for the morphine and hit the button. Unsatisfied, I open the bottle I've hidden under my pillow and take two pills, needing my mind to rest. To not scream reminders of my pathetic life at me.

I manage a smile when a nurse opens my door.

"You're awake," she says, stating the obvious.

My fake smile grows, and I look back at the clock, realizing it isn't even four in the morning yet. "Couldn't sleep."

"Hospitals are noisy. Lucky for you, you're going home today."

My head bobs up and down a couple of times, not really caring. I extend my arm for her while she takes my blood pressure, but I pull away when she tries to remove the tape holding my IV in place.

"What are you doing?" I bark, my eyes narrowing into slits.

An amicable smile spreads across her face, making my jumbled nerves somersault toward hysteria.

"You were very fortunate, Mr. Riley." She grips my arm, and with one quick tear, she strips the tape off my skin and removes the IV, quickly putting a Band-Aid in its place. "Your burns aren't anywhere near as bad as they should've been, so the doctor ordered us to remove your morphine drip."

"But I'm in pain." Even to my own ears, I sound desperate.

She pats my shoulder, sympathy washing over her face. "I know, honey. I'll bring you some ibuprofen after I clean your burns and put on new bandages."

Meticulously, she cleans each burn and chatters softly in my ear. I bite the inside of my cheek, not listening to her. All I hear, all I understand, is that I'll no longer be getting morphine.

Fuck.

My brain buzzes with the new information, and bile rises to my throat, but I swallow it down. I close my eyes and count the seconds as they tick off the clock.

One.

Two.

Three...

"You have someone looking out for you," the nurse says when she finishes dressing my burns. Once again, she pats my shoulder before she leaves.

The very idea that some holy being is out there, looking out for me, is laughable, but I don't bother telling her. I'd rather let her live out her life in blissful denial than tell her the truth. I'm not lucky. If I were lucky, the fire would've consumed me and left me for dead.

When she returns and offers me ibuprofen and apple juice, I take the two pills and swallow them.

"Now, try to get some rest," she advises.

Alone again, I close my eyes and let the drugs coursing through my system take effect.

FIFTEEN

CAMDEN

Like a terminal disease, I'm draining the life out of the very people I wanted to save when I left seven years ago. But Santiago and Carmen won't let me go, not for a second time. Although I know my existence will eventually debilitate them, I follow them out of the hospital and back into their home.

They are my peace in this cruel and unapologetic world. They are my one hope of becoming the man they see.

They are the parents God mocked me with, dangled in front of my face, making me believe I could have them for my own. But they aren't mine to keep.

I belong to my own parents, to their vices that I all too happily obliterate myself with.

Shortly after Santiago and Carmen left to see what Yanelys had done to get herself imprisoned, Pastor Floyd gave me two bottles—one full with anti-anxiety pills and the other with two different types of opiates. I ignored Pastor Floyd's disapproval as I placed the time-release pill on my tray and smashed it into powder.

"Camden." Pastor Floyd's voice was distant, but I could taste his bitter disappointment in the back of my throat just after I snorted the powder.

Leaning into my uncomfortable pillow, I closed my eyes and thought of nothing. Longing for the indifference I found at the bottom of a bottle, I waited for the pill to take effect.

Emptied by the world, I held hands with destruction and opened my eyes just in time to watch Pastor Floyd's tired body turn and leave.

Every day, Santiago and Carmen would come to see me at the hospital, never once speaking of Yanelys or the trouble she'd gotten herself into. Carmen stayed by my side and held my hand when my doctor ordered my first skin graft.

Yanelys, on the other hand, stayed away. Every day, I'd look at the door whenever it swung open, and every day, when she didn't walk through it, disappointment would run over my face. It hung on my shoulders, weighing me down, as I waited for the girl who had finally given up on me.

Growing up, I held on to the idea that, one day, my parents would love me with the same ferocity they hated. I watched them, I silently pleaded with them, and I waited for them to be parents, but I loved them, no matter what they had done to me.

Now, that energy and affection is focused on Yanelys. She controls my heartbeat. Every thump is for her.

I have no right to ask her to see me, to beg her to love me, but as I sit in Santiago's car and listen to Carmen talk, I know that's exactly what I'm going to do. Yanelys touches me. Her warmth wraps itself around me, despite the days or years that have passed since I last saw her.

Tired lungs breathe in a sigh, and I try to remember what it was like not to live in tragedy. I was granted five years of peace with the people who still call themselves my family.

Carmen's hand rests on Santiago's as he drives, their love filling the empty space around us. I want that. I want to experience it for myself.

"I want to see Yan," I say from the backseat, interrupting whatever Carmen was saying. I cough. "I mean, can you drop me off at her place, so I can speak to her?"

"Not today, Cam." Carmen turns around and squeezes my knee. "There's so much about her you don't know."

"Is she seeing someone?" Fear grips my heart like a vise.

Carmen laughs a humorless laugh and shakes her head. Still, the tension in the car rises, and I wonder what they aren't sharing with me.

"Please?" I ask again, turning my attention to Santiago.

Santiago sighs and glances over at Carmen. Her lips form a thin, straight line, but she doesn't reply to his unspoken question.

"I'll call her," Carmen offers. "If she says no, then you'll wait until she's ready."

I nod, swallowing the lump in my throat.

"He wants to see you," Carmen whispers into the phone in place of a greeting.

The silence in the car grows thick, and I fidget with the single pill in my pocket. With the bottle hidden in the bag the hospital gave me to keep the few items I own, I have only this one companion to comfort me.

"I know, sweetie. It's up to you," Carmen finally replies.

The pill in my pocket grows heavy, its secret screaming louder than the silence. My jaw tightens as I wait for an answer.

"Okay." Carmen sighs. "I love you."

The complexity of my situation slams itself into my stomach. Overflowing with confessions I'm not ready to share, I avert my eyes when Carmen turns around in her seat and looks back at me.

"Okay." She smiles a watery smile. "Yan said you could come over."

Relief. Joy. I haven't felt those emotions in a long time. I hardly recognize them.

"There are some things you should know first." Carmen eyes Santiago, and he nods.

"What?" I ask, preparing myself for the worst.

"We'll talk about it over doughnuts," Santiago says.

Although he smiles back at me through the rearview mirror, apprehension glosses over his eyes.

"Tell me now," I push.

Santiago lifts an eyebrow. "Son, when you walked out on your family, you lost the right to demand things from us." His grip on the steering wheel tightens, making his knuckles whiten. "We'll talk at the doughnut store. And, Cam"—his voice is laced with warning—"you weren't here. You don't know what Yan went through. You can be upset with what you missed out on, just like she has every right to be disappointed with your decisions, but these emotions aren't going to get either of you anywhere."

"What do you mean, Yan has a daughter?"

Anger poisons my heart, and without thinking, I take the pill from my pocket and swallow it dry in front of Santiago and Carmen. I pretend not to see their quick exchange or the worry creasing their foreheads.

I see red.

And a baby who isn't mine.

"How old is she?"

"Six," Carmen replies.

"Six?" I laugh, bitterness slicing through me. "Didn't take her long to get over me," I spit, "and get under someone else."

"Listen here!" Santiago roars, slamming the palms of his hands on the table.

Carmen flinches and sends an apologetic look to the patrons in the shop, but my eyes remain on the man I've loved since I was a boy.

"You will not disrespect my daughter." Santiago keeps his voice dangerously low. "I don't care what you think or how hurt you are, you will respect her, Camden."

Rage spreads throughout my body, destroying common sense, and for once, I don't want to love the man and woman before me.

I want to hate them. As much as I hate myself. As much as I hate loving Yanelys.

When I stand to leave, Santiago's hand grips my arm and holds me there. I stare back at him, unflinching.

"Whose is she?" I ask, ready to kill the man who thought he was worthy of touching Yanelys.

"She's Yan's," Carmen answers while Santiago and I continue to stare at each other.

My eyes flit over to Carmen, and after registering the fear behind her eyes, I release the tension in my body and sit down, scraping the bottom of the chair over the floor.

"Who's the dad?"

"Cam"—Carmen places a hand on my wrist—"you left her. You were gone so long."

"I'm disappointed in you," Santiago interjects, taking his seat in front of me again. "You of all people should stand by Yanelys and not tear her down."

The sound of Santiago's words grate on my chest and will haunt me to my grave. But I've only begun disappointing him. I hate the looks in both their eyes, and I know I'm the only one to blame.

"I'm sorry." The threat of tears blurs my vision so I stare at the table.

My bandaged hands run over my face over and over again. But still, the condemnation of her forgotten love remains, alienating me even further.

"Her name is Olivia," Carmen says, her eyes brimming with pride. "She is a beautiful little girl, looks just like her mom."

The idea of Olivia looking like her mom brings me a hint of joy. Yanelys's beauty should be shared, and there's no better tribute than with a little girl who looks just like her.

"She has Yanelys's oomph for life." Carmen laughs, and despite myself, I join her.

How I've missed the oomph Yanelys brought me.

"And her dad's intensity," Carmen adds.

I wince, connecting with the sorrow her words bring.

Stripped of everything good, my bleeding heart welcomes her truth. Carmen's sympathetic eyes roll over me, so I look away, but curiosity forces me to know.

"Who's the girl's dad?" I ask through clenched teeth.

"You," Carmen says barely above a whisper.

Confusion fills me, and I catch Santiago's unrestrained gaze.

"You didn't just leave us"—Santiago waves a hand toward Carmen and himself—"or Yan. You left your daughter."

I hear his words, my own thoughts echoing in my mind, and reality sets in.

By leaving, I thought I was giving Yanelys a chance at a real future. I thought I was hurting only myself. But sharp edges aligned our broken love, and the pieces continued to shatter as I stayed away and broke us even more.

My heart, the part that still cares, throbs with regret, all the broken pieces flowing together to slice through my chest. And I wonder if I can even remember my life without the heartbreak. Without this searing agony.

I'm back, but there's no one to come back to. There's no home, no place where I belong.

I mask the pain with an uneasy smile. "I have a daughter?" I swallow.

As I nervously tap my foot under the table, sweat begins to build at the base of my neck. With trembling fingers, I lift a hand to Carmen, not wanting her to go on.

But I drop my hand in my lap and clench it closed. Frustrated, I unwrap the bandages, exposing the angry red marks.

The shop is too quiet, too loud, too much.

My pills, just one more pill, would grant me the escape I need. My fingers itch, but I remain planted on the seat with heavy legs I can't move.

"You have a daughter," Santiago confirms.

Relief floods me. And hope.

The mangled wad of napkin that somehow ended up in my hand is taken from me by Carmen. She closes a tight fist over it and smiles slightly.

"Did you honestly think there was ever anyone but you?" Small tears roll down her cheek, and she wipes each one away before they drip off her chin. "I won't lie to you, Cam. I kept praying there would be, so she'd get over you."

I wince again but understand. The idea of Yanelys hurting alone brings me nothing but misery.

Unease advances on me, the air buzzing anxiously around us, making sweat pool down my cold skin. Nausea hits me, and I swallow hard to keep it at bay. The itching in my fingers increases and spreads across my hand to my arms. My foot bounces as Carmen tells me about my daughter, but my rattled nerves make it difficult for me to sit still. Without giving a reason, I excuse myself and go to Santiago's car where I'll find my pills inside the hospital bag.

Outside, the gravel crunches beneath my fast-paced steps. The peaceful sky spans around me, the scattered white clouds uncaring of the storm brewing within me. I pull on the car door handle and cuss when it doesn't open.

Wild with desperation, I spin around and crash into Santiago's broad chest. He grabs my shoulders and steadies me as my legs grow heavier.

"Cam."

My name echoes in my head.

"What's going on?"

"Migraine," I lie, keeping my eyes on the ground.

"Okay, take it easy, son."

Santiago squeezes my shoulders once, and I hunch over when he unlocks the car door and opens it. Rummaging through my bag, he pulls out the bottles Pastor Floyd gave me and shakes them after reading the label.

"Your doctor didn't prescribe these."

"No."

My shoulders hunch over even further as reality exposes me as a liar. A junkie.

"Where'd you get them?" he asks.

Unable to meet his eyes, I fidget with a tear in my shirt.

"I asked you a question, Camden." His firm tone slaps me.

My face inks red with embarrassment, but I try to laugh it off.

"I need them." I shrug.

"These aren't migraine pills, Camden!" Santiago shakes the bottle inches away from my face. "They're drugs! Fucking drugs!"

"Santiago," Carmen pleads when she walks up to us. She places a calming hand on his shoulder, which only seems to infuriate him further.

"Drugs, Carmen," he hisses. "Our boy left us to become a junkie." Santiago runs his hands over his face several times.

Shame weaves itself into my soul, darkening me even more. It's a battle I can't win, and as each second passes, the need for another pill increases.

"Santiago," I breathe his name softly. "I need another pill."

The turmoil whipping its way around us makes me tremble. Understanding crosses Santiago's face, and he opens up the bottle. Putting a pill in his palm, he extends his hand. When I take the pill from him, he grips my wrist and pulls me to him.

Santiago wraps his arms around me in a tight embrace. "We're gonna get you clean, Cam. You and me—we're in this together, and we're gonna get you clean."

I hug him back, and my rapid breaths fall on his shoulder as he runs soothing circles over my back.

"Take your pill, go see Yan, and meet your little girl. Then, we'll go away. It'll be our first men's trip, just the two of us."

When Santiago lets me go, I take the pill—my worst enemy, my loyal companion—and I prepare myself to see Yanelys…and my daughter.

SIXTEEN

YANELYS

Through all the fights and bad dreams, through the abuse and lies, I loved Camden. I stayed faithfully by his side. I never wavered. No matter what his parents did to him or said to him, I was proud to stand with him. To fight with him.

I loved him in the truest way.

When he left me, pregnant and alone, I hated him in the truest way, too.

It took months of my parents and me searching for him to realize the truth behind what my mom had always said. We were too young. My feelings, though very real, were too much, too consuming, and when he left, I was numb to everything but the pain of my gaping heart.

Countless tears were shed over the loneliness I felt for both myself and the little girl I thought would never meet her dad.

How many times did Olivia ask about her dad? Still, I told her what a good man her dad was, how strong he was, how much he loved her. She'd listen without understanding because all she knew to be true was that her dad was missing. *And how could someone who loved her not be around?*

I locked away my anger and grief, and every morning, I smile at the little girl who gave me life. Mom, dad, teacher, nurse, and friend—I've played those roles with pride. Despite the constant ache in my chest, I've given every part of myself into being a mom. Because, in the end, Olivia looks up to me to give her a happy childhood.

But hope lingered, and now that Camden's back in my life, my love for him clashes with the hate.

I don't want to love him. I don't want our love to cease either.

I don't want to see him. But I don't want him to leave me again.

Hearing the doorbell ring, I pat the top of Olivia's head and run my hands through her long dark hair before I answer it. Her light brown eyes follow me, and I stick my tongue out at her, making her giggle, before she focuses her attention back on the television.

My fingers toy with the fabric of my shirt as I walk through the hallway of my house toward the door. My chest tightens as I grip the doorknob, and air escapes from my lungs when the man I both love and hate stands between my parents. I nod once, promising my heart I won't let it get hurt again, and I step back to let them in.

Camden's throat bobs, and his lips part, as if to say something, but he shuts it when I cross my hands over my chest. I clench my fists and hug myself tighter when I see the visible bruises on his face. His hands, marred red by his own mother's doing, fall limply to his sides. The air in the room closes in around us, and I swallow hard, trying to get rid of the lump forming in my throat.

Even as a teenager, Camden looked strong. But the man standing in front of me is small. Although he still has broad shoulders, he's too skinny, too withdrawn, too much like a stranger.

My Rottweiler runs toward Camden only to stop once she's on top of his leg. His eyes fill with fear and dart in my direction. So he doesn't see me smile, I cover my mouth with my hands but I can't hold back the laughter.

"That's Nisa." I pull her off of him and pat her head when she simply leans onto him. "She's a bit needy, so if she gets on your nerves, just push her with your foot. Not hard or anything," I instruct. Having lost the ability to shut the hell up, I continue speaking, "She's already traumatized enough."

Camden's mouth turns down, and the memory of his lips pressed against mine floods me, drowning out all common sense.

"When she was a puppy, a guy I'm no longer friends with came over for a barbeque. He was going through a bad divorce and drinking," I ramble.

When his tongue peeks out and caresses his lips, I turn my attention to the wall behind him.

"When he started crying, my friends and I tried to console him, but only Nisa was able to get him to stop when she curled up on his lap."

I bite my lip, wanting but not able to prevent the words from spilling out of my mouth. Needing to occupy my hands, I let my hair down from its ponytail, only to put it back up into a loose bun on the top of my head.

"It was going fine at first. He was just petting her, but then she got up and licked his face. Before we knew it, her tongue was all over his mouth. I don't know why he let her, but there was a lot of tongue."

A disgusted sound comes from the back of Camden's throat, and I put both my hands up and fake a smile for his benefit.

"I know. But none of us knew what to do, so we just kind of left them and went inside. It was wrong—I know that—but what do you do in a situation like that?"

Rather than responding, he blinks at me. That's it. He just blinks. I'm such a tool.

"That was a really weird thing for me to say to someone I haven't seen in seven years. Can I start over?" With my tongue still too loose, I don't wait for him to reply. "This is Nisa," I make unnecessary introductions again. "She's a sweetie, but she can get too friendly sometimes."

"Is she going to try to slip me some tongue?" he asks.

His blue eyes search mine, flickering with his emotions. My face heats up when he licks his lips again, and I look around my house for a hole to crawl into.

My dad laughs at our awkwardness and pats Camden on the shoulder. My mom crosses over to me and kisses my cheek. My dad quickly follows suit.

"We'll take Olivia out back," my mom says.

Hearing the word *out*, Nisa lets out an emphatic bark and runs to the back door.

"That way, you two can talk privately," she adds.

I nod, breathing through the knots growing in my stomach.

"Can I meet her first?" Camden asks.

With his shoulders slumped and his eyes downcast, I can hardly see the boy I once knew. But he's in there somewhere, and every part of me wants to find him. More than that, I want Camden to find himself.

Whatever I've been through without him is nothing compared to what he's been through. Forgiveness creeps into my heart, slightly freeing me of the weight I've carried for seven long years.

I can't hate the boy who left me any more than I can prevent my lungs from breathing.

"Sure."

Smiling broadly, I take Camden's hand, and although he winces in pain, he still laces his fingers through mine.

Warm familiarity sears into my skin while butterflies explode in my stomach, expelling the knot I just had moments ago. Turning on the tips of my feet, I spin around to face him. He arches an eyebrow, and I laugh.

He's still my Camden. He's also Olivia's dad.

He might have left me, but he also gave me the best parting present imaginable.

Without reservation, I tightly wrap my arms around his stomach and rest my head on his chest, listening to his erratic heartbeat.

So skinny, I think when I reach around and clasp my hands behind his back.

Camden doesn't hesitate as he puts his arms around me, leaning his head on top of mine.

"You left me," I whisper into his chest.

He lifts his head and takes my hair out of the bun. He begins to comb his fingers through my hair and I hold back a sigh. "I know."

Two words. That's all it takes to break my resolve.

Face flushed with resentment, I push off of him and square my shoulders. "You left me with just a memory!" I accuse. "You tore me to pieces, and now? Now, you want to come back into my life. No. No, no, no, Camden! You don't get to pick and choose when I'm convenient."

I shove him again, each shove getting harder, until his back is against the wall. Tears stream down my face, the witnesses of my despair. When I move to walk away from him, Camden takes ahold of my hand and brings me to him. He wraps his arms around me, pressing my body to his, until we are flush with one another. Struggling in his grasp, I lift my head to yell at him, but he crushes his lips against mine.

"I'm sorry," he murmurs against my mouth. "I'm sorry, Yan. I'm sorry," he continues to whisper between the light kisses he presses into me.

The taste of his despair is my undoing, so I kiss him back. Harder, wanting to take away his pain.

When we finally separate, we look at each other, breathless. Words go unspoken as our panting settles.

"So," my mom says, her voice nonchalant.

Our eyes dart to my parents, who we had forgotten about in the heat of the moment. Embarrassed, I slide my bare foot against the cool tile and squirm away from their watchful eyes.

"Do you still want to meet Livvy?" I ask Camden.

"Yeah," he whispers, taking my hand in his.

Drowning in the misery and compassion I find in his eyes, I squeeze his hand. Our fingers entwined together feels natural, like an extension of myself. I guide us through my house and breathe deeply when we enter my living room.

"Livvy," I call out.

At the sound of her name, Olivia hops off the couch but not quick enough. I turn my lips down into a frown and look at her while she dances in place with an overabundance of energy.

"What were you doing?" My lips twitch.

"Watchin' TV." Olivia bounces on the heel of her foot.

"On your head?" I ask and she nods. "Is that how ladies are supposed to sit?"

"Ita thinks it's funny," she answers me, and I throw my mom a sideways glance as Olivia launches herself into my mom's arms. My mom holds her close to her body and brushes her lips over Olivia's hair. Her unmanageable, wild hair. Just like mine.

Pride spills from my heart every time I see her, and I'm reminded that she's mine. She was born from a love that lifted me. A love I hunger for. The pain from it's still visible in the scarring of my heart.

"Olivia," my dad says, pulling her into his arms for a hug as well, "we want you to meet someone."

My dad gestures to Camden, and Olivia narrows her eyes at him in speculation. Camden stiffens under her perceptive gaze and his throat bobs several times. Nervous hands shove into his front jean pockets and his anxiety reaches me.

"This is one of your mom's oldest friends," my mom explains, placing a hand on Camden's shoulder. "Her very best friend growing up."

Olivia's face lights up as an innocent smile spreads across her face. She wiggles out of my dad's arms and runs to Camden, who waits for her on his knees. When Olivia puts her arms around his neck, Camden burrows his face in her hair.

"You're Cam," Olivia confidently tells him.

My face flushes, my eyes widening in shock. The little brat pays more attention to what I've said than I ever realized.

Camden's eyes meet mine and he laughs. His laughter floods into the room, becoming a living thing that bounces off the walls.

"I am," Camden agrees, facing his daughter and the lines of his face soften as contentment gentles his features.

Heat rises up my neck when he winks at me.

"Mommy has a picture of you in her room. Wanna see?"

"Uh...I, um..." I stammer.

Everyone looks at me, my dad smiling a devilish smile, and they all wait for me to continue.

My heart stutters. Even after all this time, after all the heartache, I want him with a desperation that possesses me and a ferocity that both terrifies and excites me.

What was broken could be mended. We could love one another again. We need that love, the vitality of our existence. The only thing that would continue to hurt is if we held back from one another.

87

"I have a picture of your mom, too," Camden whispers into the ensuing silence.

His fixed gaze meets mine, and I open my mouth in shock.

"Want to see?"

Olivia's head bobs up and down as she rocks on her heels in anticipation. Camden pulls out his wallet, and his fingers explore the crevices for a short moment before he brings out a tattered wallet-sized picture.

Shifting away from the picture, I close my eyes as small tremors shake through me.

Olivia giggles when he hands her my picture, but I don't turn to see which picture he kept.

Strong hands touch my shoulder and turn me. After a reassuring squeeze, Camden places his hands on either side of my face, brushing his thumbs over my cheeks. In turn, I grip his shoulders, needing to hold on and hoping he won't let go this time.

As he leans toward me, the air between us shifts, making me shiver. His hands cup the back of my head, and I tilt upward, anticipation of his silent promise building in my stomach. His mouth, warm and soft, touches mine, kissing me slowly. My chest explodes with a whirlwind of emotion slamming against my rib cage. His body presses against mine, and my fingers roam over his back, feeling his muscles tense under my touch.

Too quickly, he pulls away. My eyes stay on his as his lips spread into a small smile.

"I also kept this." He tucks a piece of paper in my hand.

Turning my attention to what I'm holding, I open it and blink back tears when the fake airplane ticket I made him for his eleventh birthday stares back at me.

My mouth widens into a small O, an ache building in my heart. From the corner of my eye, I see my parents usher Olivia out of the room.

"You kept this?" I whisper.

"Did you think I wouldn't?"

I shrug. "You didn't keep me."

My words are out before I can stop them, and I immediately regret them when pain flashes over Camden's features. His agony takes me suddenly and quickly. Camden covers his face with his hands, so I take them in mine and bring them to my lips.

"It doesn't matter," I whisper, kissing the side of Camden's mouth. "We're starting new. Right now."

He searches my face, his eyes roaming, seeking, finally finding the truth behind my words. I stare at his lips as they curve into a smile, and the need to kiss him is intolerably intense. My tongue sneaks out and passes over my lips. His eyes regard me with an infectious joy, and I return his smile, but I back away from him and the need to feel his lips on me again.

SEVENTEEN

CAMDEN

Sweat gathered on the palm of my hand when I stood in front of Yanelys's door with Carmen and Santiago beside me. Words I wanted to tell her jumbled on my swollen tongue, but I was unable to get them out so I could speak. But when Yanelys and then Olivia wrapped their arms around me, I exhaled the breath I'd been holding in for seven years. My heart, mind, and soul rejoiced.

It felt too real but also like a sweet fabrication. I couldn't even remember anything but my rattled nerves from the time I got out of Santiago's car up until the moment Yanelys was in my arms. When her arms wrapped tightly around my body, my reality stopped feeling like the ill-fated nightmare I'd been living through most of my life. My mind became overcrowded, but I thought of nothing. Needing more, I kissed her. My heart thumped erratically. I felt peace.

Our emotions run so thick in the air, we can touch it. So, we touch each other. A stray hair pushed behind her ear. A tender caress over my battered face. Worn knuckles over her delicate skin.

I touch her, needing a reminder that I'm loved. I touch her again to soothe the wounded part of me that'll always believe there's nothing left in me worthy of love. Worthy of saving.

When we sit on the couch in her living room and our knees knock against one another, I kiss her again, loving her with the same ease I've loved her with my whole life.

"My beautiful Yan."

My forehead meets hers, and I breathe her in.

"Am I yours, Cam?" she whispers, her voice laced with anguish.

"If you'll let me back in. Please let me back in." My lips press to her tear-stained cheek as my throat burns with emotion.

Yanelys pulls away and bites her bottom lip when it trembles. "What if you leave again?"

"I won't," I promise. "Even if you don't love me anymore, if you don't want me…" My voice breaks at the thought of her not wanting me.

She backs away a couple of inches, anger crossing over her features. "Why would you say that? I'm not the one who left. You did."

"And I left you with a daughter to raise on your own. I've given you the perfect reason to hate me." The palms of my hands itch, so I close them into tight fists. "I don't blame you if you do, Yan. Every day, I hate myself a little more," I admit.

Yanelys takes my face in her hands, and although her lips still form a thin line, her eyes reveal how she really feels, and I'm met with a love I've longed for, starved myself of.

"I love you. I want you," she says.

She wants me. After a lifetime of knowing what it is not to be loved, not to be wanted, her unrequited devotion glows like a beacon signaling me home.

"I always will," she admits, her eyes filling with tears.

"I'm sorry. Forgive me. Please forgive me," I plead.

She rests her forehead on mine.

"I'm here. I'm not going away, not ever again." I kiss her tears as they fall. "I have a daughter I want to get to know and a woman I've missed every second of every day for seven long years."

She breathes in the words I exhaled.

"You have a little girl." Yanelys's lips turn up into a radiant smile that I return.

"She looks just like you. Beautiful like her mommy."

My hands trace over her face, and Yanelys does the same, bringing her fingers to my cheek. Skin on skin, she restores my empty soul. The pills rush through my system, and it gasps for more as her fiery touch ignites my skin. Rough and healing.

"She looks like you," she counters. "Her eyes are dark like mine, but they have your shape. Her hair is as crazy as mine, but it's dark like yours."

The tips of her fingers wander over me as she describes our daughter. Each caress leaves a trail of the love I turned away from. Of the love I never lost.

Already, Olivia knows of life's imperfections. Already, I'm one of those imperfections. But I'll right my biggest mistake and slowly become her dad. In an instant, my life no longer belongs to me but to her. And to her mom.

Always to her mom.

"Tell me something about yourself," I say.

Yanelys tilts her head in question.

"Where do you work?"

"I'm the volunteer coordinator at our local animal shelter," she answers.

"Do you like it?"

"Yeah." She nods, her eyes glowing in their excitement. "It's hard, seeing all those animals without a home, but it's also rewarding." Her lips spread into a smile. "Even on the crappiest days, I get to go inside a dog's kennel and play with him or her, and my day immediately gets better."

My eyes trace her face, taking her in. Her eyes, her lips. My fingers run through her hair, playing with the soft tips.

"Your hair's darker."

She looks down, all self-conscious, and when her eyes meet mine once again, she bites her bottom lip.

"I colored it a few months ago." She shrugs. "I wanted something different."

"I like it."

Red tints her cheeks as she blushes under the intensity of my stare. Toying with the bottom of her shirt, she looks up at me through shy eyes.

"Haiti, huh?" Yanelys asks. She pulls away so that we're no longer touching, breaking the awkward but sweet moment between us.

Mute despair escapes my lungs, my spirit breaking at the thought of Jocelyn Marie and Yvon. Two beautiful souls that filled the void inside me.

In Haiti, my days were full of games I'd never played before. Through sticky fingers, dirty faces, tender hugs, broken toys, scraped knees, and wet kisses, we learned the basics of what being a kid meant. We became a family, a unit, and I promised them I'd take care of them, that I'd be their constant.

The weight of that broken promise crushes into itself.

Yanelys takes my hand, molding hers with mine. My heart beats wildly in my chest, calling her name with every thump.

Compassion spills from her eyes as she places our united hands to her chest where I can feel her heart beating just as hard as mine.

"I hurt when you hurt." She brings my hand to her mouth and brushes her lips over my knuckles. "Talk to me, Cam."

Supposedly, a person can die only once in their life. But I've died several times in mine. Once, when I left Yanelys. Again, when I woke up in the hospital after Haiti. And a third time, when I went back to nothing.

It's only when I feel her heart beating for mine that I've come back to life.

"It's messed up, Yan." I comb a hand over my face, squeezing the bridge of my nose, before I continue, "I don't even know where to start."

Yanelys rests her head on my shoulder, and I breathe in the smell of her shampoo, it's a delicate scent with a hint of lavender. Not quite the girl I remember, the woman sitting beside me is better. Sinfully sexy without even trying. Compassionate and caring. Beautiful, inside and out.

Rubbing my bandaged hands together, I start at the beginning. My time with Pastor Floyd, learning Creole and prayers that I'd later recite when I still held on to hope. Haiti and the secret beauty she held deep inside her. My voice catches in my throat when I get to the part about the earthquake, about the all-encompassing heartache and loss that followed.

The remnants of all the yesterdays wordlessly cut through the air. It bounces off the walls, crushing me each time it returns to me, hitting my chest.

"We'll find them," Yanelys whispers.

My body stiffens, and Yanelys sits up, taking my face in her hands.

"We'll find them," she speaks softly, slowly.

I look away, knowing she believes her lie.

"Cam…"

"I can't do this right now, Yan." I abruptly stand up.

Yanelys follows. "Okay"—she holds her hands up—"we'll talk about something else. Do you want me to tell you about the day Olivia was born?"

While her words are meant to soothe me, they slice right through me. I missed my daughter's birth, her first words, her first steps, her first birthday. I wasn't there to hold Yanelys and assure her that everything would be okay when the idea of having a baby got too big.

Just another failure to pile on top of the others.

"Yeah"—a forced smile crosses my face—"tell me."

Taking a seat back on the couch, I reach out to Yanelys, and when she closes her hand over mine, I pull her to me. She resists for only a moment, but inch by inch, her apprehension unravels in front of me, and I sit her on my lap. She rests her head again on my shoulder while I run lazy circles over her back, my tension easing as her breath falls on my cheek.

"I went in for a scheduled ultrasound that morning. There'd been quite a few at that point that I told my parents not to worry about going. I let my mom slept in, and I drove myself. While the technician did the scan, I knew something wasn't right. She wasn't her normal chatty self, but I was too scared to ask her anything."

My hands stop tracing small circles, and I tighten my hold around Yanelys's waist.

"Everything turned out fine, Cam." She kisses my cheek. "You saw Olivia yourself."

"But you were scared." My voice comes out hoarse, so I cough to clear it. "You were alone."

94

"Even when you weren't here, you were never so far away that I couldn't reach you. I always felt you with me. I'd talk to you." Yanelys laughs, and a light blush creeps up her neck and stains her cheeks.

I'm reminded once again that, while our bond is strong, we're still strangers to each other. I hate seeing her battle between her love for me and the discomfort and sadness I bring her.

"Every day, I'd talk to you and tell you about my day and about Olivia. You were never completely gone."

"How? After everything I've done to you, how can you still love me?" I ask for what seems like the hundredth time.

"How can I not?" she replies, shaking her head against my shoulder. "It'd be easier if I could hate you. A part of me wants to. Anyway, back to my ultrasound." She laughs. "After the technician finished, she patted my leg, told me to get dressed and that my doctor would be in shortly. I wanted to call my mom, but I didn't. I didn't know what was happening yet, and I didn't want to worry her, so I waited. It felt like hours had passed before the doctor arrived." She laughs again and softly kisses me on my cheek. "She told me that the amniotic fluid was low, and she was sending me to the hospital, which was thankfully right next door, to prep me for an emergency C-section. I'm not gonna lie to you. I was scared, Cam. I needed you."

A choking breath slips through my lips, and unable to take back any of my previous decisions, I rest my head on her.

"I still need you. Don't leave me again, or I won't be as forgiving the second time," she warns.

"I'm not going anywhere," I promise, knowing Yanelys might very well kick me out of her life if she knew about my addiction.

My empty chest sighs out a millennium of pains. But with Santiago wanting to help me get clean, maybe I won't have to tell her until I'm able to stand on my own.

"Just"—I close my eyes—"no matter what, please don't turn away from me. I'm messed up, but I'm trying. For you and Olivia, I'm trying. I swear it."

Yanelys turns and wraps her arms and legs around my shaking body. I try to fight the tremors, but in Yanelys's embrace, I weaken further and further into the memories of the destructive life I've led. The boy Yanelys knew is gone, invisible even to myself.

"You're strong, Cam," she whispers into my ear.

I shake my head, denying it.

"You are."

"And you?" I ask with wonder in my voice. "You had our daughter by yourself. You've raised her, loved her, given her laughter. You, my Yan, are the vision of strength. I admire you. I look up to you. I love you."

Yanelys's quick intake of breath makes me realize that she hasn't heard those words from me in so long, too long.

Framing her face with my hands, I repeat them, "I love you." Still caressing her face, I pull her down to me. "I love you for the woman you've become." I kiss her lips. "I love you for loving our daughter." I kiss her again. "I love you for how you make me feel." Again, our lips touch. "I love you for you."

When our lips meet once again, Yanelys opens her mouth in invitation, and my tongue slips in, tasting her.

Lost in her, I find myself. My heart. My salvation.

As she runs her hands through my hair, I deepen the kiss, telling her everything I'm not quite ready to speak of yet. I empty myself into our kiss, and when our lips part on a loud smack, I stare at her swollen lips and smile.

"So, you went to the hospital?"

Confusion crosses her face before she realizes what I'm asking.

On a breathy laugh, she starts again, "Yeah, I called my mom right after I registered at the hospital. I hadn't shaved my legs in a couple of days, maybe weeks." She scrunches up her nose, making me laugh. "I was huge, Cam. I couldn't bend down to shave my own legs. When I got to my room, one of the nurses came in and shaved them and my, uh…private area." A sweet blush spreads across her cheeks while she sucks on her bottom lip. "Anyway, that's not important."

"Every part is important," I counter. "Don't leave anything out."

"There really isn't much else to the story. What was supposed to be an emergency C-section got pushed back eleven hours because my doctor had another emergency. Olivia was born just before seven p.m. on July twenty-first, nine months after you left." Her voice quakes, gripping me with urgency.

Too scared to speak, I hug her closer to me and press my lips against her temple. I'm aching as the room grows dense, the sharp edges of life whispering all the wrongs I've done. All the wrongs I need to make right.

Her love will carry me, make me stronger, so I can break free and finally be with them.

I swallow around the lump in my throat and sink my face into the side of Yanelys's neck, kissing her soft skin. My unshaven jaw rubs against her, and then I pull away, so she can see me and all the promises I intend to keep.

"Never again," I say.

Her light-brown eyes flash to mine, hope and despair intertwining with one other.

"Never again will you celebrate another birthday without me. Christmas, Thanksgiving, the Tooth Fairy—I'm gonna be here for all of that."

"Okay." She nods. "School functions, too."

"School functions, too," I agree. "When she knows me and you're ready, we can tell her I'm her dad. I won't push it, but, fuck, Yan, I want her to know me. I want her to know she has a dad and that he loves her so, so much."

"When I'm ready." Yanelys's eyes glint with fierce tenacity when she nods her head again, her throat bobbing as she swallows. "Meanwhile, I want her to get to know you. Next week, she has a show at school. She's singing a solo for the Thanksgiving show that we've been practicing for close to a month now," she says, her tone that of pure amusement.

My eyes meet hers, dancing with joy, when reality slams into me.

"Next week…" I begin, but I stop when her confused eyes rake over me and she gets off me, leaving me empty without the pressure of her body pressed against mine.

She crosses her arms, shielding herself from me and the inevitable pain I might bring her. Her eyes narrow, her sweet mouth turning down into a grim scowl. "What's wrong with next week?"

"Nothing. I'll be there," I amend. "And every day before then."

I dig my fingers into her sensitive skin, already feeling her slipping away.

"Prison, huh?" I ask as nonchalant as I can. I can't help but wonder what could've possibly happened for her to end up behind bars even if it was for a short time.

"My dad's friend has a weird sense of humor," she replies, her eyes downcast to my shoes.

"Right." I suspiciously eye her but let it go because what right do I have to ask her anything when I'm hiding everything?

Claustrophobia settles in as I stand between the narrow walls of Yanelys's hallways, just outside her bathroom. Heat gathers in my chest, the tension between Santiago and me growing, as I wait for him to give me another pill. The hardness in his eyes steals the breath from my lungs, and I cock my head to the side, hoping he won't give me away. The man I've worshipped my whole life, who now holds the fate of my future in his hands, regards me with silent disapproval.

On a long sigh, he reaches into his pocket and gives me a pill.

One single pill. My prison. My sanctuary.

A malignant companion that makes my skin itch.

With shaky hands, I take it from him and pop it into my mouth, swallowing it dry.

"We need to get you clean, Cam." He holds my gaze, my disease spreading into his veins, seeping out all the good. "Two weeks is too long to wait. We leave tomorrow."

We leave tomorrow.

Marking an end of lies. The finality hits me.

"Livvy has a show next week. Then, Thanksgiving's a week after that. I've missed too much already." My voice begs with him, my emotions reprimanding me for the unspoken words that scream the truth. "Please, Santiago. Two weeks with my girls. Let us get to know each other. Then, you and me—we'll leave. I'll get clean and come back home to them."

Infested with guilt, I conceal the other truth and conform my thoughts, hoping Santiago will take pity on me and let me have a two-week reprieve before we battle my demons.

"You can't stay here. Not with your addiction."

"I won't hurt them," I plead, needing to be near them, for them to give me purpose. "You have to know I'd never hurt them."

"Two weeks," he concedes. His chest heaves, his eyes narrowing. "But I'm keeping the pills with me. I need to know how much you're taking, because I'm not putting you, my daughter, or my granddaughter in danger."

Helpless to my addiction, I chase my deceit and half-truths with a strained smile.

Reading the emotions crossing over my face wrong, Santiago cups the back of my neck and squeezes. "I'm not going to let you fail, Cam."

My eyes cut to him, faith resurfacing, only to be resigned by an addiction I'm powerless to control.

EIGHTEEN

YANELYS

Night clings to the darkness of my bedroom as an impossible silence hangs over Camden and me. So many unknowns remain between us, driving us apart while we continue to pull our bodies closer to one another.

We don't know how to talk to each other—not really. This invisible divide pushes us away yet draws us closer to each other.

I love him. My heart recognizes that love, but I hurt because of him. Olivia will hurt because of him, too, and that's the hardest part for me to face. I want her to get to know him.

Her open spirit and easy nature have already accepted him in our lives. When I took her to the side after my parents had left and explained how Camden was going to stay the night, I thought she'd ask questions, but my daughter simply twirled a couple of times and asked if Camden could tuck her in. As we left her bedroom, I took his hand in mine and led him to my bed where we've been trying to talk before he has to go back into his bedroom. I've asked him questions that have gone unanswered, and felt him inch away from me through the silence.

Dropping his face to the inside of my neck, he pulls me closer to him, and I feel his heart beating against mine.

"Cam," I say.

He releases a desperate breath that brushes over my neck, making it tingle.

"I just want to know what's going on." Fisting my hands into his shirt, I hold on to him.

We used to sleep like this, our bodies molded against one another, and in each other's arms, we'd find rest. But tonight…tonight, restlessness vibrates off his skin, making cold sweat drip down his back and chest.

"Migraines." His voice quakes.

I move my face closer to his, placing a tender hand on his chest.

"They come on suddenly like this. I just need my pill."

Worry drapes over me while my blood races as he trembles beneath my touch.

"Where are your pills, baby?" I whisper, my lips grazing over the stubble on his chin. "I'll get them for you."

"No!" he shouts, the word filled with ferocity, as his fingers wind around my wrist. "I'll get them."

Unsettled, I turn on the lamp and track him as he stumbles off the bed to the bag he brought from the hospital. His hands search frantically through the bag until he pulls out the same jeans he wore earlier. His face crumbles, and he shuts his eyes just before he puts the pill into his mouth and swallows it dry.

Seconds tick by, the pulse in my throat keeping time while I wait. His blue eyes, dark from his pain, search my face.

"Come to bed, Cam," I say. When he looks at my bedroom door, I turn off the light. "No more questions," I promise before he can escape. "I just want to sleep with you."

On shaky limbs, he comes back to bed where he drapes an arm around my waist and brings me close to him. Feeling him shiver, I pull the sheets over us and run my fingers through his long hair. Rather than close his eyes, he watches me, the weight of his intensity making me blush.

"You always take care of me," he murmurs. "I've never asked you to, but you do it anyway."

Hurt flashes in his eyes, crushing me, as the flame behind them dies out.

"I've given you every reason not to," he whispers, misery pulling his lips down.

His eyes flutter closed when I trace a gentle finger over his lips.

"We take care of each other," I say.

He shakes his head, denying all the comfort he brought me growing up.

"I've done so much bad in my life, Yan. Things I don't want you to ever know. It scares me, what I'm capable of. Even now, I'm ruining your life, but I can't leave you. I can't survive again without you. Without Livvy. But with all this bad"—his eyes open, intense and raw—"I don't know how to be with you, how to breathe the same air as you."

"You're doing it right now." Swallowing hard, I pull him impossibly closer to me, thankful when I notice he's shaking less.

"I don't deserve to."

"You deserve happiness and love. The unfiltered kind only we can give each other."

"No." His pained voice tears at my heart, stealing the beauty of today, the day Camden came back into my life.

"Why don't you let me decide what you deserve?" My whispered voice blends with the darkness cloaked around us, spoiling our night.

My slender fingers glide over his skin, his scars, marred by an abusive past neither of us knew how to escape. Still my fearless knight, he places a hand to my chest, squeezing them to a fist over the thumping of my heart.

Where his wounds are visible, mine lie just below the surface. But with him back, my cracked heart fills with the love we've always shared. And although my heart warns me to be careful, I know I'm already in too deep for caution. Where Camden's concerned, I've always been in way too deep.

A rush of air flees from my lungs when Olivia jumps on top of me. Still groggy from a restless night, I roll her to the side, hoping she'll give me a few more minutes of sleep.

"Time to wake up, sleepyhead." Her melodic voice rings out, making my lips curve into a small smile. "Cam's already making us breakfast."

My eyes flutter open, and I take in the morning with newfound exuberance. The sun caressing my bedsheets shines more radiant than ever. The haze of dawn is more blissful than yesterday's. Magic impresses on us, making Olivia bounce in anticipation.

Camden's home. Her daddy's finally here.

I take Olivia with me when I jump out of bed, twirling her in the air once before I set her back on her agile feet.

"He makes the best chocolate chip pancakes." My eyebrows raise.

She giggles at the expression on my face.

"I'll race you to the kitchen. Whoever loses cleans the dishes."

Not waiting for her to reply, I sprint toward the kitchen, her laughter chasing me, filling me, just like it always does. When we round the corner, Nisa barks at us, her butt wiggling in greeting.

"That dog"—Camden points the spatula at a grinning Nisa—"is gonna give me a heart attack."

"You'll live." Moving past him, I pat his shoulder, and he sends me a lingering glare.

Losing myself to him all over again, the ground shifts, caving beneath my feet. For a moment, our eyes narrow in on one another, and he cocks an eyebrow when my cheeks redden. He sets the spatula down, and after one long stride, he's standing next to me, invading my space with his scent. Without hesitation, he stretches his arms and places his hands against my waist.

"Never knew a blush could be so sexy." His voice rasps against my cheek, making my blush deepen.

Raw anticipation builds in my core, and I exhale a sharp breath when he rubs his rough knuckles over my cheek.

"So beautiful," he whispers, his breath tickling my lips as he draws near them.

With his hands back on my waist, he tugs me to him, and I fall onto his chest. A strong rhythmic heartbeat thumps against me while I place my arms around his thin waist.

"Are you gonna kiss like Ita and Tito do?" Olivia asks, calling my parents by the nicknames she gave them when she was a year old. "'Cause that's really gross."

Camden's laughter erupts from his chest, and I press a hand to my lips, savoring the sound as it ruins me in the most amazing way.

"Livvy, sweetie"—Camden kneels down in front of her and gathers her in his arms—"I plan on kissing your mom a whole lot. I hope you're okay with that."

Olivia settles in his arms without any misgivings and peers up at him with the innocence of youth. His fingertips brush along her jawline. As our daughter slowly accepts her dad into her life, my heart crashes behind my rib cage in violent happiness.

Walking back to the forgotten pancakes, I let Camden and Olivia have their moment. There'll be questions when we finally tell her the truth, but we'll get to those in time. For now, my family is complete. Joy radiates off every inch of my kitchen.

Chewing on my bottom lip, I watch them interact once he places Olivia on the kitchen counter, farthest away from the stove. Adoration pours from his eyes as he devours her constant chatter. The pangs of the night before disappear as the purity of the moment seeps in its place.

Olivia peeks around Camden to me, shifting her eyes when she catches me watching them. When he pushes away her overabundance of wild hair and whispers something in her ear, she giggles.

"Whatever you two are planning, it isn't going to work," I warn.

Neither of them pays me any attention as they conspire against me.

"I feel like an intruder in my own home," I say.

A trace of a smile lifts at the corners of Camden's mouth when he finally turns to face me.

"Can I take Livvy to the grocery store after breakfast?" Camden asks, his sweet smile a direct contrast to Olivia's devious one.

"Please, Mom." Olivia bounces off the counter and dances in front of me.

"Well..." I draw out. My teeth clamp down over my bottom lip as my eyes narrow at my little girl. "Who'll do the dishes while you're at the grocery store?"

"I'm a kid, Mom, not your maid," she sasses, her lips spreading into a huge grin.

"You're a brat." Twirling her around, I lightly smack her bottom.

She sends a glee of giggles and squeals into the open space of our kitchen. Out of breath, I sit on the floor and gather Olivia onto my lap.

"Is that a yes?" Camden asks.

I arch a brow at Olivia, who makes a show of rolling her eyes.

"If you do the dishes this time, I'll do them after lunch and dinner. Deal?" Olivia asks, her voice begging me to give in this once.

"I can live with that," I agree.

"Can we try some of Cam's world-famous chocolate chip pancakes now?"

"World-famous, huh?" Camden questions.

Olivia scurries around him, putting place mats on the kitchen nook.

"Don't let it get to your head." After grabbing a kitchen towel, I throw it in Camden's direction, but he catches it before it hits his face.

"I can't believe I'm gonna have chocolate for breakfast," Olivia whispers, awe spreading in her light-brown eyes.

There's a lot I can't believe, starting with Camden.

He's here, yet it's like he's occupied somewhere else. Fading. Sometimes slowly. I keep waiting to turn around and find him gone, but then he comes back.

He smiles at Olivia, grounded by his tribulations and her tender love.

I hold on to him, wanting to bind him to us, to have him worn into the fabric of our souls. I want him for a lifetime, but I'll take whatever fleeting moments he has to offer.

NINETEEN

CAMDEN

Cramped, the walls of the grocery store push against me, and I brace myself, placing my hands on Olivia's shoulders. Eyes bore into me, staring, judging, circling around me and the little girl I helped create.

"Livvy"—I lick my dry lips—"why don't you look at the flowers we're gonna buy your mom while I talk to my friend?"

Pure and good, she puts her undisputed belief in me and the notion that I'm a trustworthy man, and she ambles off toward the flowers. A current of cold air whips around me as the store's air conditioner kicks on. I put my hands in my jeans pockets and stare at anyone but Pastor Floyd.

"You have a daughter," Pastor Floyd accuses.

Emotions grow thick between us, and I turn my eyes to my child. My daughter.

"I didn't know." I swallow the lump in the base of my throat. "I swear, I didn't know."

"You know now." His eyes narrow, and his cheeks flush. "This?" He takes out the bottle of pills I asked him to bring me and shakes it in front of my face. "This has to stop. I can't do this anymore."

Pastor Floyd paces in front of me, waging his ongoing war between what's wrong and what's worse.

Yanelys thinks she's seen the worst of me, the worst of my parents, but only Pastor Floyd has. He was there the day my world crumbled with truths I'd have rather stayed hidden. And he's been there every day since.

He doesn't want to enable me; he wants to help me because he's seen my tears and anger and helplessness. He's seen me grow from that pain, only to have life knock me down again. And again. And again.

"I'm gonna get clean, Pastor Floyd," I promise and his eyes widen in shock.

Never, in all the years I've been with him, have I ever uttered those words. Because never, until right now, have they been true.

"I'm gonna get clean," I say again.

Pastor Floyd's chest heaves as he sucks in a breath. He closes his eyes, squeezing them so tight that a small tear drips from the corner. Scared, desperate, but hopeful, I place my hands on his shoulders and tighten my grip so that he looks back at me.

"I'm sorry," I whisper when he opens his eyes, "for everything I've done. For everything you've done to help me. I'm sorry." With shame filling my soul, I hang my head.

"I know," Pastor Floyd replies. "I want the best for you, Cam. I do. But I don't know how to help you."

"You can't." A small smile tugs at the corner of my lips and I shove my hands into the pocket of my again.

Yanelys. Only Yanelys can help me.

"Santiago knows about my problem, and we're going on some guys' trip in two weeks. He says he's going to help me get clean. Until then, he's keeping the pills and only giving me one every four hours." My hand twitches in my pocket, so I close it into a tight fist. "It's not enough." Defeated, my voice rises barely above a whisper.

"Okay." He nods once and hands the bottle to me. When I move away, he grips my wrist, gaining my attention. "Get clean, Cam. Not for your daughter or for Yanelys. Do it for you. Because you deserve it."

My feet feel heavy when I take my first step away from Pastor Floyd and toward Olivia. The weight of the pill bottle burdens me, pulling me down, willing me to tear open my heart and leave it bleeding.

On one knee, I gather Olivia into my arms, aching for her gentle embrace to heal my sick soul. But my sickness remains, forging its way to Olivia, blemishing her goodness.

"What do you think about the lilies?" I ask, pointing at the white flowers Yanelys favors.

"Mom loves these." Her fingers caress the petals with the same tenderness as her mom.

I pick out two bouquets, and with Olivia's small hand in mine, we go to the cash register and pay with the money Pastor Floyd gave me. Outside, a cool breeze greets us, the blue and white sky spanning like an endless dream. Rather than head to Yanelys's house, I lead us to a nearby playground where I place both sets of flowers on a bench under a wide tree and then turn to Olivia.

"Did you know it's good luck to catch leaves?" I ask.

She shakes her head.

"It is," I say.

The wind blows harder, making her hair swirl, as the tree shakes above us. Small leaves free themselves from it, floating and dancing their way to the ground. Turning, I open my arms and close my fist when a leaf falls into my waiting hand.

I position the leaf so that I'm holding it by the stem, and I show it to her. Her eager eyes trace my every movement, and my pulse quickens with her wistful heart.

"You want to make a wish with this one or catch your own?"

"Catch my own!" Olivia's lips curve into a radiant smile, her eyes glowing with joy, as she runs beneath the tree. Her feet crash into small piles of leaves, sending them into the air. Elated giggles paint the sky as she jumps, twirls, and catches as many leaves as her small hands will allow.

"Okay, Cam!" Breathless, she jogs toward me, stray leaves falling from her grasp. "Now what?"

"Make a wish."

With my eyes closed, I throw my leaf in the air. And wish I weren't alone. That the emptiness could somehow be filled. I wish for a life I'd left behind but never wished away. For the love of a little girl who didn't even know who I was.

Leaves fall on my face, and when I open my eyes, I find Olivia spinning in circles with her eyes closed and her arms open wide. On a whim, I scoop her into my arms, and together, we spin.

And spin.

And spin.

Like a circle, without beginning or end, we spin and spin until we grow dizzy. The ground rocks, shifting on its axis, so I place Olivia on her feet while I lie down on the cool grass. Within seconds, she lies down next to me, nestling her head in the crook of my arm.

I hesitate before I grip her closer to me. Streaks of light flash behind my eyes as the dizziness squanders away. Sad thoughts and the rough edges of life unblur, making my heart thunder in my ears.

"What'd you ask for?" I ask.

"I can't tell you." She angles her face toward mine, her nose scrunching up at my question, as her eyes glint in merriment. "Then, it won't come true." A small blush creeps over her neck to her cheeks.

"You and your mom." I laugh, kissing the top of her head. "You two are a lot alike."

"Mom loves you, you know?"

"I love her, too."

"And me?" Her eyes peek at me from the corners, and I lick my lips while I collect my thoughts.

Echoes of my past fade to today, my load constantly narrowing my life. As Olivia's small body curls into me, my vision clears and stretches along with the sky. In every direction. Unconfined and limitless. Unconditioned to the hard nature I've harbored for far too long.

"And you, Livvy. I fell in love with you the minute I saw you. And I keep falling every second I spend with you."

"Even though you don't know me that good?" Her eyes well up and my heart crashes against my ribs.

"I know you well enough." I touch her nose with my finger. "I know you like chocolate, that you help your mom out around the house and make her laugh. I know you make me laugh, too. You can run really fast and spin better than me. And I know you have a bouquet of lilies to put in your room when we get home."

Her eyes grow big, and she scrambles to her feet, pulling my hand up with her.

"You got me flowers, Cam? For real?" She jumps in place, her face illuminating with the simplicity of her pleasure. "We need to put them in water. They can't die. Let's go, Cam." She tugs on my hand. "Hurry, let's go!"

"Okay." I laugh. "Okay."

Hand in hand, we walk away from the playground—Olivia holding her bouquet of flowers while I cling on to her mom's. A terrain of love spreads before me as I listen to Olivia chatter about the flowers I bought her. How I'm the first person to ever buy her flowers. And I know...I know it in my achy body that I want to be the first of many good things in her life.

The wind continues to play with her hair, leaving her cheeks flush from the rush of cool air and the short walk to Yanelys's house. New dreams and new thoughts break into my heart when I walk through the door to find Yanelys sleeping on the couch with a paperback resting on her chest.

With a slight tilt of her sweet head, Olivia smiles and asks, "Will you put my flowers in a vase for me?"

My heart stutters in my chest, my throat growing thick. My charming girl, a beautiful blessing from a god I thought had left me. I nod once, knowing I don't stand a chance. Already, she has me eating out of her hand.

"Thank you, Cam." Olivia's hands clasp together behind my neck after I've filled a vase with water and put her flowers in them. "I love them. I love you," she whispers.

A piece of my broken heart slides into place, and for a fleeting moment, I'm complete.

TWENTY

CAMDEN

There's a place beyond us, beyond the sky and earth, and even beyond heaven that stretches infinitely, not allowing any of our yesterdays to hurt us. Where only we exist. Where the only thing that counts is us and our heartbeats thumping as one.

Yanelys's fingertips run circles over my heart as we sit on her bed facing each other with our foreheads touching. My hands comb through her hair, and she exhales her sweet breath on my face. Inches away from her, my lips linger over her mouth. She parts her own lips, inhaling and exhaling me.

Quiet, so quiet, the room stands still, and I hear the hope her breaths whisper across my face. Through jumbled nerves, I move my lips closer to hers, my eyes trained on them. Plump and soft, they quiver in anticipation.

My heartbeat rises but then collapses when Yanelys pulls away.

"Yan?"

"We slept together last night," she says on a rough exhale of air. "But that's all we did. Sleep. I want more, Cam. I really do. But I want more than just sex, too."

Her eyes meet mine, and when I don't respond, she closes them.

"Open your eyes, sweetheart."

She does, and I'm taken aback by the love shining from them. Or maybe it's my own love I see reflected from her soulful brown eyes.

"It could never be just sex with you."

"It was though. Maybe you didn't mean for it to be. I know you thought you were protecting me, but when you left, you turned the most indescribable and delicate moment of my life into ugly sex. I can't go through that again." Her tongue sneaks out of her mouth to wet her lips as her eyes skirt away from my face. "I don't think I could survive it a second time."

Guilt braids itself around my conscience, fear and doubt tangling with its tendrils. Silence thickens the air, separating us, when all I want is to keep her as close to me as possible.

"Forgive me, Yan." My eyes search hers, my jumbled nerves running amok when she doesn't reply. "I'm sorry for leaving you. I'm sorry for hurting you. I'm sorry for making my love something ugly that you're afraid of. I'm not promising you an eternity because you wouldn't believe me. But I will spend every second of every day showing you all the love of my forever."

Her body draws closer to mine, her apprehension clearing and making room for the hope that's been burning in her soul since we were kids. Joy teases her lips as she glides a gentle hand over my cheek. She leans into my face and our lips touch. A wave of passion builds in my core, and I slip my tongue across her lips. My body presses further onto her so that her back rests on the bed. She arches when I lift the thin fabric of her pajama shirt and trail soft kisses over her curves.

When I remove her pajama shorts and panties, I place a gentle kiss on the scar from her C-section, and she exhales a sharp breath, our abandoned hearts finding one another within the whirlwind of lust and love.

"I've only ever been with you, Yan." The admission shocks her, and I close my eyes, hoping to hear her utter the same words even though I know I don't deserve them. "It's always only been you."

"It's always only been you, too, Cam," she whispers, her breath falling across my cheek and lips, warming me from the outside in.

The pressure in my chest intensifies, but I pull away, worry drawing my eyebrows together. "I don't have any condoms."

"It's okay." She exhales heavily, and I shake my head, pulling further away from her. "I'm on the pill. It's okay." Her hands fist my shirt, and I willingly let her pull me back to her.

Piece by piece, I discard my clothes and throw them to the floor. Our heated tongues meet when I go to her again. Her body moves beneath me, urgent, letting me in. I align myself with her opening and slip inside her. Her small gasp breaks our kiss, but she pulls my face back to hers, our bodies molding against one another. Slowly, I sway my hips back and forth, not wanting to lose control and jostle her sacred heart.

"Don't stop," she whispers, her lips moving against mine.

My fingers stroke the stray stands of her hair from her forehead while her nails dig into my shoulder. I'm throbbing with need. My hand and then my mouth travel to her breast, savoring her, as she consumes me. My eyes close as I listen to the soft moans slipping from her lips. Tension builds inside of me, and my thrusts become more erratic. I open my eyes to meet hers as she pulls me closer to her, trusting me, as her body trembles.

Our eyes hold, and I see her. My reason, my purpose.

"Cam," she moans my name. "Don't stop. Don't stop."

Like a hundred orgasms, her words hit me, rocking me, as my motions become harder, faster. Her hips move with mine, a synchronized dance of love and lust and fire and passion.

Reaching between her breasts, I place my hand on her chest and lean into her, so my lips caress her right ear.

"I need you, sweetheart. Yesterday, today, tomorrow. I love you."

Undone, she embraces me, our hearts beating against one another. She clings on to me, our limbs mixing with one another. Silently, I promise us a future where our pasts readjust, making us inseparable.

After she reaches her peak, my name crosses her lips in a frenzy of kisses that she places against my jaw. As I lose myself in her, with her, because of her, my ecstasy rises in perfect waves. I crash into her, Yanelys leading the way with her light. Seconds expand into a beautiful timelessness, and all I see is Yanelys, her bright brown eyes, her alluring smile, her tender heart.

Morning light spills from the shades, its radiance showering over the soft blue covers of the bed. The warm glow of Olivia nestled between Yanelys and me puts my sleeping dreams to rest and brings me to a reality that makes the everlasting darkness of my soul disappear.

Finding my love in them, I reach over Olivia, who snuck into our bed after midnight, and trace a finger over Yanelys's arm. In her sleep she murmurs, filling my voids, making living less terrifying.

A new day, a new hope.

The recognizable tremble of my fingers reminds me of my addiction, crushing my hope to the destiny I paved when I caved to my destruction, believing it would cure my every pain. Stumbling out of bed, I cross Yanelys's room to the bathroom where I hid the pills Pastor Floyd had given me in a small sandwich bag and then placed in the air vent. I stand on the edge of the tub and slide the vent cover. I reach my hand in there until I feel the bag and then pull it out. Taking a small pill in one hand, I slide the bag back into its hiding place and step off the tub.

With closed eyes, I whisper a prayer, my faith crying, my spirit dropping. Looking forward, I put the pill on my tongue, swallowing the emptiness, as my gaze meets my reflection in the mirror. Disgust builds up in my heart, the embers of my hatred burning my skin.

When the door opens, I turn toward it and sink into Yanelys's arms when she comes to me. Her head rests over my racing heart, and she squeezes my lean frame closer to her.

"Livvy's going to ask you for more chocolate chip pancakes." Her eyes, twinkling with happiness, meet mine when she leans her head back. "You're going to say no."

"What?" My eyebrows shoot upward. "And disappoint my daughter?"

"Yep." She nods her head. "It's a school day, and I have a strict no-sugar rule on school days."

"Oh." I lean down and nip her bottom lip. "That's why you have a hidden stash of Lucky Charms, huh?"

"I don't go to school, so that rule doesn't apply to me."

Her laughter brings out mine, misting over the ugliness that clung to me moments ago.

"You always find a loophole."

I rub my nose over the crevice of her throat as she brings her arms around my neck. Her goodness fills the air, taking away the tension that threatens to linger. Not wanting to break the illusion, I pretend that I'm okay. That I don't already wish I'd taken two pills instead of one.

Taking ahold of Yanelys's hand, I guide us to the kitchen and take over breakfast, chopping onions and bell peppers for an egg omelet. I pretend I don't hurt, that the wars I lost haven't left battle scars on my heart. I pretend I'm a warrior, that my hidden rage is locked away. I hide it all with the calmness and smiles that quickly fade away when I'm alone.

My emotions churn, anxiety taking precedence in the pit of my stomach. The disquiet rumble of needing more pricks at my skin, coiling my muscles.

I steady my breath and listen to my girls argue over the shoes Olivia wants to wear to school.

After whisking four eggs, I pour them into the frying pan and sprinkle the chopped onions and bell peppers into the middle along with a few leaves of spinach and shredded cheese.

"That's a big omelet," Olivia says from behind me, peeking at the pan that's slowly cooking one side of the omelet.

A smile spreads across my face when I notice Olivia is wearing the white shoes she insisted would go perfectly with her white-and-pink dress.

"It's a monster omelet." I wink at her, making her giggle.

Pretenses fade away, replaced with the darkness that floats into my soul, when I spot Santiago and Carmen coming into the kitchen. Olivia bounces toward her grandparents, a flurry of exuberant innocence, while my sickness claws at me, edging me toward the tranquility I can only find with another pill.

My eyes meet Santiago's, and he slightly nods his head, leaving the kitchen and heading to the back patio with two steaming coffee travel mugs in his hands.

"I have to talk to your dad," I tell Yanelys, who takes over the stove after planting a kiss on the side of my lips.

When I sit next to Santiago on Yanelys's wicker chair, he hands me the coffee mug that warms my skin and a pill that ices my veins.

Weak, pathetic. A constant circle of doubt, survival, hatred, I surrender to the angry daze of my reality.

And I wait for the sadness to quiet so that, for just a little while, I can forget what it feels like.

TWENTY-ONE

YANELYS

The way he hides his pain only intensifies my need to protect him. From himself, from his past. I see it but can't reach it. Can't reach him. So, I hold him closer, squeeze him tighter.

He scans his eyes over the auditorium, sweat building on the base of his neck, his muscles twitching. His need to leave the school we had gone to as kids grows inside of him, but still, he stays because he promised Olivia he'd be here, that he'd never miss a single one of her shows or school events.

"They don't start for another fifteen minutes." I squeeze his hand. "Why don't we go outside and get some air?"

He nods once, his eyes unbridled when they land on me, and he licks his dry lips.

"We'll be back," I tell my dad whose wary eyes track us as we stand up to leave.

Through the halls, I try to keep pace with Camden's hurried strides. Our loud footsteps fall on walls littered with school-age drawings, echoing down the long hallway. His hasty, jerky movements unnerve me, but I keep my hand tucked in his, holding on so that I don't lose him entirely. When he opens the door, cool air greets us, and the scent of fall hits my nose.

"Cam," I call to him when he continues to walk away from the school and toward my car, his worried past trailing behind his heels, the expansive blue sky stretching before us. "Come back to me," I whisper, tugging on his hand.

His body stills, and when he spins around, our eyes meet. His are clear blue. Raw. Damaged. Pained.

He crushes his lips to my mouth, and my lips part from the force of his kiss. His tongue dances with mine, unyielding, as he pours his desperation into me. His fingers dig into my shoulders as mine fist in his hair, tugging, pulling, demanding even more. On a painful sigh, Camden pulls away from me, expelling a heavy breath over my face. Tormented eyes seek mine, and I place a hand over his cheek, his sadness washing over me, as I search his face for the boy I love.

"Where are you, Cam?"

He drops his hands from my shoulders, his gaze scouring the ground around us. Even in the cool air, his sweat continues to drip from his forehead.

"Nowhere. I'm nowhere, Yan." Blurred bloodshot eyes meet mine. "I don't exist." Grief-stricken, his tone is raspy and barely audible.

At his words, my entire body goes up in flames and I hope the burning light in my soul will help him find his way back to me and away from the memories of his tormented youth.

Moving my hand from his cheek, I place my hands around his neck and bring him closer to me. Our bodies flush against one another, I feel the pounding of his battered heart against my own chest. A cold wisp of air surrounds us, and I bury my face into his neck, wanting to tell him just how good and beautiful he is. How he doesn't have to run away anymore.

"You're home, baby. You're home," I whisper, desperation edging my voice. "I'm your home, remember?"

"Yeah." Agitation coils through him, making the muscles on his face twitch.

He steps away from my embrace, brushing his hands over his face and squeezing his eyes shut, staying that way for only a second before he opens them to look back at me.

"You, me, and Livvy. Okay?" I take a step forward and meet his frown with a gentle smile.

The blue dimming, his eyes are like an endless meadow of infinite fear. I hold his gaze, a prisoner to the sadness behind them.

"You don't have to stay to watch the show," I finally say, sad for our daughter and the disappointment she'll feel when she doesn't see him in the crowd. "I'll record it, and we can watch it on the TV back home."

"I promised Livvy." His frown deepens.

"You can make it up to her with chocolate chip pancakes for dinner."

"No!" he shouts, anger rushing through him.

I startle a few steps away from him.

"I need to be here for Livvy, for you, for myself. I can't let my parents continue running my life. Once, just once, I need to win."

118

"Okay." I nod, again putting my arms around his neck and holding on to him, hoping he'll hold me back.

"They took my childhood," he whispers into the crevice of my neck, "scarred it so that the weight of it still pushes me down. And every time I get this little glimmer of hope and I start to feel happy, they rip it away from me. Being with you makes it hurt a little less. Since we were kids, you've made living hurt a little less." A small sob escapes from his throat, and I stroke the back of his head, my fingers combing through his unruly hair. "Don't make me do this by myself."

"I wouldn't." Framing his face with my hands, I make him look back at me. "Never, baby. I'd never leave you."

"You say that now…" He trails off, averting his eyes away from me.

"I say that now and tomorrow and a hundred tomorrows from now."

His chest lifts on a slow inhale, pain taking over his features as his jaw clenches and unclenches. Emotions spill from him, his silence thickening the air between us.

"Being back at this school brings back memories," he finally says on a broken whisper. "Good and bad, but so much bad that I feel myself choking on it."

Out of the shadows of our childhood school, his silent screams for inner peace rake over me as we both remember the endless lies of Camden's youth. We can't hide from them; we never could. So, we continue to put on masks in the hopes of making the other feel better because I know…I know, I know, *I know* I can't love away his scars. I can only heal his heavy heart when he's finally ready to let me in.

"So much good, too, Cam." I kiss the side of his head. "We owned the hallways when we were kids." A soft smile spreads over my lips when he chuckles. "There wasn't a kid in our class who didn't want to be us."

"Your delusion is scary," he jokes, his voice trembling.

He places his warm lips against my neck as I encircle my arms around him again.

"We were totally the coolest kids here."

"That's even scarier if you believe that." His body goes limp as he relaxes in my arms and peers down into my face. Guiding strands of my hair behind my ear, he rubs his callous knuckles over my cheek. "We weren't even close to being cool."

"By high school, we were," I retort. "Kind of. I mean, no one ever made fun of us after you beat up a couple of kids."

"And no one ever dared to ask you on a date for that same reason," he informs me.

119

I throw my head back in appreciative laughter. "I knew it! You always denied it, but I knew Johnny didn't ask me out because of you."

"Joey," he corrects.

I narrow my eyes at him.

"And he didn't ask you out because he knew he wasn't good enough for you."

"Did your fist tell him that?"

"No, common sense did." He winks.

Undeniable joy surrounds me when he tightens his arms around my waist. His warm breath falls over my face when he presses his lips to my forehead, lingering there, savoring me. Our hearts beat against one another, gentle and soft.

"Let's go back," he says, holding me a little tighter before he drops his hands and takes a step back.

The corners of his eyes crinkle when a smile paints across his sad face, ringing out as a sweet song through a gentle breath. Beautiful, so beautiful, it hurts my chest to look away from him.

My hand reaches for his, and our fingers interlace with one another. The walk back to the auditorium is quiet yet peaceful, as I escape deeper into my lost boy. Olivia shouts Camden's name as soon as we walk into the room, and he waves back at her, his smile growing when she waves at him again. Seated next to my parents, he puts his arms around the back of my chair and curls the tips of my hair with his fingers.

Ripe desire blooms in the pit of my stomach. I turn my head to face him, my eyes open, bold, telling. His fingers run over the back of my neck. Slow, delicate, awake to the same longing. His soft eyes darken with the oncoming storm, his lips forming a thin line, before he plants a kiss on my cheek.

His wandering mouth travels to my ear where he whispers, "It's good to be home."

Those words stir me, the warm rays of our love igniting my passion. Molten and ferocious, it flows through my veins, filling my soul, consuming me with pleasure and his irresistible heart.

When Olivia takes the stage, my heart drums in my chest, strong and proud. Feathers from her costume fall from the top of her head, trailing past the brown paper-bag dress she made that covers the pale green dress she's wearing beneath it.

This morning I styled her hair in long ringlets that now fall and frame her pretty face. A radiant smile stretches and reaches me, and I lift my cell phone, already in camera mode, and take pictures of my little girl dressed as a Native American.

Grief eases from Camden's face, the firm lines of his forehead smoothing as he watches Olivia's performance. Her voice is low, but her body sways to the music, free and joyful, as she keeps her eyes trained on the four of us—her family.

When the first dance is done, Camden rises from his chair, applauding and hooting her name, but I tug him down, knowing the show is nowhere near over. He brings my hand to his lips while his blue eyes watch me.

"She's incredible, isn't she?" he asks, his voice filled with wonder.

My head bobs up and down in agreement, but I keep my eyes trained on Olivia. The kids in her class go back to their seats while she bounces on her heels with a microphone in her trembling hand. Camden gives my hand a comforting squeeze.

Once she stands on the stage by herself, the beginning of the song she's been practicing comes on. Her eyes dart to us, and I give her a quiet nod of encouragement.

My chest tightens when she stays silent on her cue to sing. As she shuffles feet, her eyes bore into mine, and I give her a thumbs-up when her teacher starts the radio again. Tears swim behind her eyes when she misses her cue again.

Her teacher whispers words of reassurance that Olivia doesn't seem to hear. I lick my dry lips and hold my breath when the song starts again. On her cue, Camden stands up and loudly sings the words he's heard us practice tirelessly. Bodies shift as the parents gape back in shock at Camden.

A shy smile crosses her face, and she joins Camden in his offbeat song about wobbling and gobbling.

TWENTY-TWO

CAMDEN

After my impromptu performance, the kids in Olivia's classroom go back to the stage and continue their show. Strumming at my heartstrings, Olivia pulls me in with her melody and fills the gaps of my soul. While her voice remains soft throughout the show, her magic reaches me. My darkened shadow hides for a while, allowing Olivia's innocent exuberance to consume me, and her mom's delicate light to ground me.

Once the show is over, Olivia bows once before she runs toward her mom, who picks her up for a quick embrace. Happiness crashes into me when she turns to me and lifts her arms for a hug. When I pick her up, her arms and legs wrap around me. Such a simple gesture, but still, it strips me bare, one by one putting back the pieces of my tattered heart.

"I'm so happy you're here, Cam." Olivia's fingers brush over my chin, pulling at the beard I've been keeping short.

Setting her back on the floor, I reach beneath the chair I sat on during her show and pull out a bouquet of white roses. Eager, she takes them from my outstretched hand and spins circles in front of us as she holds her flowers. Her laughter rings freely, her hair tousled in all directions, and I drink in the sound as my lungs press firmly against my chest. Olivia's like the warm sun and I bask in her glee and the love that pours so easily out of her.

Tears well up in Yanelys's eyes, a quivering finger running small circles over her bottom lip, as she watches our exchange. My heart stutters before it lurches forward, making me fall in deeper and deeper and deeper into the lives that matter most.

My two beautiful girls cleanse me. Their essence seeps into my soul, and for just a little while, I relish in the healing and allow my heart to feel the good rather than the bad.

Santiago claps his hand on my shoulder, his never-ending smile full of hope and belief. He nods his approval once, and I'm forced to bite back the threatening tears. He's always believed in me, never turned me away. God, I hope he doesn't ever live to regret me.

In the car, I sit in the backseat with Olivia, my fingers twisting her curly hair, as she chatters on about the show, and Yanelys peeks through the rearview mirror to watch us with fierce adoration. Olivia keeps her flowers close to her chest and only stops talking to smell their fragrance.

Once we get back to Yanelys's place, Nisa pushes her big body against my leg while her butt wiggles in excitement.

"Is she always this happy when you come home?" I scratch the back of Nisa's ear, and I swear, she smiles at me.

"If we're gone for anything longer than a minute, yeah. I'm pretty sure, in dog years, each minute counts as long as a month," Yanelys explains with a serious tone that makes me chuckle.

With one last pat on Nisa, I follow Yanelys, who puts Olivia's flowers in a vase and lets her choose where she wants to place them. Not too surprising, she puts them on the dining room table where she does her homework and we eat dinner together.

When my skin begins to crawl, I excuse myself to the bathroom, stopping on the way to ask Santiago for a pill. With him going out to his car, I go to the bathroom and slip open the vent door where I retrieve a pill from the baggie hidden behind it. The acid in my throat rises as I swallow the pill and sit on the floor, hoping my trembling limbs will stop shaking once the poison has worked its way through my body. My blood runs cold, and I only stand up when someone raps on the bathroom door.

"Coming."

On my feet, I walk to the mirror and stare at the figure standing in front of me. I clench my hands into tight fists when my eyes mock me, telling me I'll never be able to get clean. That I'll always be a slave to my shame. Not even Yanelys or Olivia can love me as much as these pills do.

"Everything okay in there?" Santiago asks through the locked door.

"Yeah," I call back, closing my eyes to the demon standing before me. I rub my hands over my face.

I tap the vent door to make sure it's closed properly and then open the door to Santiago and another pill. Taking the offered glass of water and the pill, I swallow them and lean against the hallway wall.

I haven't even started trying to get clean, but already, I know I want to quit. Beaten by the memories I can't shed, I want my addiction to win, so I don't have to feel.

Exhaling a harsh breath, I clap Santiago's shoulder, squeezing it once, before I speak, "I can't do this anymore."

Santiago scans my features, taking in the distressed emotions passing through me.

"Today," I stammer, my heart beating in rapid succession against my chest. "I want to get clean today."

My fingers squeeze deeper into his shoulder, grounding me, as my legs shake, threatening to give.

"Okay." His voice bleeds through his lips.

Every nerve in my body explodes.

He rubs a shaky hand over his face, and I do the same with mine. My eyes cut to the wall, to the floor, to Nisa wagging her butt at us before I find the courage to look at him. Empathy pours from him in waves, washing over me, soothing me like a balm to the burning flame within me.

"Okay, son," he repeats.

Strong arms go around me, holding me, while I shake in his embrace.

"After dinner, we'll go to the beach house."

His words grate against my chest, a warning for me to flee, but I swallow it down, silencing it, and meet his bleary red eyes before I nod once.

"We'll get through this, Cam, I promise."

"What are you two up to?" Yanelys asks, her eyes growing wide when she takes in the tears in her dad's eyes. "What's going on?"

Soaked in guilt, I go to her, two calculated steps forward, but I don't touch her. My hands twitch on either side of me, unease latching onto me, as I dispense a hot breath.

"I have to go away for a little while, baby." My voice shakes, and my heart trembles.

"Where?" She steps away from me, her hands going up to cover her heart. "Why?"

Tears build and spill from her eyes, my guilt growing with every tear she sheds.

"Just for a little while," Santiago tells her, his eyes roaming her face for understanding. "We'll be back in time for Thanksgiving."

My body shifts, my lips pressing against one another. Thanksgiving is only nine days away. Rubbing my hands over my face again, I go to Yanelys and make her a promise I hope I won't break.

"Thanksgiving," I whisper, my voice low but rough.

Brown eyes glare back at me, confused and hurt. Desperate, I lean into her and place my lips on her, soft and sweet, letting her breaths fall onto me, into me, to resurrect me.

"I love you, Yan," I murmur against her mouth.

"Thanksgiving?" she asks, resting her head on my chest.

"Yeah."

"Whatever's going on, Cam, I need you to know, I believe in you." She cups my face in her delicate small hands, holding my gaze with eyes full of love and tenderness. "I believe in us, in the love we share. In your strength and the goodness I see in you."

My body shifts, uncomfortable with her unwarranted trust in me, and I drop my head to her shoulder. "How?"

How can she see any of that when my own demons darken her spirit? When the horrors embedded in me taint and ruin everything I touch?

I swallow the lump forming in my throat. My eyes drop, scan the hallway, and finally land back on her. The only girl who could ever touch me. The only one who could piece together this screwed-up puzzle.

"Because I don't know how *not* to," she says simply.

"When I come back, I'll tell you everything." And I can only hope she'll feel the same way.

With our hands clasped together, we go to the dining room. Our hands separate after a small squeeze, and Yanelys goes to the kitchen with Nisa a few steps behind her while Olivia and I set the table for dinner.

"The forks don't go on that side," Olivia informs me when I've placed a fork on the left side of the plate.

"To be honest with you, Livvy, I don't get why we need forks and knives for pizza."

She scrunches her nose at me. "They're not for the pizza, silly. Mom always gets salad and spaghetti when we order pizza."

"Sounds like quite the feast."

"She even lets me have soda on pizza nights."

"Soda?" My eyes widen in mock shock, and it makes her giggle.

With twinkling eyes, she nods her head. "Sometimes, if I'm really good, she'll let me drink two cups of soda."

"Wow!" I pat the top of her head and bend down to plant a small kiss on her forehead. "Think I can have a bit of your soda, too?"

"Sure"—her eyes narrow, and she places her hands on her hips—"but don't hog it all."

Laughter builds inside of me, and Olivia joins me with her warm giggles.

After a short bath that flooded the bathroom, I soak up Olivia's mess before Yanelys can see it. Olivia twirls circles in front of me, her green pajama dress fluttering against my face with each spin.

Affection coils around my body as this cute little girl dances over my heart, marking it as hers.

"What is this?" Yanelys's voice rises above Olivia's singing.

We both freeze, but laughter spills from me when Olivia slants her eyes at me.

"It's almost clean, Mommy. See?"

"Yeah, I can see that." She narrows her eyes at Olivia, who squirms under the intense stare. "Get to bed, and I'll help Cam finish."

Olivia scurries off, and I catch the humor in Yanelys's small smile.

Peace wraps its arms around us as we clean the bathroom floor in communal silence.

"I'm gonna go say bye to Livvy." My hands rake over my face, and then my fingers tighten as I grasp on to the strands of my hair and pull.

A sigh mumbles from her throat, and I feel her sadness simmering.

"You're really gonna go?"

"I have to. If there were any other way…"

Taking her hand in mine, I lead us to Olivia's room. Yanelys stands by the door, giving me time alone with the daughter I've just started to get to know.

I climb into Olivia's bed, pulling her small body to me, and bury my nose in her hair, memorizing her. "Livvy, baby, I know we've only known each other for a short while."

"Almost a full week," she supplies, her smile showing off a crooked tooth.

I chuckle. "Almost a full week. That's all it took for me to fall in love with you."

Small hands go to my face, caressing my beard, before they wrap around my neck.

"I love you, too. Kinda like I would if you were my daddy."

Air wheezes out of my lungs, my heart pounding in my ears. I bring her closer to me because her love is stronger than my weaknesses.

"Yeah, just like that," I whisper. "Just like that, baby girl." I pull away from her so that she can see my face, the honesty behind my words. "I have to go away for a little while. Not long," I add when her bottom lip trembles.

Emotions stir inside me, clawing their way through my body, exposing me to all the feelings I've tried to hide from. I swallow hard, my breath wobbling.

"Stay, Cam. Please don't go."

"I'll be back, baby girl. I'll be back," I promise, scattering kisses on top of her head, combing my fingers through her thick hair. "I'll be back. Then, you and me? We're gonna plant the prettiest flower garden with whatever flowers you want. And every time you see them, you'll know I love you, and I'll never leave you again."

"White roses?" she asks, her eyes peeking up at me. "Like the ones you gave me today?"

"Just like those," I agree, kissing her one last time before I get out of her bed.

Walking the distance from her bed to Yanelys, waiting for me by the door, drains me of all my energy. Disbelief crashes into me, and I lean against the wall while soft fingers caress the base of my neck. Scared, I turn around and wind my arms around Yanelys's waist, my hands running circles over her back.

"I'm gonna get better." My lips graze the crevice of her neck. "For you and Livvy."

"For you, too," she adds, her fingers combing through my hair. "I believe in you, Cam."

"Thank you." I exhale. "Thank you for always seeing what I never could."

I kiss her, my tongue dipping into her mouth, and she takes me, all of the broken pieces, and welcomes me, strengthens me.

I've been running from my past, from the pain, for so long that I don't know how to stop. But I need Yanelys and Olivia. And they need me.

Tormented brown eyes watch me leave, and the shadows of my sins obscure the beauty of the only girl who can save me.

TWENTY-THREE

YANELYS

On loose limbs, I walk to Olivia's room and climb into bed with her. Without hesitation, she goes into my arms, her eyes searching for the same reassurance I need.

"He's coming back, Livvy."

My heart quivers, my skin buzzing with the threatening storm. I'm falling again, my heart plummeting with the pressure. The gloomy shadows surround me, and numbness spreads over my body, but somehow, the pain from my shattered heart remains intact.

"I told him I loved him." Overwhelming misery spills from her lips and takes ahold of my heart. "I thought maybe he could be my dad."

"Oh, sweetie," I whisper into her hair, rocking her in my arms, the same way I did when she was just a baby. "He's coming back. He's coming back," I repeat as much for her as for myself.

He's coming back.

He has to.

"Why'd he leave?"

"I don't know," I answer honestly. "But he went with Tito, and you know Tito will take good care of him."

"Tito would kick his butt if he didn't come back." Olivia perks up, flashing a cautious smile in my direction.

I laugh. "You're probably right."

"He seemed sad when he said good-bye. Like maybe it was forever."

"Yeah." I sigh, a tear freeing itself from behind my eye. "But Cam's always been a bit intense, even when we were kids."

Olivia's eyes widen, her lips forming a thin line. "Was he always sad, too?"

"Not always. He had mean parents who did a lot of horrible things to him," I try to explain the complexities of Camden's life to innocent ears. "Ita and Tito took him in when he was twelve, and we became his family. After that, he was a lot happier."

But still, the horrors he'd endured lashed out at him every chance they had and eventually drove him away.

"Is that why he's leaving? So, he can find happiness again?"

"I think he found his happiness right here." I trail a finger down her nose.

"Then, why'd he leave?" she asks, confusion contorting her face.

In love, we find hurt. In late hours, we find restlessness.

My head lies on my tear-soaked pillow, and I close my sore eyes to the early morning rays of sun spilling through my window shades. Memories of Camden and me surround me, an avalanche of what I already miss. Wrapped in my warm blanket, I lift my tired body from the bed and steal one last breath of Camden's pillow before I start making breakfast for Olivia.

Startled, I take a step back when I find my mom sitting on the living room couch.

"*Mi corazon.*"

Sympathy and understanding wrap itself around me, and I go to her.

My mom brushes my hair away from my face and hugs me close to her as she murmurs words meant to soothe me.

"He left." My heart cracks open, the tiny pieces slicing its way through my chest.

"Only for a short time," she reassures me.

"But why? Don't I get to know why?"

"You will. He'll tell you everything when he comes back."

"When he comes back?"

Anger builds in my stomach, thrashing and pulling me in all directions. My mouth twists, and I rub the nape of my neck as I try to gain control of my shallow breaths, but I know it's futile, so I embrace it. Lost in the chaotic pain, my heart grows tense. Burning, devouring, destroying me.

"When he comes back?" A humorless laugh radiates from my chest. "And then what? He'll leave again?"

Nerves rumble inside me, seeking a way out, and I stand up to pace in front of my mom.

"It isn't like that," she insists, standing up so that she can hug me again.

I shake away from her embrace and pin her down with a stare that encompasses all the hurt and frustration.

"How would I know?" I shout. My vision blurs, bleeding and fading. "I don't even know what's going on! I tell my daughter he's coming back, but how do I know that's true? How do I know how long he's going to stay until he breaks our hearts again? Don't I get a say in any of this?"

"Yes," she whispers. "You've always had a say, but even when he wasn't here, you still chose him."

The truth of her words takes my breath away and I hunch over in pain. My chest spasms, and I suck in a greedy breath, my heart refusing to stop thinking, hurting, beating.

"Mommy?" Olivia's soft voice echoes inside my ears, bringing me back to reality.

"It's fine, sweetheart. I'm fine." I turn to her with a forced smile and plant a kiss on her forehead. "Why don't you let Nisa out?"

Nisa runs from the kitchen and bounces in front of us before she runs to the back sliding glass door, barking her impatience as she waits for someone to open it.

"Go ahead," my mom coaxes Olivia, who finally listens. She closes the small distance between us and places a warm hand against my cheek. "Yan, I want to tell you, I do, but I think it'd be better coming from him. You two have always understood each other."

"He didn't tell me though. He didn't try to make me understand. He just left. So, you tell me, Mom. Please." My eyes water, begging for an answer I'm not sure I'm ready to hear.

"Yan…"

"Please," I whisper. "I need to know."

A heavy sigh falls on my cheek.

"Cam made a mistake. A bad mistake that has followed him since the day he woke up in the hospital after the earthquake in Haiti."

My mind spins and lands on Camden's mom as my mom tells me about his addiction.

"An addict?" My voice bleeds, the tone slicing through the tension in the air.

I back away from her, from the lies and deceptions. A dull ache roots itself in the pit of my stomach, spreading into my chest. It throbs, twisting my heart, trying to force him out of me.

"He's getting clean." Scared, my mom steps forward, grasping my arms with trembling hands.

"He's an addict." My lips quiver, so I suck them between my teeth and clamp hard.

Tension continues to builds, and the air becomes saturated in it. Suffocating me.

"Yanelys," my mom warns.

I lift an arm in her direction, halting her movement. "Don't." My eyes, shining with their betrayal, bore into her. "You should've told me. Instead, you chose him over us and put your granddaughter in danger," I speak slowly, each word pouring out of me like poison.

"It's Camden we're talking about." Her body inches forward but stops when I take another retreating step away from her.

"You don't know him!" I accuse, my voice vibrating with my temper. "You knew the boy, not the man. The addict," I hiss, bracing my arms around my chest, protecting my fragile heart from the only boy I ever loved. "I'm not doing this." I step back further, my back pressing against the wall, leaving me no room to escape. "I'm not letting my daughter have his childhood."

"He'd never hurt Olivia," my mom insists, her lips parting in distress as she inhales a sharp breath of air.

"He already has."

"Yanelys, you have to understand…"

"No." I shake my head, the throbbing inside making me queasy. "I don't. I have to let him go."

"He's getting help. For you," she emphasizes.

"He's an addict, Mom. He's just like his parents. I can't—" I stop, interrupting myself, "I won't raise Livvy in that same toxic environment."

On weak knees, I retreat back to my room where I burrow myself into the bed. My heart rate intensifies, shallow breaths falling onto my pillow, and I cocoon myself into the despair. With no end in sight, sorrow hits me with all the dreams Camden shattered. My soul screams, grief rising as bile, and I rush to my bathroom where I dispense all my unwanted thoughts.

I gave him every part of who I was. I tried so hard, willingly handing him my heart. Now…now, there's nothing left of me. Because there's nothing left of the boy I knew and loved. He's gone, too. Maybe he was never really here. Maybe he was always his parents, and I was too young, too naive, to see it.

Blinded by my fear, I stumble back in bed, and when I find Olivia under my covers, I lie down next to her and pull her to me. Delicate fingers trace my jaw, outlining my face. Her eyes are wide as a pensive smile spreads across her face.

"Ita said you're mad and to leave you alone."

"And, of course, you didn't listen." I wiggle my eyebrows.

"You always make me feel better when I'm mad." Her tongue skirts out of her mouth, and she takes a small breath. "Are you mad at Ita?"

"Yeah."

"And Tito?"

"Him, too."

"What about Cam?"

I close my eyes, not wanting to hear his name.

"You can be mad at him. That's okay, Mommy."

"He made a bad mistake, sweetie. I don't know if I can forgive him."

"Remember when I painted your face with permanent marker while you were asleep, and you had to wear it for, like, a week?" she asks.

I nod, the memory of my little mischievous girl lifting my spirits.

"I thought you'd be mad at me forever, but you said you couldn't because your heart loved me too much. Maybe your heart loves Cam that much, too."

Her cheeks rise with her smile, and I rub my fingers over her tender skin, absorbing her warmth. Her eyes watch me, waiting for an answer.

"I think my heart loves him that much, too," she says, her voice pleading with me, breaking me even further.

My heart thrums, wild but strong, and I close my eyes to her wisdom. My breath stutters, and a rush of heat creeps up my neck, casting a flame over my cheeks.

Every time I told him I believed in him, I meant it. I still do. I believe in his love and the goodness rooted inside of him.

But his deceit and the danger it poses to our daughter weigh on me. And, for the first time, it clouds the overwhelming love I have for him.

I inch closer to Olivia and cry. Because I can't see past this pain. This sorrow.

My foolish heart remembers him. The boy I gave my heart to. The boy who loves me without restraint. And the vision distorts my doubts. My deceitful heart twists, turning his lies into truths. Believing him because he is my truth.

Silence brushes over me like silk, and I give in to the embrace, closing my eyes, not wanting to think or feel or love.

TWENTY-FOUR

CAMDEN

Crisp fall air rushes over me when I step out of Santiago's beachfront house on Carolina Beach and make my way to the shore. Nerves hum around me, pricking my skin, as I take in a deep breath of the salty air. Letting it out slowly, I bring my coffee mug to my face and let the steam warm my skin.

"Ready?" Santiago's voice comes out hoarse, his eyes scanning over the white sand.

My knees knock together, and sweat builds in the center of my hands, so I wipe them on my cargo shorts.

Am I ready?

The waves keep time on their own terms, the ebbing tide rising with the sun. Speckles of gold reflect in the distance. A gull breaks from a tree, its cry echoing over the rumbling waves, neither realizing nor caring about the war I'm set to wage on myself. I shiver.

The sea foams, slapping the cool sand with surging waves. Swell after swell, it heaves, taking what it wants. Never giving in return. Plunging, pummeling, expunging.

In a muted plea, the wind stills, the electricity resonating in the air passing through me.

"Yeah," I mutter, the extended perfection of the beach stretching before me with towering dunes.

Another wave swells, a solitary mercenary whose soul stirs with each crash, frothing before it retreats back to sea.

"I'm ready," I whisper into the cool air.

I turn around, my footprints in the sand following me home.

The mirrored wall can't hide the devil pulling my strings, clawing at my skin. With my fingers gripping the bathroom sink, I look away from the image, a wordless message of all my many flaws and disappointments.

On lead feet, I shuffle to the bed where I sit and hide my face behind my hands. I hurt. Everywhere. Like a thousand needles pricking my flesh. Already, I know I can't do this, and it hasn't even been twelve hours since I had my last pill.

The day slowly ticked by, each second weighing on my resolve, on my spirit. Santiago spoke about fishing, about collecting shells for Olivia, about sunsets and the surf. I listened with a haphazard ear, the only sound resonating being the clamoring pulse of my heart. The tide rose and fell. Lunch and dinner came and went. Too nauseous to eat, all that my stomach claimed was the cup of coffee I'd drunk earlier this morning.

Shame rises, and my spirit lingers…barely, wanting to retreat from the radiating aches of withdrawal.

I ease my body onto the mattress and press a pillow to my stomach, hoping to ease the nausea.

The back of my head throbs. My stinging eyes sear into the ceiling. Anxiety creeps up my spine, so I roll over and stand up. Rough hands rub my face, and I take a step away from the bed. My feet continue to move, each step falling unheard on the bright walls.

Emotions, raw and tender, flood me, my past and future mixing together so that all I see is the horrifying idea of living my life without relief. The boy who felt too much and the man who can't stop running from the agonizing misery, clash and mold into one trembling figure.

My shoulders drop, bitterness moving over me, as my back hunches over, and I lean my hands onto my knees. Hatred silences me, pours freely from me, as I gasp for air I can't find. My disease taunts me from the inside, demanding a way out, to expose me as the fucking disaster that I am.

The walls quiver and begin to close in on me, so I rush to the door and turn the knob with an unsteady hand. Lost in my aching body, I hang my head, my heart pounding with every painful thought, as I leave my room and walk to the living room.

Santiago stands when he sees me, his eyes wide with worry. I look back at him in a blank stare, silently pleading with him to help me. The sharp blade of his disappointment cuts into me, making me bleed.

Quitting without weaning myself from the pills I've habitually taken for years was a bad idea. He warned me against it, but when I refused to take another pill, wanting them all out of my system as soon as possible so that I could go back to Yanelys and Olivia, he flushed them down the toilet.

My eyes shift to the sofa, and after he nods his head once in my direction, he sits back down. I sit on the spot next to him, on the other side of the small couch, and wrap my arms around my chest as we turn our attention to the blinking television in front of us.

This life…this life I've been living with a broken heart, a broken mind, a broken soul tugs at me so that I can't see beyond the despair. Or the damn loneliness.

And I remember a time I was so alone that even the sky cried. Stormy clouds hung over me as I wandered the streets, trying to escape Yanelys, Pastor Floyd, and Haiti. My tattered, wasted existence with no hope for an easy escape. I screamed, my lungs burning from the exertion. The clouds opened and shed the tears I'd struggled to hold on to.

Steely brown eyes watch me, and I squirm on the sofa with my knees shaking. On a soft grunt, Santiago leans forward and grabs something from the coffee table, which he hands to me without uttering a word. My fingers run over the glossy finish before I open my hand to find a picture of Yanelys and Olivia smiling back at me, the vibrant color of their souls gripping me.

For a long time, I sit there, taking in my girls, with a smile painted on my face. Even though I hurt, even though I'm being torn apart by grief and uncertainty, I smile. And I feel them, their love, their light, their trust.

I reach deep inside myself to where a tiny flicker of hope remains, and I know I'll survive. My life will not come from the years of my existence but through the damage that kept me alive.

TWENTY-FIVE

YANELYS

A white double-wide trailer stands in front of an open field with a volleyball court on its side. Children run, their laughter chasing after them, while adults talk among themselves. An older man, about my dad's age but with a head full of gray hairs, walks to me with a knowing smile.

"You're Yanelys," he says, putting his hands in his jeans pockets.

I nod. "You must be Pastor Floyd."

With the necessary introductions out of the way, the awkwardness of the situation claims the confidence I mustered up on the drive over.

"Camden carried your picture with him everywhere he went," he explains.

I dig the toe of my shoe into the ground.

"Do you want to talk in my office?" His blue eyes shift toward another double-wide that sits behind his church.

I bite my bottom lip but nod again.

His steps are small and cautious as we make our way over the well-manicured lawn. Although old, the trailer homes are tidy, the sidings still white with a light yellowish tint running along the edges.

"Once a week, Camden cleans both homes and goes over the sidings to keep them looking clean," Pastor Floyd tells me when he sees my appreciative inspection of both homes.

My eyes dart and roam the grass when he says Camden's name. "They're very nice."

"He's painted them once already, but they're old, and up until Camden came, no one really took care of them. He also mows the lawn and cleans up after services."

"That's great," I say, easing myself onto the two steps to the trailer home that houses Pastor Floyd's office. I take in both homes and the open field surrounding it.

And it is. Camden maintaining a place he must love is great. And completely Camden. I don't know why I'm surprised.

When I walk through the door, a somber teenager greets me from a couch in the reception area. His eyes barely meet mine, and I see the same insecurity that looked back at me when Camden and I were kids. I give him a hopeful smile that he turns away from, and I follow Pastor Floyd to his office.

Taking an offered seat, I put my hands on my lap and fidget.

Pastor Floyd coughs. "What can I do for you, Yanelys?"

I fold my hands and take a deep breath. "You know my dad and Cam went to my parents' beach house?" I ask.

He nods, his eyes watching me with caution.

"Do you know why?"

Pastor Floyd leans forward, the wrinkles on his forehead deepening. "Yanelys—"

"So, you do know," I interrupt. "You know he's an addict."

He lets out a grunt and leans back on the chair. "Camden is Camden. A good man with strong morals. He's loyal and kind, and when he lets his guard down, he can be funny. He loves deeply." He pins me with his eyes. "You know how much Camden loves."

A blush creeps up my neck, and I look away. Camden loves without reserve, as if he's never been hurt.

"He has an addiction, but that doesn't define who he is as a person. Calling him an addict takes away from everything else that he is, from all the good he's done, and everything he still has to offer."

My heart pounds, wild but without escape, and I press a hand to my chest, trying to keep myself from bleeding. A soft sigh brushes over my lips.

Camden is Camden.

"I was only trying to help him. He was in so much pain after Haiti," he rushes on, not seeing the shock on my face. "And when we couldn't find Jocelyn Marie and Yvon, it was like the world had crushed him."

"Wait." Blood drains from my face. "How did you try to help him?"

Pastor Floyd's mouth hangs open, and when I stand, his eyes dart across the room to the closed door.

"Yanelys," he says my name, pain and anxiety rolling off each syllable.

Resigned, he hangs his head, and I sit back down.

"Camden…he's been through too much. When the doctors stopped prescribing him pain medication"—his voice quakes—"his pain…I couldn't watch that boy suffer like that."

"So, you fed him pills?" My words splinter the air.

His face pales. "It wasn't like that. I just wanted to help."

"Are you helping that boy sitting on your couch the same way?" Angry, my hand slices in front of me as I point at the door.

"No." He shakes his head. "No, Yanelys, no. Please try to understand. If I didn't give it to him, he'd have found pills or other drugs from somewhere else. He was so lost, so sad. At least I knew what he was taking. I'm not saying I was right—I know I wasn't—but I didn't know what else to do. And then it got out of hand." He shrugs, his shoulders reaching the sides of his face, as he exhales a long breath. "I begged him to get help, but he wasn't ready until you came back into his life. You and Olivia—you've brought him back, and he's willing to feel the bad, so he can feel the good you bring him."

A tear falls down my cheek, and I brush it away. "That doesn't excuse what you've done to Cam."

"Camden did this to himself. Yes, I made it easier, but I'd like to think I also made it safer."

I scoff, looking at the man I thought had taken care of Camden when he left me, when he left his family.

"My dad would never have let him do this to himself. He would've made Cam see past the hurt."

"But he wasn't here. Neither were you. I was what Camden had, and I did my best for him."

The planes on my face soften, and I take Pastor Floyd in. A man who took a lost boy in and tried to give him a life where suffering didn't exist. I want to hate him, but I can't any more than I can blame him.

"When Cam came to you, how bad was he?"

Grief washes over every part of his face, and I suck in a breath, the tremor in his hand crushing my heart further. He leans forward, and after opening a drawer, he shuffles through it and gives me a plain envelope.

"What is this?" I ask.

"You only know bits and pieces of Camden's story, of why he left you and your family. You know he ran into his dad at the mall, and a few days later, he left. You know his dad left him money and asked him to take care of his mom, but that's only a part of the story. Before he walked away from his dad, his dad slipped this letter into his jacket pocket. It took Camden three days of sleeping on that couch"—he points at the closed door, toward the couch I saw the boy sitting on when I first came in—"to read it. That was the first and only time I've ever seen him cry. He shut down after that."

Toying with the sides of the envelope, I roll it over in my hand.

"Read it, Yanelys," he urges. "Afterward, I'll tell you about Haiti."

I open the envelope and swallow the lump in my throat. My hands shake as I unfold the paper, and through wet lashes, I read the words that have haunted Camden for so long.

Camden,

I don't know where to begin with you. I never have, and that falls on me and your mom. It's our shortcoming, not yours. It's our insecurities that we blamed you for.

This isn't some sort of near-death revelation. I've known this for a long time, maybe since before you were born, and there have been many times in my life that I wanted to love you, but I couldn't. Even now, as I near my death, I can't love you.

But it's not because of anything you did or didn't do. Again, this is on me and your mom, our problems that you were born into.

You see, before your mom got pregnant with you, she cheated on me with my brother. It was a betrayal that went beyond what your mom had promised me when we got married because it involved my brother, my best friend, my fucking hero.

My brother wanted to take a paternity test and take care of you and your mom as his family, if you were really his. So, we did. Camden, you're his son. Not mine. Never mine. But I took you anyway. I made your mom lie to him and live out the nightmare that was our home with a boy I couldn't stand the sight of.

He would've been a better dad to you than I was. I've known that since the moment he laid his eyes on you at the hospital. He loved you even though I told him he wasn't your father. I hated him for it. I hated you for tying the woman I loved with the man I hated.

I banned him from our lives, and every day, I punished you for sins you hadn't committed. I lashed out at your mom for things she couldn't take back. I should've let you both go, but sometimes, you fight your monsters for such a long time that you become a monster.

I'm not asking for your forgiveness. I don't deserve it any more than I want it. Your mom, though, is as much of a victim as you are. Under different circumstances, she would've been an incredible mom. I robbed you both of that chance. I robbed my brother of that, too.

Don't forgive me, Camden, but forgive your mom. Find your real dad, and make a life with him. He'll help your mom. He'll heal her. The three of you can hate me together while I spend eternity burning for my sins.

The letter wasn't signed, but his dad left an address with the name Edward Riley.

Bile rises, burning my throat, as I fold the letter and carefully put it in my purse. Pastor Floyd opens his mouth, but I put a hand in the air, stopping him before he can speak. I can't hear anymore. Not about Camden or about Haiti. On wobbly legs, I thank Pastor Floyd for his time and walk back out to my car. The sun beams down on me, warming me, as the hatred that Camden lived through trickles down my spine.

Some people are born fractured. I used to believe Camden wasn't one of them. That he was born whole. Pure. And that life and its circumstances made him jagged. Intense.

It wasn't until now, when I read the truth that had slipped carelessly from Herb's fingers, that I learned Camden's truth. Camden was born from hatred. He's lived with that same hatred, and it's splintered his version of reality so much that all he's wanted to do was hide from it.

"Go wash up, Livvy," I call from the stove as I pull the fish out of the oven.

Olivia runs into the kitchen and bounces on the heels of her feet. "Ita's in there."

I rustle her already unruly hair. "Then, use my bathroom."

She spins twice before running to my bathroom with Nisa close behind her. I make Olivia's plate, cutting up the fish and mixing it with the rice and vegetables, and when my mom steps into the kitchen, I lean my body onto a nearby wall.

"What will you do now?" my mom asks, having read and cried over the letter Camden had received so many years ago.

"I'm going to Carolina Beach. I want Cam to know that I know and that I'm going to stand by his side."

Wrinkles deepen in the corners of my mom's eyes when she smiles at me with a decisive nod. "Good. He needs you. And Livvy."

"Livvy needs him, too." I sigh. "I wish he had told me himself, but I guess it worked out better this way since he didn't have to see me lose faith in him. I shouldn't have done that." I shake my head, repulsed with myself for giving up so quickly on Camden, who doesn't have a bad bone in his body.

"You were surprised and disappointed. We all were." My mom takes my hand and pulls me to her for a hug. "I knew you'd come around. You love that boy too much to let him go."

My cheeks warm as a blush creeps up my neck, and I look at the floor to hide my smile.

I do love Camden. With every single beat, my heart loves him more and more. Despite what I thought earlier, our story isn't over. We were robbed of several chapters, but this? This isn't our end.

"I'm gonna go get Livvy," I say, my thoughts still clouded. "Make sure she hasn't started a flood in the bathroom."

Not bothering to knock, I open the door to my bathroom and stumble toward Nisa when I see her chewing on a torn plastic wrapper. I look up at Olivia to ask why she let Nisa eat plastic when my heart stutters to a stop.

I fall to my knees in front of the toilet and push Olivia's head over the rim. The small pill Olivia spit out when I walked in swirls down to the pit of the toilet, and I shove a finger down her throat, making her gag. Not understanding, Olivia squirms in my firm hold while I scream for my mom.

My tears trickle down and soak the back of Olivia's head as I coax her to vomit, wanting her to get rid of whatever poison she swallowed. Our bodies tremble together, feeling the pain of Camden's destruction.

TWENTY-SIX

CAMDEN

Sleep evades me, and with nothing to numb the pain, my emotions swim inside me, suffocating me. For the first time in years, I feel the pain of everything I've lost and the joy Yanelys brings that I don't deserve.

With the pounding in my head worsening, I lie in my sweat-soaked bed and wait. Wait for the aching to stop, for the nausea to subside, for the remnants of my sins to cycle through. I wait to feel human again.

Restless, I tug the sheets off my heated flesh and shove it aside until it hangs off the bed. A disarrayed quiet settles on the bright walls and all that I hear is what's going on inside of me. My heart pulses, each thump echoing in my hypersensitive ears. My breaths come out as needy whispers as the orange embers of the falling sun pour through my open window.

I close my heavy eyelids and sigh as I kick my feet off the bed, knowing sleep will continue to elude me.

I've fallen apart several times in the past forty-eight hours. Each minute that ticks by is another minute I get closer to crumbling. I feel it, the desperation growing inside my bones. But every time I've wanted to give up, Santiago has been there to build me back up. He refuses to leave me, so I refuse to run away.

Instead, I'm embracing the pain because he says it's a reminder that I'm alive. That I'm a survivor. The dull hollowness I sought through drugs still pulls at me, reminding me that with emotional pain, less is more when more becomes too much, but I'm fighting it.

God, I'm fighting it, fighting myself, fighting the mess I created.

I rub my tired eyes and then run my hands over the stubble on my face. The constant cycle of wanting to fight and wanting to give in makes my head swim, so I turn to the notebook Santiago gave me, and I sit on the edge of my bed to write the words troubling my heart, etched in my soul.

But, right now, overwhelmed with conflicting emotions, I tap the pen to the paper, unable to form a single word.

My hand shakes, and my mind threatens to slip me away into a frenzied panic. I scribble the only words that bring me peace.

Yanelys Sanchez + Camden Riley = 4-ever

So many times in our past, Yanelys doodled the very same words, and like her, I encircle it with a heart. A hopeful smile forms on my lips, but I startle when my door bursts open.

Addled eyes, large in their resentment, settle on me seconds before Santiago jumps on top of me, pushing us off the bed. We land with a hard thud on the wooden floors, and Santiago's heated screams fill my ear as he holds his hands in tight fists that rain their torment over my face

My nose erupts in pain and blood, and while I don't know why Santiago's hitting me, I let him, somehow knowing I deserve it. I don't wince in pain or block his assailing fists because I can't. I've been hit, beaten, and abused countless times, and I never fought back out of fear.

But, this time, it's different. I'm not scared of Santiago, just unable to fight the man I idolize. I bite back the adrenaline coursing through my veins so that I don't lose my temper with him. Instead, I watch him lose control. And my soul shatters pain with every hit.

With the same silence as when he stormed into my room, he pushes himself off of me and surveys me as I lie still on the floor. His hands run across his face, his shallow breaths wheezing out of his lungs.

"You did this." Acid drips from his lips, and he points a shaky hand at me before he stomps off.

Santiago leaves the door open, and I can hear him slamming the pantry doors in the kitchen. Unmoving, I stare at the ceiling, the never-ending pathetic show of my life playing in slow motion in my mind.

I want to feel betrayed, to be angry with Santiago, but I know who I am. Gently lifting myself from the hard floor, I go to the bathroom and wash my face, spitting blood into the sink a couple of times before I leave. Testing my jaw, I open my mouth and click it. Disgusted, I turn away from the mirror and the swelling starting to show on my face. Emotions churn inside me, but I push them aside and leave my room to look for Santiago, whom I find outdoors, putting his small suitcase in his car.

I don't know what's happening, but whatever it is, I know I deserve it.

"What's going on?" I ask, making him turn to face me.

Wild eyes roam over me, finally seeing me for who I am.

"I tried to help you, Cam." He shakes his head.

My eyes dart to my bare feet.

"I gave you pills to help you get through until you could get clean." He steps forward.

Anger rolls off of him like a crushing tidal wave, and I drown in it.

"You lied to me! Now, Livvy's in the hospital because you—"

Advancing on him, I grab his arm, squeezing tighter than I intended. "Livvy?" The world tilts and spins, and my hold on Santiago hardens.

He growls, his eyes meeting mine, "She found the pills you'd hidden in Yan's bathroom. Livvy swears that she didn't take any, but Yan's taking her to the hospital because she walked in to see her little girl spitting out one of *your* pills into the toilet."

Relief floods me, and I close my eyes. "Good." I sigh. "That's good."

Santiago pushes me away from him, and I stumble on the steps behind me that lead to the house.

"Not good, Camden!" he shouts in my face. "What would've happened—"

"It didn't happen," I cut him off again, desperation taking over me. "It didn't happen. She's okay. She's okay. Livvy's okay," I repeat, letting the words wash over me like a balm.

"Stay away from us."

Angry, hateful eyes look past me, his decision already made. My head grows dizzy, and the world around me distorts as realization hits me.

I lost them. I lost them. I fucking lost them.

I swallow, my life in ruins by my own hands, and watch Santiago walk around his car and open the door on the driver's side.

"No!" I run to him and close the door he just opened. "You can't leave me here!"

"The hell I can't," he spits his words at me.

"Please, Santiago, take me back with you. Just to see Livvy." The threat of tears blurs my vision so I turn my face down. "And to say good-bye to Yan."

Our eyes meet, and when he nods his agreement, tears spill from behind my eyes. For the first time in seven years, I cry, dampening my exhausted heart.

Just as the automatic hospital doors open for us, I spot Yanelys and Olivia leaving the emergency room. Olivia's eyes immediately find Santiago and me, and she rushes to us, leaving her mom trailing behind.

After hugging and kissing Santiago, she leaps into my arms, and I hold her close, rubbing her back in comforting circles.

"I'm okay, Cam," she says, pulling away so that she can put her small hands on my face. "Nisa and I thought they were candy, but it tasted so bad that I spit it out, and I'm okay."

"That's good, sweet girl." My eyes lift and meet Yanelys's hurt eyes.

She offers me a gentle smile that I can't return, so I ignore it and focus on holding Olivia, committing her to memory so that I can keep her with me for the rest of my lonely eternity.

"Nisa had to go to the vet because she ate a lot of them. Ita's with her, but she says Nisa's going to be okay, too."

My stomach clenches, knowing how quickly my selfish acts could've destroyed the family I love. The family I don't deserve and was never meant for me.

Everything seems out of place, out of focus. Lost without a clear vision, I take in a greedy breath, my hope disappearing with every second that brings me to my last good-bye.

"I'm glad you're both okay."

I offer her a smile, but already, I feel the stupid tears welling in the back of my eyes, so I put Olivia down and stand up.

"Livvy, why don't you go with Tito? I'll meet you at our house in a bit," Yanelys whispers, her eyes searching mine.

Yanelys pats Olivia's head and then kneels down to give her a hug before my little girl spins two enthusiastic circles and takes Santiago's hand, who leads them to his car. I bite my bottom lip, watching her leave without being able to give her another hug.

"You're leaving?" Yanelys crosses her arms over her chest and lifts an eyebrow in question.

"I'm sorry, Yan." With my eyes closed, I rub my hands over my face several times but open them, so I can look at Yanelys and remember everything about her one final time. "I'm so fucking sorry for everything. This is all my fault."

"It is." Her eyes bore into me, making me squirm with the truth. "You screwed up bad." Her bottom lip trembles. "You leaving isn't gonna make it right though."

"My staying is only going to make it worse. I'm an addict, Yan. I'm always going to be an addict. Every night I go to bed, it follows me. It stays with me and waits for me every morning. It doesn't stray or give me five minutes of peace. It's just there, all the damn time. I can't control that."

"You're a coward," she counters. "You run, pretending you're doing it for everyone but yourself. But that's not true. You're doing it for you." She shoves a finger into my chest. "You're doing it, so *you* won't get hurt, not us. Stop thinking with your pain, and follow your heart. Let us help you." Her eyes plead with me, her lips forming a tight line, as she waits for my response.

When I stay quiet, she narrows her eyes, her simmering anger boiling, stopping the flow of her tears.

"Let us help you before I finally listen to you and turn away from you for good, which is what I should be doing! I'm tired of giving you chances because all you do is screw them up."

"Look at me, Yan!" I step away from her and let her look at my bruised face, torn shirt, and bare feet. "I'm a mess. And all I'll bring to your life is more messes. I've never been the white knight you—"

"Forget about the white knights in shining armor," she interrupts, stepping closer to me so that I can feel the heat from her skin on my own. "That's nothing more than a load of crap. You're a warrior, Cam. You fight, you lose, and you keep going. So, get off your ass and fight. You fight for us, and don't you dare give up."

Her fists slam into me, tearing through my chest and exposing every broken piece of who I am. My heart skitters, reminding me that the blood coursing through me is made up of nothing but my mistakes.

Yanelys moves even closer, leaving a tiny gap between us, and places a gentle hand on my cheek. I lean into her, placing my hand over hers. As angry as she is with me, as much as she wants to hate me, I know she's not ready to give up on me.

She's my hope, the light in my darkened life. And every day, I love her more.

I should've chosen her. It was always supposed to be her.

"Don't leave."

Her eyes, swollen and red, spill over with tears, and I lose my footing at her words.

"Fight for me."

I open my mouth, gasping for air, but drown in her accusatory tears.

I don't bother explaining. None of the words I have for her will undo the damage I've already done.

She closes her eyes to me and the future we could never have. Her head turns away, and she hugs her arms around herself, misery casting shadows over her features. Her despair grips my chest, crushing us both with its iron fist. The quiet between us is so loud that I can hear her every thought damning me for giving up on us.

Her face crumples when she turns away from me. The ill-fated tragedy of our relationship mocks me.

"Yan." I reach for her, but the words stop there.

I can't think. I shake my head, defeated once again by the world and its sharp edges.

TWENTY-SEVEN

YANELYS

Pain is a surreal thing. You think you've felt the worst of it until, one day, real pain hits you, and you find yourself gripping on to the bathroom sink as tears pool down your cheeks, begging your reflection in the mirror to be strong. To hold on a little while longer.

My breath hitches, and I turn my face away from my reflection, not wanting to meet my puffy red eyes.

Crawling into my bed after a cold shower, I can't keep the image of Camden giving up out of my mind. His sad eyes no longer a luminescent blue, the deepened creases surrounding his grim mouth, his slumped shoulders, the weight of the world rolling down his spine.

With my heart scarred, I curl into myself when I feel the side of my bed give.

"He was right to leave," my dad says, his voice gruff and seemingly louder in the quiet of my room. "He's not the same boy we knew. The Camden we knew would never...he'd never..."

"He'd never what?" I whisper into my tear-soaked pillow.

"Fall so hard. He's unreachable."

Callous hands stroke my back and shoulders as I sob into my bed, praying Camden feels each tear so that maybe he'll fight. If not for himself, then for me. I hope his heart won't scab over before I have time to reason with him and force him to see what I've always seen.

Gripping the pillow with a tight fist, I peer up at my dad and blink back the tears. "He isn't unreachable." I sit up and look past him. "I can get to him. He'll listen to me."

Together, we'll face his pain and dark memories and let them go. We'll face his demons so that he can stop running, stop hiding. Even if it takes a lifetime because I can no longer fathom a single day without him.

"Yan." My dad takes in a long, slow breath.

I look back at him in time to see him shaking his head.

"The boy you knew doesn't exist. He died the day he sold his soul to his addiction." He grips my shoulders with tense fingers and squeezes. "Don't romanticize this with thoughts of saving him. He's gone."

Although my head hurts and my body aches from the stress of the day, I shoot up from the bed and turn away from my dad. "He's not gone." With my arms crossed, I slowly turn around and face my dad.

"He gave up, Yan! The boy I love as my own son chose to give up and gave in to his parents' destruction." My dad's eyes reflect the same agonizing emotions churning inside of me.

"Dad"—I move to him and put my arms around his waist as I rest my head on his wide chest—"he's still there. I saw him. He's so much more than all the bad in his past. He just has to see it." Pulling back, I wipe away a stray tear falling down my dad's cheek. "Tomorrow, I'm going to find him, and I'm going to show him how his family will never give up on him."

My dad's eyes leave my face, and he rubs his hands over his face. "It's too late, Yan." He sighs, his eyes closing in resignation. "I already told him to leave you and Livvy. He agreed, Yan. I'm sorry."

"You're sorry?" I whisper, my heart thundering in my ears, cracking with each deafening beat.

"The pills he kept hidden from all of us could have killed Olivia!" His voice booms inside my small room.

He walks to my nightstand and every one of his angry steps reverberates in my chest.

"And now, you've probably killed *him*," I accuse, my voice sounding stronger than I feel.

Rage connects us like a strained thread, and I feel it snap when my dad reaches for the picture of Camden that I keep by my bed.

"Dad!" I shout, advancing on him seconds before the frame slams against the wall, the glass shattering to pieces and landing on the floor.

TWENTY-EIGHT

CAMDEN

Tears fell long after the morning sun had kissed my bruised skin, and I continued to cry until I felt hollow inside.

Brushing the dirt from my knees, I walk to Pastor Floyd's church.

When he opens the door and sees me, he murmurs, "Son," draping me in a tight embrace.

Stepping out of his hold, I walk inside his office building and let myself fall onto the couch. Rather than waiting for him to ask me what happened, I tell him. Words pour out of me in violent desperation.

"Why'd you leave her?" Pastor Floyd asks when I finish.

"Because I'd ruin her. I couldn't give our relationship a chance to breathe or grow because, eventually, it'd fall apart. I'd destroy her and Livvy. I can't live with that."

We sit in silence, and it isn't until Pastor Floyd's eyebrows draw together that I know he's about to throw some spiritual crap at me.

"Yeah, I get it," I cut off his words before he has a chance to form them. "God only gives his hardest battles to his strongest soldiers. The devil's only fighting me because he knows I'm going to win." Sarcasm drips off each word.

My heart teeters, anxiety fogging my mind, but Pastor Floyd watches me with an amused grin on his face.

"I'm tired of hearing that shit. It doesn't mean anything to me. You've wasted years on me, and still, I'm nothing. My journey in life doesn't mean a damn thing."

"Your journey was never about becoming something, but unbecoming everything that isn't you. These insecurities and self-hatred you hold on to so tightly are destroying you. You can't be who you're meant to be until you let them go."

"I can't."

"You can!" Pastor Floyd shouts, startling me. "You're not your past. You're not the sins of your father or the scars on your skin. You're not the heartbreak or abuse you lived through."

Taking a deep breath, he sits on the couch, and I watch him with the same intensity he watches me.

"You're Camden Riley. And it's time we found out who he really is."

We're silent for a long time, and I feel his agitation with me vibrate in the air. I run my hands over my face and tug on my hair that fell into my left eye.

"Before I became a pastor, I was a businessman. I was smart, savvy, and ruthless. I had a big house and a beautiful wife who I ignored. Over and over again, she'd ask me to work less hours and spend time with her." Sighing, he scans the walls of the room before his eyes land back on me. "She wanted to start a family. I wanted a chance at being something great. It wasn't until she left me and found someone who could give her what she wanted that I realized I'd already had something great when I was with her." Pastor Floyd stops and stares at me with eyes swimming in apprehension and pain. "If you give up and refuse to find yourself for your daughter and the woman you love, Yanelys will eventually find someone else to raise your child and give them the life you should've been giving them."

Greedy for air, I suck in a deep breath, but with his words swirling in my mind, I find I can't fill my lungs. My jaw twitches, the muscles in my body tightening, as my poisonous friend summons me, reminding me of the reprieve a couple of pills can give me.

My eyes lock with his—mine hard and unyielding, his brimming over with the same concern I've taken advantage of for years.

"Pastor Floyd," I say, knitting my brows together.

Misery overflows from his eyes, mixing with his love and hope for me.

"Don't ask me to do this, Camden," his voice, hoarse and uncertain, pleads with me. "I can't keep giving you pills."

Taking him in, I bow my head in shame and stare at my knees.

"It's okay," I tell him as I stand up from the couch. "It's okay."

His expression tightens when I step around him and toward the door to leave.

His hand grips my arm, trembling, as his emotions play on his face. "Don't go, Camden."

I step away from him, from the security he offers me, and with a failing heart, I leave the church and edge toward the desolate friend that pulls my strings.

Realization grips me, making my stomach turn, while the fear and pain of what I've thrown away consumes me. Loss spirals through me, fusing with the regret and self-loathing. Each emotion presses into my lungs until I can't breathe.

I cling to my chest, fisting where my jagged heart once beat, and wonder how it can still hurt when it's the very part of me that's missing. It throbs and aches and reminds me that I can never escape the pain of loving and leaving Yanelys.

Without thought, I walk and only stop when I reach the debris of the building Santiago found me in. The desire to have died in that fire overwhelms all common sense, so much so that I don't even feel the rubbish or ground cutting into my bare feet.

"My boy," a familiar voice says.

I spin around to see my mom's worn face. Her lips pull into a scowl as she narrows her eyes at me and turns her head to one side in silent speculation.

Disgust spreads through me, and I turn away from her, not wanting to see myself in her or the future that beckons me every time I take a pill.

"You've nowhere else to go," she calls after me, "or else you'd still be with that silly little girl."

"Don't ever speak of Yan." I turn around and peer into her cold dark eyes.

"She's finally realized the truth, hasn't she? I told her you were a junkie, no better than me, but she didn't believe me." My mom points a shaky finger at me and smiles, exposing a cracked front tooth. "She knows now, huh?"

Confusion crosses my face before I can disguise it, but still, I go to her and shake her small frame.

"When did you see her?" I ask as her eyes, glazed and unfocused, look past me. "Tell me!" I shout, shaking her again. "When did you see Yan?"

"Yan?" She furrows her eyebrows in question. "The girl you left us for?" She sucks in her bottom lip and bites down. "I could've been a better mom to you if you had given me a chance."

Frustrated, I let her go to run my hands over my face, and she stumbles back a few steps but regains her footing so that she doesn't fall on the unforgiving hard ground.

"Just tell me when you saw Yan." Anguish pours from my lips, clearing my mom's muddled mind and she looks back at me with momentary clarity.

"The day after the fire," she whispers, her eyes tracing over the ground, as she wrings her hands together. "I didn't mean it. I mean, I did, but I wasn't thinking straight. I needed money, and you wouldn't give me any." She lifts her face, remorse and fear crossing over her features. "I didn't have a choice…" Her words trail off, her eyes scanning the fallen building.

Understanding creeps in, and I repel from the ugly truth. From the devastating hatred I've fled from for years.

"That was you?" I ask, backing away from her.

She takes a step in my direction.

"You set the fire?"

"Cam…"

"You tried to kill me?"

Losing my footing on a rock, I fall to the ground, and my mom kneels down in front of me.

"I…I…Cam, I can't…" Averting her eyes, she reaches into her pocket and pulls out a clear plastic bag and lighter. "Take it." She extends her hand and waits.

"What?" Bewildered, I look at the offered bag, my fingers itching to reach for it. "You're giving me heroin?"

"It's all I have."

Sad eyes watch me as I take her drugs and lighter from her and put them in my own pocket.

"Maybe this is it." Subdued, I stand up and begin to walk back to Pastor Floyd's office with a sudden calming peace passing over me. "Maybe this'll finally be what kills me," I mutter into the cool air.

With earnest hope, I stalk toward the madness sitting in my pocket and catch a glimpse of death and the promise of a new horizon.

The door to Pastor Floyd's church office creaks open after I unlocked it with the spare key he'd entrusted me with years ago. Although I hadn't wanted to come back here, I'd had nowhere else to go when the weight of what was in my pocket hefted me further into a bleak oblivion. I craved a sense of familiarity. Needed it, so here I am.

Smothering the tension inside my gut, I sit on the same couch I sat on earlier with Pastor Floyd. With a definite purpose, I swallow the heartache clogging my throat and reach for the small plastic bag in my pocket. I toy with it, looking at the brown substance, before I stand back up.

On tired knees, I go to Pastor Floyd's office and rummage through his drawer for one of the spoons he keeps in there for the canned soups he's so fond of. After finding it, I go to the medicine cabinet in the bathroom and find one of the many sealed syringes he keeps stowed away in case he needs an emergency injection of insulin for his diabetes. I also grab a few cotton balls. My hands shake as I turn on the faucet and suck a bit of water into the syringe.

The disquiet in the air follows me as I go back to the couch and take in a ragged breath. The promise of tranquility pushes forward.

After putting a small chunk of heroin onto the silver spoon, I squirt water over it and then use the back of the syringe to mix it together before setting the needle on the couch beside me. My heart hammers inside of me and I close my eyes as I pull out a lighter from my pocket and heat the bottom of the spoon.

My eyes narrow, my left leg shakes, but still, I press on, and I roll up a small piece of the cotton and place it over the solution on the spoon.

My eyes dart to the door, a part of me hoping for some sort of divine intervention. When God continues to ignore my silent plea for salvation, I push the tip of the needle into the cotton and pull back the plunger, watching the syringe fill with all the regrets of my sorry life.

Again, my eyes dart to the door, but I know no one's coming for me. I'm alone, not worth the trouble I've caused the people I love.

I angle the needle and insert it into my arm. My breath catches in the back of my throat, and after a few small wiggles, I pull the plunger back. When I see blood trickling into the syringe, I let go of any lingering hope and inject myself. I hold the shame and guilt close to my center as I wait for my heart to stop, for my body to stop fighting.

Resting my head on the back of the couch, I stare at the yellowed ceiling eager to leave this beaten and broken life behind.

A picture of Yanelys holding Olivia crosses my mind, and I hold on to them, wishing I could have been what they needed. I offer God my last prayer, knowing He'll hear me because they deserve happiness. Olivia deserves a dad, and Yanelys, a good man who'll be everything I couldn't.

A soft sigh brushes over my lips as warmth spreads throughout my body seconds before my eyes close, and the world goes black.

TWENTY-NINE

YANELYS

There once was a boy who was strong and kind and caring. He was courageous but sad. Sorrow and destruction followed his every misstep.

There once was a boy who loved a girl and protected her from harm, even when it meant alienating himself so that she could be safe from him.

There once was a boy who followed a path full of seduction and deceit. False promises were made that kept him away from the people who loved him most.

There once was a boy who one day woke up as a lonely man, away from his life, his family, his home.

Neither the boy nor the man knew the true value of love. He reached for love, but his own feelings of disapproval destroyed every chance he had of letting love in.

I grip the man's hand and plead with the boy to find his way back to me. To fight and stop underestimating himself or the love we share.

"Be strong, Cam," I whisper, brushing the loose strands of hair out of his face. "Come back to me."

After we hounded the nurses, Camden's doctor finally spoke to my parents, Pastor Floyd, and me and reassured us that Camden would make a full recovery although he had experienced respiratory arrest while en route to the hospital in the ambulance Pastor Floyd had called when he found Camden unconscious this morning.

They had been able to bring Camden back.

Now, all he has to do is open his eyes and choose to live. Really live, not just breathe and go through the motions of daily life. I want Camden to live and experience, and love and laugh. I want him to hurt and feel, and scream and cry. I want him to do all of that and more right beside Olivia and me.

"I'm waiting for you." I press my lips to his forehead. "We all are. You have a new life to live, but you have to fight for it."

"I'm tired of fighting," Camden groans.

My lips twitch, relief flooding me at the sound of Camden's voice. "Dig deeper inside of you, Cam, because you're gonna fight. We're gonna fight."

Camden's eyes flutter open, a pair of blue eyes looking back at me. "You're so beautiful, Yan. You know that?"

"Figures you'd almost die, and those would be the first words out of your mouth."

His eyes dance, his lips lifting for a second, but then another soft groan fills the room when he takes in his surroundings. "I'm in the hospital?"

I nod. "Do you remember what happened yesterday?"

His brows knit together, a tight frown painting over his lips. He takes in a sharp breath of air, and when his eyes meet mine, he nods once.

"That's behind you, Camden." I take his hand in mine and intertwine our fingers together.

"You can't fix me, Yan." He watches me, waiting for my response, as fear and pain play behind his eyes.

"But I can stay with you."

I sit on the edge of his bed, and he moves to the other side to give me room. When I lie down next to him, he pulls me to him and kisses my forehead.

"Olivia," he whispers his daughter's name, making my heart skip several beats. "What about her?"

"She's with my parents."

"Tomorrow—"

"Tomorrow will come," I interrupt. "And we'll face it together. One day at a time, Cam. That's all it takes."

His arms tighten their grip around me, and I lean my face toward his, so I can kiss the stubble on his jaw. He tips my chin and places a soft kiss on my mouth. His fingers caress my cheek and I lean onto his hand, needing the same comfort I'm giving him.

"Together, we'll make sense of it all," I promise.

"I'm no good for Livvy."

"You're enough, Cam." I take his hand and kiss the palm before I tighten my fingers over his. "You are so enough. It's incredible just how enough you actually are."

My words bleed into him, and I watch his walls give and begin to shatter behind his eyes.

"Stop betraying yourself with lies, and open your eyes, so you can see just how important you are. We all have something that destroys us and makes us flawed." I lick my lips, our eyes connecting us, and I can feel his pain as my own. "It strangles our hearts and keeps our emotions raw, so we can't move past them. We all have something we can't take back that cripples our souls."

"What destroys you?" he asks.

"You do. Every time you leave me."

He balks at my words, but I press on.

"So, stop leaving me, Cam."

His lips form a thin line as he presses them together. "I don't know how to stay and not ruin everything."

"One day at a time, remember? Forget about what could or might happen weeks or months or years from now. We're only focusing on today."

"Since we were kids, you've always tried to save me, but what if there's nothing left to save?"

"I'm not trying to save you. You can do that on your own. I just want to make it hurt less." The sides of my lips tip up, remembering the very same conversation we had when we were kids.

He draws in a small breath, both of us lost in the memory of our youth and the bond we've shared for years.

"You're wrong," he stammers, dropping his eyes to his lap. "I can't save myself. You're my knight, my warrior, my everything. You're the one who made me fight when what I really wanted to do was give up." Bright blue eyes look up at me, begging me, as they darken with his intensity. They overflow with emotions, with the never-ending sadness framing his thin face.

My tongue sneaks out, wetting my lips, as we stare at each other. The man I love, hardened by life's many blows, watches me with all of his vulnerabilities exposed.

His hands reach out and take my face, his warmth emanating the same fierceness he has to find internally. His voice comes out raw, the expression on his face rigid, as he says, "When I left, I gave up. The only time I felt even the tiniest bit of hope was in Haiti, but when I lost that…"

"Your world came crashing down." With tender fingers, I touch his hands, acknowledging his pain, wanting to carry some of his load for him. "I'm sorry, sweetie. I'm sorry for everything you've lost. I'm sorry I wasn't there to help you."

He leans his head forward, and I bring him to my chest, tightly hugging him, swearing I'll never let him go. He trembles at my touch and lets out a loud sob. With his restraint gone, I hold him, both of us experiencing the same excruciating pain that plummets into our chests, leaving us breathless.

"I'm here now. And, Cam, I need you to get clean. Livvy and I—we need you to get clean. Livvy needs her dad, and I need my soul mate."

"Okay." His grip around my waist tightens, and he exhales a long breath. "I'm gonna do this right though. I have to go away again."

My chest constricts, and he looks up at me with bloodshot eyes.

"I have to go to rehab, Yan. It's the only way I can do this."

"Okay," I agree, leaning forward so that I can kiss his forehead.

He closes his eyes, and when he opens them, he gazes at me with determination. "I'm going to get clean—for you, for Livvy, for myself. I just need you to promise me something."

Our eyes meet, and I nod my head, licking my lips.

"Promise me you won't bring Livvy to see me. I can't have my daughter seeing me in a place like that." Emotions rake over his face as he waits for my reply.

"Okay, but you can't keep me away, Cam. We're in this together."

THIRTY

CAMDEN

I always knew whatever path I followed would somehow lead me back to Yanelys. She's my destination. My hope, even when I thought I'd given up on that. My heart, mind, and soul still guide me to her.

Her words, her promises, hold me together. One day at a time is a lot less daunting than picturing endless days of trying and fighting. Those words spoken from her lips reached me, breathing life and faith back into my lungs. The terror of wanting to live for her, for Olivia, doesn't have as tight of a hold as it did before.

Because we're doing it together, one day at a time. We'll grow together— not through the years that we spend with one another, but the experiences that bind us, the wars we wage and win. Together. And I will win.

One day, when I leave the rehab center I was admitted to two days ago, I'll wake up to my beautiful girl and greet the sun with the same determination Yanelys fills me with. Every night, I'll go to bed, knowing I fought and won another battle against my addiction.

When I leave the confines of my small room and step into the front office, familiar shame slams into me when I spot Santiago waiting for me by the receptionist's desk. My chest heaves, and I gasp.

Santiago's throat bobs as he swallows and turns his brown eyes to the floor before they settle back on me. He clears his throat, his body tensing with every step he takes toward me.

"I'm not leaving her again," I say before he has the chance to speak. "Or Livvy. I've screwed up," I rush on, blurting out everything I feel and know to be true, "so many times, and I'll probably keep on screwing up, but leaving her, leaving them, has been the biggest mistake I've made. I can't do it again." My chest lifts and drops in rapid succession. "You can hate me." My heart constricts, moisture collecting in the corners of my eyes, and I run my hands over my face. "But I'm not leaving my family, not ever again."

He purses his lips and nods once. "I was wrong to tell you to leave. I gave up on you the minute things got too hard." He takes a few steps toward me and puts his hands on my shoulders. "*I gave up on you.* I'm sorry, son."

A sense of joy and guilt weave together as I watch him hold himself together through his own feelings of remorse.

I put my hands on his wrists and squeeze. "You were looking out for your family," I whisper, ignoring the curious eyes of the workers at the center.

"You are my family, Camden." His eyes, puffy and rimmed in red, meet mine. "You're my son in every way that matters, and I turned away from you. And you…" His voice breaks as his eyes wildly dance over to the couch resting in the far corner of the front office.

"Don't." I shake my head. "I took the heroin because of who I am. Because of the stupid choices I've made. This isn't on you. It's me. I need help."

I look around, my eyes scanning over the walls of my self-imposed prison, and I know I've made the right decision in coming here. I need professional help. This isn't something I could do alone. I know that.

Every minute that passes by is a reminder of how dependent I am on the pills that numb me. Even with the medicine the center's been giving me, it's hard. Because of the medicine, the side effects of withdrawal aren't as strong as they were at Santiago's beach house, but they're still there, lying in wake with the constant need for just one more pill and its false promises.

"Your family —we will help you. I swear it. I won't ever push you away again. You're my son. You've always been my son, and I'm going to fight for you even if you don't want me to."

Gratitude pumps through my veins, and a small smile crosses my face. The fear of Santiago's disapproval has weighed heavily on my shoulders. Knowing he still cares, that I'm still his son, frees me.

He takes my hands to his face and touches his forehead with mine. Tears clog the back of my throat, and I shut my eyes, allowing my emotions to squeeze and torment and eventually alleviate the tension in my chest.

"I love you," I choke out and when Santiago drops my hands, I grip his wrists with tight fists. "You and Carmen—you're my parents. And"—I'm unprepared for the turmoil swimming inside me, and tears fall from my eyes and down my cheeks—"thank you."

Santiago pulls me to him, hugging and consoling me, while I struggle to find a breath.

"We love you, too. You know that, don't you?"

Unable to speak, I nod my head and close my eyes tightly, forcing more tears to escape from the corners.

My whole life, I've reached for love but never gotten a proper grasp on it. But I can't back away from it anymore. I can't continue to live on empty when the girl who is my world has asked me to live and love by her side. For too many wasted years, I lived my life in denial and lost everything that was important to me because it was easier to hold the devil's hand than risk the chance of Yanelys turning her back on me. But she's finally seen the worst in me, and for some crazy reason, she's still holding me close to her heart.

THIRTY-ONE

CAMDEN

"Happy Thanksgiving," I whisper into Yanelys's hair, bringing her closer to my bare chest when she murmurs a sleepy response.

Several days ago, I started to live again. One day at a time.

It hasn't been easy, but change in its inevitability never is. Mistakes and regret form in its wake. Repercussions follow us that haunt us, never loosening their hold. At least, not really.

But I know it's well worth every hardship when Yanelys's eyes flutter open, and her lips lift into a radiant smile. Delicate hands trace over my back, sending shivers down my spine. My mouth covers hers, taking and giving, offering and demanding.

Earlier this morning, Santiago picked me up at the rehab center and dropped me off at Yanelys's doorstep. She was shocked when she opened the door, but she didn't ask further questions when I explained that I had been granted a day pass from my twenty-one day program. We took advantage of Olivia sleeping and went straight to Yanelys's bedroom where we held each other until we both fell back to sleep.

The story of us unravels, spinning its tale through our limbs and into our souls.

Our mouths stay connected as I bend my knees and climb over Yanelys. I press a long, urgent kiss against her lips. Breathless, we separate, and I trace kisses over her chin, down her throat, and onto her naked breasts. Her lean muscles twitch, and she grips the back of my head so that I lean back and gaze into her tender brown eyes. Minutes pass with us just staring at one another, anticipation and need growing and stirring inside us.

When she leans her head into her pillow and arches her back, I align my cock with her entrance and kiss her neck as I go inside her.

"So beautiful," I whisper. "You're so beautiful."

Her hands go to my stomach and wrap around my waist, pulling me closer to her. Her eyes watch me with the same faith she restored in me, and my heart thunders behind my chest.

I thrust inside her, filling us, and when she moans my name, my mouth covers hers, demanding and pulling every inch of who she is. Yanelys opens to me in invitation, and our tongues dance together as I fist her hair. Fast and hard, I lose control of myself, and together, we conquer each other. Unrestrained pleasure encompasses me with every jerk. Moaning my name again, she shudders once before her body goes languid beneath me.

Emotions run rampant when her dark eyes meet mine, and I slow my movements, so I can take her in. This woman, this incredible woman who loves me through my flaws, has my heart and has somehow saved me with her unwavering gentleness.

When I tip her chin up, her eyes never leave me, and I gasp when her hands touch and caress my face. My own hands grip her face as I continue to move inside her. Her eyes open in shock, and she lets out a joyous cry when I thrust one final time.

Arms wrap around my neck, bringing me to her so that our bodies are flush together. I rest on my elbow and touch the outline of her face.

"Thank you"—desperation floods me and spills over—"for not giving up on me. For getting me and loving me. I always knew you'd be the one to save me."

"You're the one who hasn't given up." Her fingers trace over my jaw and lips. "I can only do so much. The rest is on you."

Her eyes soften, affection pouring from her. I inch down further and place a soft kiss to her swollen lips.

"I love you, Camden. I love every piece of you."

My eyes close, taking in and absorbing her words as the truth. Letting them shape me. Because I choose to believe in her, in us. I choose to believe in love, daunting and fragile as it might be.

"I love you, Yanelys." My voice comes out rough with the promise of forever enveloping us.

Her fingers dig into the back of my neck, and I touch my forehead with hers, breathing her in, letting her light and goodness bleed into me.

After showering and having breakfast with Yanelys and Olivia, we all piled into Yanelys's car and drove to Pastor Floyd's church.

For the past three hours, we've been working tirelessly, getting the church's annual Thanksgiving lunch ready.

With the decorations hung and the aromatic scent of turkey and mashed potatoes lingering in the air, I step back and look at the sitting area just outside Pastor Floyd's office. Small round tables fill up most of the space while the coffee table in front of the couch where I've slept countless times fills with food. Next to it, a small cooler—that I've washed after every time we've had one of these lunches—is full of soda and water.

It isn't extravagant, but it's special. And for the past seven years, it's been mine. My sliver of peace throughout all the turmoil.

Pastor Floyd didn't have to take me in, but he did it anyway. He gave me his kindness, and in return, I drained him. But his affection for me never emptied. He pushed and prodded and tried to help me reach a level of normalcy I'd never been able to obtain without Yanelys. Without my family.

As if pulled by my thoughts, she looks up at me from across the room, a smile playing on her lips. My heart thumps loudly in my chest, and I walk to her. With four long strides, I'm by her side, taking her into my arms. Her lips meet mine, making my heart steady while it continues to beat for her.

"You okay?" she asks, concern spilling from her eyes.

"Yeah." I kiss her forehead, and she leans her head on my chest. "I've never been so okay in my life."

"Get a room," Jeremy, a teenage boy just as lost as I was, grunts.

Eyeing him from over Yanelys's head, I give him a good-natured middle finger, and he chuckles, shaking his head at me, while I continue to hold Yanelys. I'll be damned if I ever let her go.

"Quit bustin' my balls," I say.

"Quit being so soft," he retaliates.

After a quick peck on Yanelys's lips, I charge after Jeremy, who runs out the front door and into the lawn of our church. Not having exercised in years and with the symptoms of withdrawal swimming inside me, I tire easily, and when I stop chasing him, I lean over, putting my hands on my knees, out of breath.

"You've gone soft, old man." Jeremy walks to me, the corners of his mouth wrinkling as his mouth breaks into a mischievous smile.

When he lightly smacks my shoulder, I wrestle him to the ground where we tussle until he's able to pin me down.

"You need to work out more." Jeremy smirks.

"Yeah," I huff out. "I'm getting to it."

"You'd better work harder before she leaves your scrawny ass for someone stronger." His grin grows, and I scowl at him. "Like me."

"Like you, huh?" I punch his shoulder.

He rubs where I punched, his smile never faltering. "Yeah, someone stronger and better-looking..." He trails off.

"Cocky little shit," I mutter without a hint of anger.

"Camden." Yanelys's voice rings over the yard.

I glance up to see her standing by the front steps, wringing her hands together.

Concern creases her face, so I stand and rush to her side just as a familiar face takes a step out from behind Yanelys. I take the girl in, the familiarity mixing with the years of her growth I've missed.

"Jocelyn Marie?" I croak, my hand covering the erratic beat of my heart.

Shy, she takes a step toward me, her face more mature than I remember. Five years have passed since I've seen that angelic face, but now, with her standing in front of me, time stills, as if it never truly existed. Overwhelmed, I go to her, kneel in front of her, and gather her in my arms.

"Jocelyn, my sweet girl," I murmur in Creole, cradling her head against my shoulder.

Her tears fall in rapid succession, so I hold her longer, harder, not able to let her go.

"Yvon?" I whisper, fear gripping me like a vise.

"I'm right here," his recognizable voice calls to me and I love the sound of it and the familiarity of the language I haven't spoken in years.

I whirl around to find his eyes dancing with humor.

With Jocelyn Marie in my arms, I go to Yvon and pull him to me, wrapping my spare arm around him. Their frames are still thin but so much sturdier than the last time I saw them.

Unashamed of the emotions washing over me, I fall to the floor, taking them with me and they nestle onto my lap. I cry as I hold on to the children I believed I'd lost. Their arms encircle me, binding us, and we stay like that, our tears blending together.

"I looked for you," I whisper, still speaking their native tongue. My voice heavy with years of devastation. "For five years, I looked for both of you."

Yvon steps back, leaving Jocelyn Marie sitting on my lap on the floor. "We weren't in Haiti." His eyes go to his little sister, the misery of the day our lives changed evident on his face. "Jocelyn got hurt, and we were air-lifted to Miami."

A ball forms in my throat, and I swallow hard to push it down.

"How bad?" I ask, brushing her hair away from her face.

She shrugs and lifts her right pant leg, revealing a prosthetic leg. Unable to look away, I stare at her artificial limb, its existence tearing at my heart.

"It's not so bad," she says in English, her accent noticeable and sweet.

With her still on my lap, I dig my fingers into my jeans pocket for a pill that I no longer carry. Agitation and unease swim inside me, so I stand up, taking Jocelyn Marie with me so that she's standing on her own.

"I can still dance," she says, spinning on her tiptoes with the same joy displayed on her face that I remember from five years ago. "My mom takes me to classes and everything."

My heart stalls at her words, and my brows crease together. "Your mom?"

Jocelyn Marie peers behind me, a small smile toying with the corners of her mouth. I follow her gaze and find a young couple standing next to Yanelys. Their hands are clasped, holding on to one another. The woman smiles at me and lifts a hand in silent greeting, so I do the same.

"While Jocelyn was in the hospital, I stayed with Daniel and Gloria," he says in the same heavily accented English as his sister. He tilts his chin toward them, peace passing between them in an unspoken vow. "Jocelyn moved in with us after the doctors let her out of the hospital. After that"—he pauses, as if he's still coming to terms with his new life—"they adopted us."

Relief slams into my gut, mixing with a hint of sorrow because, damn it, I wanted these kids for my own. On shaky legs, I walk to Daniel and Gloria with my hand outstretched for a handshake.

"You're the Camden we keep hearing about," Gloria says, bypassing my hand and giving me a hug.

After an awkward moment passes, I hug her back, patting her when she sniffles in my arms.

"They've been so worried about you. We've been looking for you for years."

"Yeah, me, too," I say, meaning that I've been looking for them as much as I've been looking for myself. "Thank you for taking care of them."

"They're our life." Daniel says, and he and Gloria exchange a warm glance when their eyes lock.

I shake Daniel's hand. "I'm glad they have you as their family," I say.

Yanelys wraps an arm around my waist, and Olivia takes my unoccupied hand.

"You were their family first," Daniel says, both of their kids settling on either side of them. "That makes you a part of our family, too."

Love swells, overflowing in my heart and seeping into my soul.

Yanelys squeezes my side, and I know I got this whole love thing all wrong. Love doesn't hurt. Losing people you love—that hurts. Disapproval and rejection from those who are supposed to love you unconditionally—that hurts. But love...love doesn't hurt. It fills those vacant spaces and softens the hardened edges.

That's what I have, what I've always had, but I was too afraid to hold on to it. So, I ran away from the love that burns from my chest and catches in my throat. It's invasive and scary, so I left it in the guise that I was protecting Yanelys when I was really protecting myself.

THIRTY-TWO

YANELYS

Each morning, with its light and the gold speckles from the sun, is a new moment to conquer ourselves. A fresh shot at becoming who we are meant to be. A unique opportunity to live in love.

That's what happens when you grow up with parents who are so obviously in love. You believe in love and happily ever afters. You believe the fairy tales with the happy endings, and you crave it for yourself.

Camden is my fairy tale. He's my warrior and dragon slayer. But more than that, he's my best friend. Having him back, even if we're not living together yet, is something I won't ever take for granted. Life is too fickle, and we don't know what any of the tomorrows might bring. We have today, so we live for today.

Nothing more. Nothing less.

"Mom!" Olivia whines.

I roll my eyes and continue to take my time with putting dinner rolls in a bowl in my mom's kitchen. Today has been hectic, but in the best possible way. What happened at Pastor Floyd's small church was...a gift. And now, after the emotional reunion, joy and gratitude warm my soul.

"We're hungry!" she shouts and I hear my dad shush her.

From beside me, my mom chuckles as she gets the last dish from the oven. Together, we walk into her dining room, and after I place the rolls in the center of the table, I take my seat between Camden and my dad.

With multiple conversations going on at once, we begin to serve ourselves.

Just as we're about to eat, Camden speaks up, "Can we say grace?" He coughs into his hand as his cheeks enflame from his blush. "It's something Pastor Floyd and I have been doing for years and…" He trails off, his eyes catching Pastor Floyd's, as Camden turns his lips into a sheepish smile.

"Yeah," I agree, taking his hand from underneath the table, "I think that's a good idea."

Without further instructions, we—Camden, Olivia, my parents along with their friend Henry, Pastor Floyd, Jeremy, Yvon, Jocelyn Marie, Daniel, and Gloria—close our eyes and bow our heads.

Camden clears his throat, his fingers interlacing with mine. "Dear God, thank you for this day you've given us. For the opportunity for family and friends to come together and honor you. Thank you for our health and for the food prepared with love. Thank you for watching over us, for guiding us, for helping us find our way."

Seconds pass by where he remains silent, so I open my eyes to find him looking at me.

"Thank you for not giving up on me and for loving me, even when I wasn't easy to love." His lips part slightly when he smiles. "In Jesus's name, we pray. Amen."

"Amen," we all say in unison.

When Camden reaches for the butter, I grab his hand and lean toward him. "Loving you has always been easy."

He lifts my hand to his lips and kisses my fingers. "Loving you has always been my salvation."

"Soft." Jeremy fake coughs into his hand.

I look back at him in question. He shrugs his shoulders and catches a roll that Camden tossed at his face.

"Children," my mom scoffs, but her smile gives her away.

As food is passed around and stories are shared, I look back at my family. New faces mix with old, and I'm reminded that blood isn't what binds a family. It's the people we want in our lives, who stand by our side, celebrating the good with happy hearts. It's the people who see us and accept us. It's the people who help us write our story and make sure we create one worth telling. It's the people who love us when we fall but push us forward, not willing to let us settle for anything less than who we're meant to be.

Because we owe each other that. Our family needs us to be ourselves, to push aside the bullshit lies we tell ourselves and listen to who we really are.

Camden pushes the food with his fork and nibbles on a roll of bread as I eye him with concern. He smiles, as much for my benefit but also with joy. Real joy, and it makes my heart rejoice.

"Tell us"—my dad's voice booms over everyone else's, and the room goes silent to listen to him—"how did you come to find Cam?"

Daniel washes his food down with a sip of water. "We just kept searching. We knew he was a part of a church in North Carolina, but no one could tell us the name of the church or where it was located. We just had Camden's and Pastor Floyd's names to go by."

"We flew to Haiti twice to see if we could find someone who knew more," Gloria offers, her eyes combing over her children's faces with warmth. "Yvon and Jocelyn Marie knew you two were alive. They never gave up hope"—her eyes meet Pastor Floyd's and then Camden's—"so we didn't either."

"We eventually got lucky," Daniel finishes. "We finally asked the right person, and he had Pastor Floyd's business card with the church's address."

"So, here we are," Jocelyn Marie chimes in, her eyes twinkling, as she looks back at Camden with innocent adoration.

"Mom and Dad wanted to call you guys," Yvon says, "but Jocelyn and I wanted to surprise you."

"You surprised me all right." Camden chuckles, his eyes flashing with the hurt of his past for the briefest of seconds. "Just about gave me a heart attack, too."

Laughter rings out at the dining room table with smiles and ease being passed around.

And, for the first time in seven years, I'm truly happy. I'm whole. My family is whole.

THIRTY-THREE

CAMDEN

Tired but content, Yanelys leans her small body onto my chest and nestles her head on my shoulder while Olivia takes a shower. I stroke her arm with calloused long fingers. My quiet love for her hangs between us, connecting us, magnified by the infinite emotion that pulls me toward her.

In moments of weakness, I tore us apart, not understanding what Yanelys and I offered each other. I lived under the weight of loneliness and walked further and further away from my true self, who I was meant to be, and my heart.

Looking into Yanelys's eyes, those beautiful, soulful eyes, I get a glimpse of the truth. Her truth. My truth. Real love lasts.

For so long, I've been scared of who I was and what I could become, but I'm getting more comfortable with the notion. After all, I'm Camden Riley. Pastor Floyd was right. It's about damn time I find out who he is.

"You're thinking too loud," Yanelys whispers, tilting her head so that she can peer up at me.

I chuckle. "You can hear me, huh?"

She nods, her eyes never leaving my face. "Are you hungry? You barely ate."

My stomach revolts at the mere sound of food, and it's hard, so damn hard, not to seek refuge in a small pill that'd make the body aches and nausea go away. "I'm okay."

"You sure?" she asks.

My head bobs up and down. "I will be." I hesitate, drawing in a sharp breath. "I don't want to leave you again. I hate the idea of spending the night away from you."

Her brows draw together, her eyes mirroring my misery. "Me either, but it's only for a short time. You'll be back before you know it."

Yanelys gives me a small smile and lets out a breath of content air as she snuggles impossibly closer. With my arms wrapped around her, I hug her to me, breathing her in and letting her sweet scent intoxicate me.

With her hair still tangled, Olivia walks to us, and before Yanelys can take the offered comb, I take it from Olivia's outstretched hand.

"I'll do it," I offer, a sheepish smile pulling at my lips, "if you don't mind."

"Yes!" She dances in place.

When she sits on my lap with her back to me, my heart stutters once before it picks up a rapid pace as I comb her hair. Soft tendrils fall to the side as I pass the comb through. The strawberry scent of her shampoo fills my nostrils, and when I finish, I pull her to me, hugging her the same way I should've been hugging her for years.

A ferocious love for my daughter pulses through me when she crawls off my lap and settles on the couch between her mom and me. Yanelys points the remote to the television and hits play, and *The Avengers* flashes on the screen. A content sigh brushes over my lips when Olivia presses her face against the side of my chest, and I wrap my arm over her shoulders.

Yanelys looks back at me, adoration brimming from her eyes. When she smiles, my heart smiles back at her.

I hardly watch the movie as my fingers caress the arm of the little girl I didn't know existed until not that long ago. This little girl who let me into her life with an open heart, and my own heart has latched on to her like the life support her mom and she are.

Olivia needs a dad just as much as I need to be her dad. While I want to shield her from seeing me at the rehab center, the idea of not seeing her daily for another three weeks distresses me.

So, after the movie finishes and I tuck Olivia into her bed with over a dozen kisses, I ask Yanelys to bring Olivia to visit me. In response, her lips stretch into a smile that reaches her eyes.

Our eyes lock on to one another when we hear the soft rap at her front door. Santiago opens the door and waits for me at the threshold. Desperation claws at me, and I hold on to Yanelys.

"I'll come visit tomorrow," she promises.

I swallow hard, hating my situation and the separation it's causing us.

"It's okay, Cam. The days will go by quickly."

"I love you," I tell her for the hundredth time today. "Don't ever forget that, Yan."

Her lips caress mine in response. "I love you, too," she says, her soft breath falling on my skin, giving me goose bumps.

I pull her harder to me and kiss her with all the emotions swimming inside me, knowing it'll be the last time I'll be able to kiss her like that for close to a month.

"I have to go," I say, my eyes darting to Santiago. "You come when you can. Don't stress yourself out with trying to come every day."

Yanelys rolls her eyes, and her hands rest on my chest. "I'm gonna see you every day, Cam. Nothing could keep me away."

THIRTY-FOUR

YANELYS

Eager feet dance around me as Nisa circles me while we wait for Camden. It's been a long twenty-one days, and every day, my desperation to have him back home with me grew stronger and stronger.

I kept my promise though and visited Camden daily. Olivia and my parents would go with me as often as time allowed, and although Olivia didn't understand why Camden was living in a hospital if he didn't look sick, Camden promised he'd explain everything to her when she was older. It was a conversation I was dreading, but I knew it would be important for both Camden and Olivia to have.

Just like she did when Camden and I were kids, my mom has filled my house with balloons and a *Welcome Home* banner. The smell of cupcakes and pizza hang the air, making my stomach rumble.

My heart stutters when I hear my front door open, and I anxiously wring my hands together when my dad's laughter bounces through the span of my house. When Camden walks into the living room, our eyes meet, and his smile spreads, overtaking his face. He's filled out in the month he was at the rehab center. Eating and working out has done him well, making him even more beautiful than the boy I remember and the man who came back into my life. No longer nervous, I chuckle as I launch myself into his waiting arms, clinging on to his neck, as he kisses me hard and urgent. He lifts his face from mine, and we both take a sharp inhale of breath.

"You're everything in this world to me," he whispers, his breath caressing my ear.

Olivia tugs on the bottom of my shirt, so I step away from him so that she can welcome her dad home. Pastor Floyd rests his hand on my shoulder and squeezes. When I look back at him, I catch him wiping away stray tears, but he smiles at me, real joy shining from behind his tear-filled eyes.

"He's okay," I reassure him, putting my hand over his, and he nods.

"It's good to have you back," my mom says, taking her turn to hug Camden.

"Yeah," Jeremy, who has become a steady fixture in our lives, agrees.

Camden takes my hand, and we make our way to the dining room table where we all take our seats. Our hands finally leave each other when my mom serves us pizza and salad.

"Look, Cam!" Olivia shouts, gaining everyone's attention. "Mom's letting me drink Coke!"

She lifts her cup to his nose so that Camden can see what's inside.

"That's good." He laughs, taking her cup for a drink.

"Hey!" She laughs, taking her cup back before he has the chance to drain it.

Easy conversation flows between us, but I notice Camden fidgeting with his napkin.

"Are you okay?" I ask, leaning toward him so that no one else hears me.

"Yeah, I just want to talk to you about something tonight." His lips touch the top of my head when worry creases my forehead. "When Livvy goes to sleep."

"Okay," I say slowly.

"Everything's fine, Yan. I promise."

Dinner continues, and everyone is content. I don't even bother scolding Olivia when she reaches for a second and then third cup of Coke.

After dinner and when everyone else has left, Camden, Olivia, and I settle on the couch to watch a movie. We fall silent as the movie plays before us, happy to just be together.

When the movie finishes, Camden picks up a sleeping Olivia and carries her to her room. Nisa follows us excitedly but stills when I put my hand on her head. I kneel down in front of her for a hug, grateful that she's still with us. That the repercussions of Camden's disease didn't steal my boisterous but sweet dog from us.

I call Nisa to the bed where she lies by Olivia's feet after Camden sets her down and covers her with her blanket. Olivia rolls onto her side, and I brush a soft kiss on her cheek. Camden takes my hand in his, and together, we walk to our bedroom.

It's ours—the bedroom, the house. Everything that surrounds us belongs to both of us. Our life, our daughter. Our trials and perseverance.

I keep a watchful eye on Camden as he undresses, his hands trembling slightly when he fumbles with the button on his jeans. His strength and determination are admirable, and I find myself falling in love with every part of him. The boy, the man, the addict, the survivor. I love every piece of Camden. The broken, scared fragments along with the parts we're starting to put back together.

Taking his hands in mine, I kiss his fingers and then help him unbutton his pants, the sound of his zipper breaking the silence. His tongue darts out and wets his lips, but he keeps his eyes trained on me.

Prickles of pleasure skate down my spine when his hand takes the back of my head and pulls me to him. My lips part, and my belly tightens. I meet his urgent, unrestrained passion with my own hunger as we strip ourselves of our remaining clothes.

When he sweeps me off my feet, my back lands on the soft mattress, making the bed bounce. Kneeling in front of me, he rubs my knees, guiding my legs to spread apart. He leans down and hovers over me, his cock twitching against my stomach. His hands tangle in my hair, and his taut muscles strain in his arms as he places his palm against my neck. Heat gathers where our skin meets and I feel his palm print long after he trails his touch to my chest.

I look up at him, and the muscles in my stomach clench with the building anticipation. Camden smiles down at me, his eyes looking into me, as he slowly goes inside me and thrusts once. He thrusts again harder, his eyes clouding, soaring, as he lives in the ecstasy. My heart lurches forward with every perfect motion, and I grip his shoulders, digging my fingers into his skin.

I sigh his name, my senses obliterated of anything but Camden. There's nothing but him kissing, touching, biting, exploring every inch of my body with his lips, tongue, and hands. Pleasure moves and flexes throughout me, setting me on fire, as I watch Camden's expression intensify.

His name rasps from my throat, and my body goes languid. He brings himself closer to me, his chest pressing against mine, his thighs against mine, with my legs wrapped around his waist. His body twitches after his final thrust, making his cock throb to the beat of my heart. I bask in his musky scent. He's all masculinity with a delicate heart.

My breasts heave, and my nipples remain hard as he lies down next to me and brings our naked bodies closer together. Shocks of electricity ignite and course over me, giving me goose bumps that he brushes over with his long fingers.

My teeth graze over my bottom lip as a small smile spreads across my face, and for the hundredth time today, I murmur a silent prayer of thanks that Camden has come back home. Sure, he's come back after one of the bleakest times of his life—when he believed himself too weak, too unworthy for any goodness to spill into his life—and we both have to fight fervently for his bruised heart.

Camden's arms tighten their hold around me, filling any gaps between us, and he plants a single kiss on my forehead.

"My whole life, you've been everything to me, Yan. My smile, my strength, my peace." He kisses my cheek when I look up at him and trace a hand over his chiseled chin. "I'm going to be the same for you and Livvy. I'll be your faith when you're feeling unsure. I'll catch your dreams and help you chase them. I'm yours. All of me belongs to you." His voice quakes, and his gaze falls to my lips before he looks up at the ceiling. "But there are some things I need to do, so I can move forward."

I inch away from him, resting the side of my face on my elbow so that I can see him better as he speaks.

"My mom tried to kill me." He purses his lips together, forming a thin line, and painfully, he closes his eyes shut. "She set the building I was sleeping in on fire because she wanted money to feed her addiction." Rough hands run over his face, and he pulls strands of his hair. Wild eyes meet mine, seeking, begging for something I'm not sure I can give him.

"I know, Cam," I whisper into the dense air. "I went to see her while you were still in the hospital."

His eyes trace over my face, confusion clear in his expression, as he takes ahold of my wrist and squeezes.

"I just *knew* she'd had something to do with the fire. After I left you at the hospital, I went to find her. I'm sorry, Cam."

"Wh-what happened when you saw her?" he stammers.

Inhaling a sharp breath, I steady my hammering heart and recount the events of our encounter, smiling a bit when I confess how I ended up behind bars because I'd attacked his mom. His face falls and grows somber when I mention how she bargained her way out of serving time.

"I got the heroin I overdosed on from her," he reveals on a loud whoosh of air.

I gasp as tears collect behind my eyes, but I refuse to let them shed. Although I want to look away from his regret, his shame, his sadness, I keep my eyes trained on his, hoping he feels my love through his inner turmoil.

"It was her way of apologizing for the fire." He laughs a mirthless laugh, his eyes darkening as even more despair creeps in.

"Cam," I mutter, the only word I can say through the lump in my throat.

Gentle fingers glide over his face, and he closes his eyes for a few beats before he opens them again. I trace the outline of his features, trying to absorb his pain so that I can carry it for him, if only for a short while. Maybe I can keep some for myself so that his load doesn't feel quite as heavy.

"It's okay." He takes my hand and kisses each of my fingers.

Warmth spreads inside my chest, and my heart races with the sweet affection.

"I need to talk to her." His eyes seek understanding, so I nod.

With bated breath, I wait for him to continue, but when he stays quiet, I ask, "What are you going to tell her?"

His body shifts away from mine, and he stares at the ceiling. "I'm going to claim my inheritance and offer her a portion of it if she gets clean and stays clean for a year."

He looks back at me, and I hold my breath, unable to comprehend the kindness that lives within him.

"I'll support her during that time—pay for her to go to rehab and live in an apartment and everything. She doesn't have to talk to me or anything." His eyes darken. "She just needs to get clean."

"Okay." I lean toward him and kiss his cheek and then his lips.

I start to back away, so he cups the back of my head and pulls me to him for a searing kiss. When he finishes, I press a finger to my tingling lips, making him grin.

"I also want to talk to Livvy. I know she hasn't known me for that long—"

I interrupt him with a simple, "Okay," and place my hand against his chest where I can feel the rapid beating of his heart. "She loves you, Cam. Maybe it's because my parents and I spoke so much about you while you were gone, or maybe she sees you the same way I've always seen you. But she loves you." Sucking in my bottom lip, I let out a thoughtful breath through my nose. "She'll have questions, and she might not understand why you left, but she'll come around. Knowing you're her dad, she'll love you more and more every day."

He nods, his eyes misting over with raw emotions. "I love her, Yan, so much. The minute I saw her, my heart claimed her as mine." He hesitates. "I'll never leave either of you again. I swear it. I'll prove it to you every day if I have to."

"You're silly." I smile. "You've already proven everything."

"There's something else." He eyes me with uncertainty.

"You can tell me anything." Sincerity falls from my lips, and he smiles, the simple joy of my words reaching his eyes.

"I want to open up a center for foster kids, like the group home I went to," he says.

My heart clenches into a tight fist.

"But I want it to be more than just safe. I want the kids to grow there and learn."

"No dull walls," I add.

"Or stained ceilings."

"Oh! We can have a pet program, too." My fervor grows along with Camden's smile.

"That's a good idea." He covers my hand still resting on his chest with his. "So many of these kids have never been treated with anything but cruelty. Bringing in dogs could teach them compassion."

"And empathy if we get the dogs from the shelter I work at."

"Yeah." He squeezes my hand, his eyes speaking to me, drawing me in, with our mutual excitement. " Does that mean you're in? I mean, I don't want you to feel like you have to leave your job…" He trails off.

"Camden Riley," I scold. "Of course I'm in! This sounds amazing."

His smile grows sheepish, and pink stains his cheeks.

"You're adorable." I giggle, crawling to him so that I can rest my head on his chest.

"You're perfect. You've always been the best part of my life."

My eyes glint as a devilish smile spreads across my face. "You're sweet. Now, tie me up and ride me hard."

Camden's eyes widen momentarily before he flashes me a wolfish grin. "Yes, ma'am," he growls into my ear.

With one agile movement, he flips me over so that I'm lying on my stomach with his erection pressing against my back, and he pins me to the bed.

THIRTY-FIVE

CAMDEN

In Yanelys's backyard, Olivia and I kneel by the privacy fence with our fingers covered in fresh dirt as we plant miniature white roses. Olivia's soft voice dances in the unseasonably warm air as she chatters on about everything she learned from YouTube about maintaining flowers.

Yeah, YouTube. How any of us ever survived without modern technology is beyond me.

After we pat the last small bush into the dirt, I lean toward Olivia and wipe my dirty fingers over her face. Agile and fast, she stands up on a squeal, and I take off running while she tries to catch me. Her laughter chases me, and when I pretend to fall, she jumps on top of me, covering my face with the dirt on her hands.

"Children," Yanelys calls out.

We both look back at her with innocent expressions.

She shakes her head on a laugh and brings out the hose to water our freshly planted garden.

"Go inside to clean up," she orders. "Or I'll spray you both down."

Shrieking, Olivia runs indoors while I walk to Yanelys, who has her back to me. When I reach her, I cup her ass that's barely covered in her short denim shorts.

"Cam." She laughs, leaning her body toward me.

Pulling her closer to me, I wrap my arms around her waist and lean my chin on her shoulder, kissing her neck. Her breath comes out quick and erratic, so I lift the bottom of her shirt, tracing small circles over her stomach.

"Livvy," she breathes our daughter's name. "She'll be out any minute."

"I'm not doing anything wrong," I tease, making her chuckle. "Besides, she might as well get used to seeing me hug on her mom every chance I get."

"And leave handprints on my butt and breasts?"

"I haven't touched your breasts. Yet." I waggle my eyebrows even though she can't see me. "But I will be later. A lot. With my tongue, teeth, and hands."

"Cam," she says my name on a sigh.

Giving her time to gather herself, I pull away after placing a kiss on her cheek.

I watch her, drink in her every subtle curve, the way the sun lightens her hair, the way she moves when she thinks no one is watching. And, for the first time, my fingers itch—not for a pill, but for Yanelys. To touch her, to own every part of her.

When she finishes and puts up the hose, she walks to me and looks at me through dubious eyes.

"What?" I ask.

She bites her bottom lip, so I repeat the same words she always tells me, "You can tell me anything."

She lets out a long whoosh of air, takes the hair band from around her wrist, and quickly picks her hair up into a messy bun. Tendrils of hair fall around her face, framing it.

"Pastor Floyd gave me the letter your dad, uh—Herb wrote you." She stays quiet, waiting for my reaction.

I keep my face placid, despite the thrashing of my heart or the feeling of betrayal that washes over me.

"Don't be mad, Cam," she pleads. "Pastor Floyd wanted me to understand better, and I did. I do. I wish you'd been the one to tell me."

She reaches for my suddenly cold hands and squeezes, so I push past the anger and manage a small smile for her benefit. Still, my annoyance settles along with my hatred for the man who was never my dad.

Claustrophobic, I turn away, ready to leave, but before I can put my back to her, Yanelys stops me, wrapping her arms around my waist and rests her head on my chest, neither looking at me nor refusing to let me go. Without thinking about it, I run my hands in circles over her back, and my frustration begins to dissipate as she calms the brewing storm.

As the tension leaves my body, she takes a step back and cups my face with her hands. I take her wrists, connecting me to her so that the fury stays at bay.

"I think you should find him," Yanelys says, her voice strong, her eyes warm.

"Don't." I push away from her, but she takes a step toward me with every step I take away from her. "I can't talk about this."

Her eyes soften, but her resolve stays firm. "Herb," she says slowly, eyeing me with sincerity, "made victims out of you, your mom, and Edward."

I flinch when I hear my real dad's name slip out of her mouth.

"You're the only one who's no longer a victim. You said you wanted to move forward, and I think talking to your mom and offering to help her is a good step." She hesitates, caressing my face with her thumbs. "So is talking to your dad."

"I don't know if I can do that." I search her face for signs of disappointment, but I'm only met with her unwavering love and understanding.

"Okay," she whispers. "Just think about it."

It's not really a request, so I don't bother answering. Instead, I pull her to me and hug her with the sun hitting our backs and Nisa sniffing the flowers Olivia and I planted. A gentle breeze swims around us, and I sway our bodies to nature's rhythm. We stay that way until Olivia comes outside and starts running circles around us with Nisa on her heel.

My lips linger a few inches from Yanelys's ear, and I whisper, "Are you ready to tell Livvy?"

"Do you want me to stay, or do you want to tell her yourself?"

"Stay."

Fear festers inside my heart, making my hands tremble. I clasp them together, and my heart stammers, struggling to beat, when Yanelys takes my hands in her cool small ones and squeezes.

"She already loves you," she reminds me.

I swallow past the ball forming in my throat.

"Livvy," she calls out, squeezing my hand again as my wild eyes meet her calm ones.

The need to run resurfaces, but I push past it, and instead, I focus my attention on my daughter skipping toward us with her dog faithfully by her side. I bend down and pet Nisa on her blocky head, and when she licks my hand, I wipe it on my filthy jeans.

"You wiped off Nisa's kiss," Olivia accuses, her lips pressing together into a thin line.

"Oh," I manage to get the single word out, but it sounded rough, so I lean down and kiss Nisa on her head.

When I stand back up, Yanelys's bright eyes meet mine, laughing at me. I bite back a smile and rub my face with my still dirty hands.

"Now, you have dirt all over your face." Olivia points out the streaks on my cheek.

"Okay, little Miss Smarty-Pants," Yanelys says. Taking Olivia's and my hands, she guides us to her patio furniture. "Cam and I want to talk to you for a minute. I want you to listen to us, okay? You can ask all the questions you want after we finish, but listen first. And"—she pulls Olivia to her lap and kisses the side of her face—"remember how much we love you. Can you do that?"

Olivia nods, uncertainty tracing every feature on her face.

I hesitate, looking to Yanelys for guidance.

"A long time ago, you asked me who your dad was and where he went," she begins.

Her words resonate in the cool air as my past hangs over us and slams its fist into my gut.

"And I told you he had to go away but that he loved you very much. Do you remember that?" Yanelys asks, her voice calm, affectionate, and reassuring.

Olivia nods.

"When your dad left, he didn't know I was pregnant with you—"

"He made a mistake," I cut off whatever else Yanelys was going to say.

Two pairs of eyes look back at me.

"He was a scared boy, and he thought leaving your mom and grandparents was the right thing to do, but he also left because he was afraid. He mostly left because he was afraid." My throat bobs, the saliva thickening, as I continue to speak, "He had bad parents, the kind who hurt him a lot growing up. The only good he had in his life was your mom, Ita, and Tito. It was a dumb decision, but he got scared one day and left them. He never called, wrote them letters, or anything. He didn't know you existed. He would've come home sooner if he had because—your mom's right—he loves you very much. I'm not trying to make excuses, Livvy. I'm just telling you what happened so that you understand. It's okay if you're angry with him, but I promise you, he'll make it up to you."

"Is my dad back?" Olivia asks, caution seeping from her sweet voice.

"Yeah." I let out a small breath of air. "And I'm not going anywhere ever again. You and your mom? You're it for me. You're my girls, my whole life. I'll spend the rest of my life making it up to you, showing you what you mean to me," I press on, the ache in my chest growing with every admission, leaving me breathless.

Olivia crawls out of Yanelys's lap and takes a step toward where I'm sitting, so she's standing in front of me with her arms crossed over her chest.

"You're my dad?" Her brows draw together in question.

"Yes." My heart derails as her eyes trace over my face, and I wait for her to hate me.

She sucks in her bottom lip and nods her head. "You're not leaving again?" Her voice quakes.

I reach for her, pulling her small body onto my lap, and I hug her to me.

"Never." I press a kiss to her temple and then pull her away, so she can see the honesty behind my words. "It's okay if you're angry with me, Livvy. Just give me a chance to make things right and be your dad."

190

Delicate small hands touch my clean-shaven face before she wraps her arms around my neck. "My heart loves you too much to be mad at you."

With my daughter in my arms, my body begins to shake as tears of remorse and relief skate down my cheeks and into her dark brown hair. Yanelys's arms go around both of us, her faith coursing through me as I finally become a part of my family.

Seconds turn into minutes, but I hold my girls, my life source. When Olivia begins to squirm, I reluctantly let her go and am met with her curious dark eyes.

"Mom said I could ask you anything." Her lips twitch, the sides lifting, as she waits for my response.

"Anything," I repeat.

"Since you're my dad, will you let me have soda at dinner?"

Laughter rings in my ears, and I join Yanelys in our shared joy as I shake my head at Olivia's question.

"I won't be overriding your mom," I tell her when I can finally speak. "But maybe we can come to a compromise."

"What sort of compromise?" Yanelys asks, her brows shooting up.

"I vote for a movie night every Friday. We can have pizza, soda, popcorn—"

"And chocolate!" Olivia interrupts, bouncing on her heels.

"And chocolate."

We turn our heads and wait for Yanelys to make the executive decision, and then we whoop in the air when she agrees. Olivia's smile stretches across her face, and she hugs my neck one final time before she runs to her bedroom to play, Nisa following close behind her.

Love overflows in my veins, making the moment feel surreal.

I wasn't there when Olivia was born. I wasn't there for any of her firsts. Hell, I wasn't even the first man she loved, Santiago rightfully taking that place in her heart.

But I am her dad, and our bond...our bond is real, our souls tied together. I have a commitment to her, and from sunrise to sunset, I'll keep my word and never for a second waver. The depth of my love for her is endless, and as long as I'm alive, she'll know it.

THIRTY-SIX

YANELYS

The road spans out in front of me as I beat my feet down into the hard pavement. My blood pumps harder, faster, stronger, and my chest heaves with every purposeful step. With my earphones blaring, I continue to jog, my body slicing through the air, as the breeze whips around my face. Thoughts of Camden cascade in my mind, unfurling and settling in my heart.

His courage, his unwillingness to give up, his love for his daughter, so effortless and true.

The horizon blazes with the rising sun, and while everything in my neighborhood still looks the same, everything is different. I'm different.

I keep a steady pace and focus on my breathing as I round the corner and see Camden waiting for me in front of our house. With his shoulders straight and his head unbowed, I see the man he has always been meant to be.

I breathe in a lungful of the morning air when I greet him and bend over, placing my hands on my knees. Sweat coats my skin, and Camden traces a light finger over it, igniting the flames I carry for him. Our eyes meet, and when I stand back up, he takes my face in his hands and kisses my lips, taking his time as his tongue prods and pulls from me.

"So beautiful," he whispers against my mouth.

"Sweaty and disgusting is more like it," I counter.

He chuckles, his breath falling on my skin when he draws closer to me and licks my lips.

"Beautiful and tasty." He smirks.

"Did you come out here just to taste and taunt me?" I raise my eyebrows in question.

He laughs again but takes a step back, his body tensing. "I've been thinking"—he brushes his hands over his face and laughs nervously—"maybe you're right." He stops, his eyes meeting mine.

"Of course I'm right," I acknowledge, taking Camden's hand in mine and leading us back indoors. "What am I right about?"

His body relaxes with my easy banter. He follows me to the kitchen and prepares a glass of water for me when I sit at the bar.

He waits for me to finish drinking, and when I put the water down, he answers, "I'm going to meet Edward." His voice breaks, making my heart squeeze in my chest. "I looked him up online while you were jogging, and he's still at the same address my da—Herb gave me."

"Oh," I breathe out the word, letting it hang in the air, as I search Camden's face.

His eyes fill with unrestrained emotions, but he keeps them at bay, so I do the same with the emotions twisting inside me.

"When?"

"Today." His hands comb through his hair.

"Okay."

"Come with me?" he asks, his voice calm, while his eyes plead with me.

"Of course. I can take Livvy to school this morning and call in sick at work. I'll also ask my parents to pick Livvy up from school and take her to their place, so we can go whenever you're ready."

"Okay." His throat bobs when he swallows.

"I'm proud of you, Cam," I say, keeping my eyes trained on his. "I just wanted you to know that."

He nods once as an awkward silence hangs between us. I smile to lighten the mood, but Camden looks away.

"I'm going to make breakfast while you shower."

"No chocolate chip pancakes," I tease.

His eyes lighten. "Don't worry, Mom." He smiles. "I told Livvy I was making strawberry waffles."

In the shower, I take my time, so Camden and Olivia can spend some time together without me. Knowing Camden can use some of Olivia's lightness, I don't bother worrying about whether she'll make it to school on time. School can wait.

Camden...Camden needs her.

It took two days for him to come to terms with the fact that he should meet his biological dad, and during those days, I'd felt his apprehension grow as he mulled it over. Fear had gripped my throat. Fear that he'd leave or that he'd give in to his addiction.

But Olivia would waltz into whatever room he had been brooding in and wash away his pain so smoothly that it was as if the pain never existed. And I pray, one day, the pain no longer exists. That it becomes a memory so distant that he no longer feels it.

After I finish in the bathroom, I call my parents and then work to let them know I won't be going in today. A part of my heart grows sad, knowing someday in the future I'll no longer be working there. In the five years I've spent at the animal shelter, it has become my second home, and leaving my friends and the dogs and cats that would undoubtedly spend their lives in that shelter hurts me profoundly.

But I want to start my new adventure with Camden. I love his idea of opening a center for foster kids, and I am delighted that he liked my idea of incorporating rescue dogs into his program.

Our program. I smile. *Our center. Our kids.*

I braid my hair as I walk to the kitchen, stopping just outside the room for a moment so that I can listen to Camden and Olivia. Camden's laughter fills the open spaces of the house, vibrating off the walls and crashing into my soul.

Feeling better, I step into the kitchen. The smell of freshly made waffles makes my stomach do happy flips, so I take two from the pile Camden's building by the stove and sit next to Olivia. I eye her as she gets the butter knife and starts to put globs of butter on my waffles. My lips twitch as she tries to spread it but ends up tearing the tender pieces apart.

"You're a good helper," I say, proud that she wants to help.

She looks back at me with pride brimming from her eyes, and my lips brush over her hair as I place a kiss on the back of her head.

"They're really good, Mom. Wait till you try them." She bounces on her chair in excitement. "I think maybe Cam should be the one who cooks from now on."

I smirk, all too happy to hand over the cooking duties to Camden. "No complaints from me."

"Except for pizza. You make the best pizzas in the world!" she says.

"The rest is on me, huh?" Camden's eyes shine back at us, his lips turning into a beautiful smile.

"Looks like it," I agree, craning my neck around, seeing the mountain of waffles grow. "There are enough waffles to last us all week. Come eat with us."

Rather than wait for his reply, I take Olivia's and my plates to the dining room table while Olivia takes her glass of milk. Camden follows behind us with two mugs of coffee. He hands one to me, and I breathe in the sweet aroma of morning bliss.

"You're not eating?" I ask.

"I'm stealing from your plate."

"You're assuming I'm going to just let you eat my waffles?"

"Yeah." He smirks.

"Wrong," I reply, pushing the plate toward him after I cut a few pieces.

When the door opens and I hear my dad's voice booming through the house, I stand up, leaving Camden more than half of the waffles and strawberries to finish.

"Eat," I order before I greet my parents.

"Yeah, eat," Olivia repeats.

I shake my head when I hear Camden reply with a, "Yes, ma'am."

That's my family. Camden and Olivia. And my parents.

We talk with them for a short while before my parents leave to drop Olivia off at school. Just as I walk my mom and Olivia to the car, I catch my dad talking to Camden. Camden nods his head several times and holds on to my dad when my dad hugs him.

And I love them even more. My dad for loving Camden, and Camden for loving my dad.

When we go back inside, Camden stands by our couch and stares off into space. I take his cold hands in mine, holding on to him with my hands, trying to warm him. When he looks at me, I offer him a small smile that he returns.

"What do you want to watch?" I ask him.

"Remember the day your parents took me in?" He pulls me to his side, his fingers caressing the exposed skin on my upper arm.

"Yeah. My mom decorated the house with balloons, and we ate pizza on the couch while we watched *Iron Man*." My heart beats wildly in my chest as I remember that day. How nervous I was. How completely perfect it turned out. How similar it felt when he came home from the rehab center.

"*Iron Man* is still my favorite movie."

"Great." I grin, standing up and walking to the television. "I have it on DVD."

I feel Camden's eyes bore into me while I put the DVD into the player. Like my dad did so many years ago, I give Camden the remote and wait for him to be ready to start the movie. I snuggle into his body, letting my head rest below his chin, and my skin fills with goose bumps as his fingers dance over my arm.

THIRTY-SEVEN

CAMDEN

My fingers tap the steering wheel of Yanelys's car as I drive us down the street of Edward's neighborhood. The trees on either side of the narrow road cast shadows in front of us. I pass his house for a second time and consider turning around, so we can go back home.

It took me most of the day and two movies to build up the courage to get in the car. Yanelys handed me her keys, letting me make the decision on where we drove. I hadn't driven in years, but even without a driver's license, being behind the wheel, having some semblance of control, centered me. At least until we reached his neighborhood.

"Cam"—Yanelys's soft voice breaks the silence—"pull over."

Without uttering a word, I do as she said, and I set the car in park beside a random driveway. Our eyes lock together. Worry creases her forehead, so I pull her to me and rest my forehead on hers. Our breaths mix together in a seductive dance, hers falling on my lips, warm and moist in the cool air of the car.

Desire burns in the pit of my stomach. Our lips touch, the burning growing, spreading. My tongue touches hers, and she moans softly in my mouth. My hands scramble to touch her, lifting the soft fabric of her shirt, and I run circles over her bra with my fingers. Just as my fingers work their way under her bra and I cup her breast, a loud knock on Yanelys's window brings us back to the present. I salute the angry man standing on the curb with my middle finger while Yanelys stifles a laugh.

A smile falls from my lips, and I turn the car around, finally ready to meet Edward.

"Okay"—I take Yanelys's hand—"let's do this."

Her fingers squeeze around mine. "I'm right here. Whatever you need."

I wiggle my eyebrows, a coy smile playing on my face. "What if I need you back there?" I gesture toward the backseat.

She bites her bottom lip. "We can do that, too. After dark."

Her cautious eyes meet mine, and need twists inside me.

"Stop looking at me like that, Yan, or I'm turning the car around and taking you straight to our bed."

A blush creeps up her neck and plays on her cheeks. She's so damn cute that I can hardly stand it. Smiling, I take our intertwined fingers to my lips and kiss her hand. Her chest lifts as her breath comes out, rough and just as urgent as mine.

I turn into Edward's driveway, and without hesitating, Yanelys opens her car door, so I follow suit. I meet her in front of the car, and our hands immediately seek each other. Hand in hand, we walk toward uncertainty.

Before we reach the door, a large figure steps out, and I stop walking. He looks so much like my dad—like Herb, and it leaves me breathless. The constant fear of my childhood creeps in, but I do my best to swallow it down, not wanting my nerves to get the best of me.

"Mr. Riley?" Yanelys asks, pulling me along with her.

Edward squints as we approach him, and then his eyes grow wide in recognition. "Cam...Camden?" His voice shakes and I wonder if he sees my dad, too.

My lungs struggle for their next breath. Yanelys's grip on me tightens and warmth spreads, chasing away the frigid despair.

"Yeah." My voice comes out rough as I take a step toward him. "I don't know how to do this." Letting go of Yanelys's hand, I rub my face before I reach into my front pocket of my jeans and hand him the same letter Herb gave me seven years ago, the one that sent my life into a tailspin of unknowns, of distress. "Just read this."

My outstretched hand shakes, but rather than take the letter, Edward steps forward and clasps my right shoulder for a few beats before he says, "Come inside."

When neither Yanelys nor I move, he adds, "Please."

Yanelys looks back at me, again giving me control of the situation and a decision that will alter my life once again. I nod once, and she gives me a hopeful small smile.

That's what Yanelys is. What she offers me. Hope. And faith. And love without conditions.

Warm air greets me when we walk into Edward's house, and we follow him into his living room.

He sits. Yanelys sits. I stand. I fidget.

On an exhale, I remove my coat and take a seat next to Yanelys. She takes my hand, rubbing her thumb in rhythmic circles.

Edward looks back at us, his eyes unbelieving that I'm here.

"It's been years," he stammers out. "Your dad..." He trails off, swallowing hard.

My jaw twitches.

"The last time I saw you was on your second birthday. Your dad...he got angry while I was playing with you, and he kicked me out. I wasn't welcome after that." He wrings his fingers into tight knots, making the tips of them red.

"Because you slept with my mom?" I ask, my eyes holding his, not letting him look away.

"Yeah," he breathes out. His foot starts tapping, but his gaze never wavers. "I know how this must look to you, but I loved your mom. I loved you."

I flinch at his words, and my own foot starts tapping while I squeeze Yanelys's fingers tighter.

"Do you still love her?"

"Camden..."

"It's a simple question, Edward. Forget Herb. Forget me. My mom—do you still love her?"

"Yes." His admission is quiet, barely above a whisper.

"Okay." I stand up, taking Yanelys with me. "Read the letter. I'll be in the car, waiting for you."

"Wh—I don't understand." His eyes dart from mine to Yanelys, confusion clear in his expression.

"Read the damn letter, Edward. My mom needs your help."

I don't wait for a response. I simply walk out of the living room, my heart thrashing inside my chest. I open his door and make a quick dash to the car. When I reach for the car door, slender arms wrap around my waist. I turn around and hold on to Yanelys.

Inhale and exhale.

Each breath falls on her dark hair as she buries her face into my chest. I sink my hands into her hair and methodically comb my fingers through the thick strands. My breathing steadies. My heart continues its rage-filled quest to beat out of my chest.

"You're going to ask Edward to talk to your mom with you?" Yanelys asks.

"I don't think I can reach her, Yan, but maybe Edward can."

"After reading the letter, what if he wants to be a part of your life and get to know you?"

I sigh, rough and loud. "I'm almost twenty-five years old. It's kind of late for him to play daddy."

"That's not his fault." Her voice pleads with me.

My fingers continue to braid through her hair. "I have a dad," I remind her. "I don't need another one."

"What about a friend?" Edward's voice hits me.

Painfully, I close my eyes shut.

"Are you going to help my mom or not?" I open my eyes and meet his from over Yanelys's head.

"Camden," Yanelys breathes my name in warning and she pulls away from me.

"It's fine," Edward tells her. "Of course I'll help your mom." He swallows hard. "How can I help her?"

Rather than answer, I laugh and shake my head.

"Let's go." I open the car door while Yanelys scurries to the passenger side. "Wha—now?"

My eyes narrow, and a humorless smile plays across my lips as the hatred I hold for my parents flows through my veins. "No," I tell him, "maybe we should wait another day and see if she finally overdoses and dies."

"Camden Riley," Yanelys scolds from the other side of my car at the same time Edward asks, "Overdoses?"

"What?" I shoot her a pained expression, and her eyes soften.

"Can you excuse us for a minute, Mr. Riley?" Yanelys gets into the car before he has a chance to answer.

After she shuts her car door, I open mine and take my seat behind the steering wheel where I drum my fingers.

"Cam," she says quietly, her hand going to my thigh and squeezing, "do you remember how well Livvy took the news that you were her dad?"

"This is different." My voice comes out raw as I remember the moment she put her arms around my neck and told me she loved me. "He's the reason my dad hated me. Why he couldn't stand to see me unless it was to hit me."

Sorrow and anger hit me hard, making my head pulse with the beginning of a migraine.

"So, you blame him for your dad being an abusive asshole?" she asks, her frustration simmering to the surface.

"Yeah!" I shout. "If he hadn't fucked my mom—"

"You wouldn't be alive," she interrupts. "You wouldn't be sitting here with me. Livvy wouldn't be alive. He slept with your mom, but it was Herb who hurt you." Her voice softens as her eyes seek mine. "Not Edward. That man"—she points to where Edward is waiting outside the car—"he cares about you. Don't be afraid to let him." Her fingers touch my face and trace over my lips. "Just give him a chance. If he's as much of a prick as Herb was, I'll take a bat to his back, and he'll wish we never stepped foot on his doorstep."

Despite myself, I chuckle, the image of Yanelys defending me playing perfectly in my mind.

"Fine," I whisper, making her smile.

I bring her to me, lightly kissing her on her lips, before I roll down the window and ask Edward to come into the car.

The drive to the run-down area where my mom lives is quiet with only the sound of the engine to break the silence.

"Stay close to me," I tell Yanelys when I put the car in park.

When I asked her to come with me, I wasn't thinking clearly. All I thought about was how scared I was of seeing my mom again, knowing she'd reject my offer. I never once thought of the dangers I'd expose Yanelys to in the dark alleys or abandoned buildings my mom called home.

Our footsteps fall on the hard ground, echoing into the darkness of the looming night. I guide Yanelys and Edward around the other homeless people living on the streets as I make our way to my mom's favorite spot.

"Maureen…your mom—she lives here?" Edward asks, his throat bobbing, when I walk through a broken door into a dilapidated building.

His fear and anguish hit me, and I stop walking to take him in. I don't know this man, but I see and understand his despair. He loves my mom. Through the years, he never stopped loving her. And, suddenly, I came into his life, without warning or preamble, and I threw him into the downward spiral that had been my life.

"I'm sorry, Edward," I say, sympathy washing over me. "I never met the woman you fell in love with. She was a horrible mom, but maybe it wasn't her fault." I stop, my voice cracking, and my hands go to my face. "She's my mom, and I don't know if I'll ever forgive her, but I know addiction. I can't help her—I know that—but Herb thought if she had any chance of being saved, it was by you. If you don't want to do this…" I trail off, not really wanting to give him an easy out.

Edward breathes heavily, taking me in. "I have to try." His words come out strangled, but he steps forward, putting a tentative hand on my shoulder. When I don't move away from his touch, he says, "I'm sorry I left. I didn't know how bad it was. Your dad…" He coughs. "Herb hated me after he found out about your mom and me, but I never thought he'd lied about the paternity test. I never imagined he'd lie about that or that he'd hurt you or your mom. I would've done something. I—"

"It doesn't matter," I interrupt. "It's done; it's in the past. I've moved on from it."

"But I just learned about it. I'm trying to come to grips with what I turned my back on, and damn it, Camden, I'm sorry. I'm so fucking sorry for everything." He looks at me, sincerity and remorse spilling from behind his eyes.

"It's fine. It's not your fault." Our eyes lock for a few seconds before I swallow the tension and turn away from him. "She should be in here somewhere," I say, wanting to get the night over with.

Yanelys's hand touches mine, and I tightly grip her fingers with my own. In silence, we pass through the corridors, stepping over a few sleeping figures. I sense my mom the moment we enter the room she's staying in. It takes a few beats of my erratic heart for me to spot her tired figure leaning against the dirty wall with a pipe pressed between her lips.

"Mom," I whisper.

Edward's eyes dart toward the figure I'm staring at, but she never hears me or sees us approach.

"Mom." I bend down in front of her.

Her bloodshot eyes look back at me, but her gaze passes over me and settles on Edward.

"Maureen," he says, crouching down beside me and taking her hand in his. "My beautiful Maureen." He pulls her to him and cradles her small figure on his lap.

"Is this real?" she asks, pressing her face against his chest. Her pipe falls to the ground with a loud crash. "Ed, are you real?" She touches a shaky hand to his face and sobs when her fingers make contact. "You're here. How?"

"Camden found me," he whispers into her thinning hair.

"Cam?" she asks, her eyes clearing when they see me.

Unease crosses her face, and she stands up on unsteady legs. Her anger hits me in waves, so I stand up as well, but I hold my ground when Yanelys takes my hand and leans her head onto my shoulder.

"Why?" My mom's eyes narrow in accusation.

"Because I want you to get clean," I answer simply.

She throws her head back in hysterical laughter, and Yanelys's hold on my hand tightens as her body stiffens. I squeeze it in reassurance, but her body stays tense next to mine.

"Maureen." Edward puts a gentle but sturdy hand on her shoulder.

She shrugs it off and directs the same heated eyes of my youth toward him.

He backs away a couple of steps. "What did he do to you?"

"Your brother?" she spits the words at him. "He beat me. He raped me. Every time he remembered how much he hated you, he'd turn his anger on me."

"And Camden," Yanelys speaks up. "Don't act like you're the only one who knew Herb's anger." She steps forward, taking me with her, and we both invade my mom's personal space. "The difference is that Camden was a child, and it was your job to protect him."

"I couldn't protect him from Herb. There is no protection from a man like that."

"You could've left him," Yanelys presses.

"No!" she shouts, her words echoing against the bare walls. "He would've killed us both if I'd tried to leave."

"It doesn't matter," I whisper, pulling Yanelys to me and wrapping my arms around her waist. "All that matters now is you getting clean."

My mom laughs again, shaking her head at me. "Are you stupid?" she asks.

"I'll give you half of my inheritance," I offer.

Her eyes widen in shock. "You got your inheritance?" She licks her lips, her eyes growing hungry at the thought.

"Not yet," I admit, "but I'm going to. You won't see a dime of it if you don't get clean."

"Camden," she whines, her hands going to my chest, pawing at me in desperation.

Letting go of Yanelys, I hold my mom at arm's length. "Get clean," I say through clenched teeth.

"You worthless piece of shit," she hisses at me, pushing my chest with the little strength she has. "Herb always said you were worthless. Stupid." She bites out the words.

I flinch, my stomach dropping, as I listen to her.

"The day you were taken from us was the best day of our lives."

"Enough!" Edward roars, grabbing her by her shoulders and spinning her around so that she's facing him. "That is your son! Our son. My son," he whispers.

My heart drums in my chest at his quick acceptance of me.

"I love you, Maureen. I always will, but I won't stand by and let you speak to him like that."

"Yeah?" She narrows her eyes at him. "Where were you to stop me when he was younger? To stop Herb from beating him to near death? You're too late." A loud slap resonates in the dark room when her hand makes contact with his cheek.

"No, he's not," I admit. "It's not too late for you either. I'm offering you half of my inheritance right now. When I leave, I won't be offering it again. I'll forget you. I won't worry about you, and I won't care when you die, and your body rots in this place. It's up to you."

"Leave." Sad eyes meet mine, and my heart hurts for the woman I call Mom. "I don't want your money. I don't want you. I never wanted you." She closes her eyes, pressing her lips together so that the outer edges grow white.

Hurt, I turn around, Yanelys's hand seeking mine, and I don't look back.

THIRTY-EIGHT

YANELYS

My body molds against Camden's as we lie awake in our bed. I kiss his bare shoulder, and he turns on his side so that he's facing me. His lips touch my temple while my hands run over his back in soothing circles.

He hasn't spoken since we left Maureen. We drove Edward back home in silence. The only words uttered came when Edward and Camden exchanged phone numbers, and Camden agreed to see Edward on Christmas Day.

It's been a rough, long day that didn't exactly end well. I know Camden hoped Maureen would take his offer and seek help, but deep down, I think we both knew she wouldn't. She couldn't. She was simply too far gone.

She endured a lot at Herb's hand, and I shudder at the thought of her being raped by the man she married.

"Do you think Edward will really come over on Christmas?" Camden asks.

My chest tightens at the hope I hear in his voice, and I say a silent prayer that Edward won't disappoint him.

"Yeah, I think he'll come," I reply honestly.

Before he even read Herb's letter and found out the truth, I saw how much he cared for Camden. After that, remorse and a desperate need to make things right were evident on the planes of his face.

"I think Livvy would like him," he says. Even with the surrounding darkness of our room, our eyes meet. "I think I could like him, too."

My chest squeezes tighter, knowing Camden's still seeking acceptance, still believing he's unworthy of it.

"I like you." I lean forward and touch his lips with mine. "I like you a lot."

"You love me," he corrects, pressing his mouth to mine, hard and full of emotion.

"I do," I admit.

"Thank you for coming with me today. I don't think I could've done it without you."

"Whatever you need, Cam. We're in this together."

His fingers find mine beneath the covers, and with our hands connected, we finally fall asleep.

Loud voices and laughter ring in my ear, waking me from a deep sleep. When I open my eyes, Camden kisses my nose and smiles back at me.

"I think your parents brought Livvy over before taking her to school."

"You think?" I groan, covering my face with the covers.

Camden crawls under the covers with me and pulls my body to him. "Stay in bed, beautiful. I'm gonna see if she wants me to make her an omelet."

"Great." I sigh dramatically. "Keep this up, and you're gonna be her favorite parent before the year's over."

Camden laughs at my sarcasm and scrambles off the bed, so he can get dressed and spend time with our daughter before she goes to school.

Through the closed door, I listen to Camden's and Olivia's animated voices, and before my parents can rush Olivia to school, I get dressed and go to the kitchen.

"Who wants to miss school today?" I ask.

Four pairs of eyes meet mine in astonishment, their forks full of eggs halted in midair.

"What?" I ask. "She only has a couple of days before school stops for winter break. What's the big deal?"

"Nothing," my mom replies. "It's just that you give her a hard time about missing school when she's sick, so..." The sides of her lips lift as she trails off.

"Whatever," I mutter. "It's not a big deal."

"Can I miss the rest of the week, too?" she asks, her eyes holding the hope of innocent youth.

"I don't know. Dad"—my eyes meet Camden's, and his grin widens—"what do you think?"

"I'm okay with it *if...*" He draws out the last word.

"If what?" Olivia asks, eager to know.

"If you let me read the Star Wars books to you."

Her nose scrunches up as she weighs her options, and I stifle a laugh.

"Fine," she huffs, "but I don't see why we can't just watch the movies."

"Better books are," Camden replies in his best Yoda voice.

Olivia looks back at him in confusion. "You're so weird sometimes." She bites her bottom lip when he laughs at her. "Can I put my pajamas back on?"

"Yeah," Camden replies. Then, he looks back at me in question.

I tuck my head down, giving him control over this simple decision, and from the corner of my eye, I see him smile.

"Just put away your book bag," he calls after her.

She quickly spins around and runs back to the kitchen where she picks up her bag and runs to her room with Nisa close behind her.

"Good call," I say when I hear her close her door.

"Eat," Camden orders, placing a plate with toast and a large omelet in front of me.

Cutting a piece with my fork, I put it in my mouth and hum in pleasure as the egg and cheese melt on my tongue. "This," I say between bites, "this is heaven."

On the kitchen counter, my phone vibrates, so I grab it and see a text from Edward flash on the screen, asking Camden how he's doing.

"We really need to get you your own phone," I tell Camden, handing him my phone.

His eyes widen when he reads the text, and pleasure crosses his face as he reads it again.

"Who's it from?" my mom asks.

"Edward," Camden replies, his nerves making him shift from foot to foot.

"When do we get to meet him?" my dad asks, putting a hand on Camden's shoulder, making the tension visibly ease away.

"He said he was going to come over on Christmas." Joy and uncertainty cross his face, and he bites his bottom lip.

"He seems like a good guy," I offer, remembering how Edward stood up for Camden when his mom verbally attacked him.

"Yeah, he does," Camden agrees, eyeing my parents for their reaction.

"We're looking forward to meeting him, Cam, but this doesn't change anything between us. You're our son. Nothing will change that. We want you to get to know Edward, and if he's a good man, we want you to have a relationship with him. If, one day, you see him as your dad, that's fine with us. It's fine with me," my dad emphasizes. "You'll still be my son."

Camden releases a long breath and nods. "Do you remember when Yan and I were teenagers, and you told me that, when the time came, you'd give me permission to marry Yan?"

My hands go to my chest, holding my heart in its place, as he looks from my mom to my dad.

"You're my parents. Yanelys is my heart."

His eyes meet mine, and I push back the threatening tears.

"She's my family. I want to marry her. I want to spend the rest of my life loving her and devoting my life to her. I want to give Livvy brothers and sisters."

Despite my best efforts, tears spill from my eyes, but still, he doesn't move toward me.

"Mom, Dad"—his voice catches in his throat—"I want your permission to marry my best friend."

"I told you our answer was yes, that it'd always be yes," my dad answers while my mom clings to his arm, shedding her own tears.

"Yes." My mom nods when Camden looks at her.

Camden walks to me, taking my trembling hand in his fingers, and he places a gentle kiss on my knuckles.

"My beautiful girl," he whispers, his voice shaking.

I sniffle, standing in front of him.

"I don't have a ring to give you right now, but you have my heart. You've always had my heart because you are my heart. I don't know how I ever survived without you, but I didn't start living again until the day I almost died in a fire, and you came back into my life. Be my wife," he says, bringing his lips to my ears, making me tremble when his hot breath touches my skin. "I'll spend the rest of my life loving and treasuring you."

"Say yes, Mom!" Olivia shouts, bouncing on the heels of her feet.

I laugh while Camden wipes my tears away. "Yes," I whisper.

"Yes?" he asks, his eyes widening in shock.

"Of course, yes!" I throw myself into his arms, and Olivia joins us.

Camden picks her up and refuses to put her down as my parents congratulate us through their own tears of joy.

"Dad?" Olivia's voice comes out shy, not at all like the exuberant girl we all know.

Hearing her call him dad, Camden's breath hitches, and his throat bobs as he fights back his emotions, but his feelings come through as tears begin to stream down his face.

"Yeah, baby girl?" he whispers into her hair.

"Can I be the flower girl?"

"I'd like that, Livvy." He chuckles. "I'd actually really love that."

"Okay," she says, kissing his tear-streaked cheeks, "Dad."

EPILOGUE

EDWARD

Nervous energy bounces in my stomach, ricocheting against my ribs, as I ring Yanelys and Camden's doorbell, holding on to the presents I brought. I've spoken several times with Camden since the evening he showed up on my doorstep with a surprise that knocked me on my ass.

I have a son, and not only did I miss his entire upbringing, but I also left him in the hands of a man who abused and tormented him and the woman I loved, so much so that I didn't even recognize the diseased woman who had taken over Maureen's mind and body.

But I'm not done with her. I turned away from her once and left her to a fate that destroyed her. Luckily, Camden had Yanelys and her family to help him pull through it. Although from the limited information he's entrusted me with, it hasn't been easy.

It won't be easy with Maureen either, but she's worth it. If I have to tie her to a chair to get her clean, I'll do it.

Camden's face greets me when he opens the door, and he eyes me with the same jumbled nerves tumbling inside me.

"Hey," I say.

"Hi," he replies, opening the door wider so that I can go in.

"Dad"—my granddaughter's voice rings from another room, and Camden's eyes shine with pride as my heart hammers inside my chest—"is that Pastor Floyd?"

"No, baby girl," he answers, leading me to their living room that is full of presents. "But it is someone I'd like you to meet."

Olivia bounces into the room and assesses me. I stand there, awestruck, staring at the little girl who's the perfect combination of Camden and Yanelys. But her eyes…her eyes and the energy behind them are all Maureen.

"You're Camden's real dad." She twists her mouth.

I kneel down in front of her. "Yeah," I agree, "and you're my granddaughter." I look back at Camden, nervous that I might've said the wrong thing.

"Does that mean I can call you Pop-Pop?" she asks.

Unable to find my voice, I nod.

"You hear that, Dad?" She beams at Camden, who looks back at me with sincerity. "My friend Kara has a Pop-Pop, and now, so do I."

Camden chuckles, and I follow suit, pushing back the lump forming in my throat. In less than a week, I've gained a son and a granddaughter and, once again, lost the love of my life.

"Mom, Pop-Pop is here," Olivia calls.

"Why am I not surprised that you've already given Edward a nickname?" Yanelys walks into the living room, followed by who I assume are her parents.

She gives me a warm hug. Then, I shake her parents' hands, who introduce themselves as Santiago and Carmen, and laugh when Olivia asks if she can finally open her presents.

"You didn't have to wait for me," I tell Camden as he watches his daughter tear into her presents.

"Yan's pretty strict about her rules, and she said none of us were allowed to open our presents until everyone in our family was here."

Emotions clog my throat, and I cough to clear it.

"Thank you for including me, Cam," I say, watching Olivia bounce from one present to the other. "You said you never met the woman I fell in love with." I cautiously eye him, making sure he's okay with what I'm saying. I only continue when he nods, "That little girl, your daughter, is your mom. Her enthusiasm and energy? That's your mom. That's the woman I love." I leave out my plans of bringing her back, just in case I fail.

"I always wondered where she got all that energy." Yanelys smiles. "We got you something," she adds when Olivia finishes opening her presents. "Livvy, why don't you hand out the presents?"

Olivia jumps from her sitting position on the floor and gives Yanelys's parents their gifts first. She waits for them to open them before she goes to the next person.

Taking advantage of her being distracted, I hand Camden his present. It's big and awkward, and I hope he likes it.

He carefully takes it from my hands, surprise crossing behind his eyes, and

I wonder how many presents he got as a kid. He unwraps it, slowly at first, and when he realizes what it is, he tears into it with the same enthusiasm Olivia exhibited earlier.

"A fishing pole." He grins.

I smile back at him. "I thought we could go fishing some day."

"Yeah." His smile grows, and he puts his arms around me in a tentative hug.

I hold on to him, my hands closing into tight fists, and I wish the moment would last longer than it does.

"Your turn." Olivia shoves her present toward me.

I gingerly take it from her outstretched hand and watch her skip away to give out more gifts. My heart stills when I unwrap my gift to find a frame with several pictures of Camden throughout the years. Yanelys stands behind me and points to two empty slots.

"I thought you could fill those on your own."

I nod and lick my suddenly dry lips. "Maybe you could take a picture of us," I say, my voice trembling through my uncertainty.

"Of course." She smiles.

Camden stands next to me, his posture as stiff as mine, and I nearly break down when he puts an uncertain hand on my shoulder. I wrap an arm around his back and we both smile for Yanelys as she takes the picture.

The man who has taken care of Camden, even when he was away from Yanelys, walks in with a boy I immediately recognize.

Jeremy.

My heart constricts and I choke on the sudden despair coiling itself around my lungs.

Carmen puts a gentle hand on my shoulder, and squeezes in silent understanding. But she doesn't understand. How can she? "It's a lot to take in, but Cam's worth it."

I nod, swallowing down the bitterness. The hands of time have shifted once again and a past life screams about a deserted yesterday I long to bury.

"Who's that boy?" I ask even though I know the answer.

"His name's Jeremy," she replies. "Pastor Floyd takes care of him the same way he took care of Cam."

"His mom, though?" I spit out, and she curiously eyes me. "I mean, doesn't he have parents?"

"The police took him away a few years ago. Pastor Floyd has been taking care of him since."

Again, my head bobs up and down. The simmering anger of a woman that betrayed me opens to the burning rage of the little boy I left behind in the guise of self-preservation. Twice in my life, I have abandoned people who have needed me and twice those choices have been proven wrong.

Leaving Camden and Maureen in the hands of my brother is something I can never forgive myself.

I watch their exchange, and once again, I'm grateful Camden has so many people in his life who love him so dearly. Yanelys was right when she told Maureen that she should've protected Camden, but what Yanelys failed to see was that, his whole life, Camden had people watching out for him and loving him while Maureen had no one.

Until now.

I'm back in her life, and I'll be damned if I allow her addiction to take her away from me. I'll walk through the very flames of hell to bring her back to me. I'll fight her. I'll fight for her. Because she's worth it.

She's my girl. She's always been my girl, and I'm not letting her go a second time.

But Jeremy…

A long time ago, I loved him as my own. For years, his mom and I dated and a month before we were to get married I found out about years of infidelity. I left her. I left the boy as if he didn't matter.

My hand braces the side of my throbbing head, and without uttering a word to anyone, I walk outside. I can't stop the thoughts swarming in my head. Thrashing, abusing, teasing the last bit of my sanity.

I left Camden, Maureen, and Jeremy in the cruel hands of fate. Those are my sins, and no matter how hard I'll try to make things right, I don't know if I can ever atone them.

AUTHOR NOTE

While *Pieces of Camden* wasn't a pretty story at times, it was a tale worth telling. Camden's strength and the love he found in the family he created was beautiful. I'm eternally grateful he sought me out, and through many tears, we were able to share his story.

So many times, we pass strangers on the street, not knowing the demons they fight or how hard it is for them to simply live. If you or anyone you know suffers from abuse, whether it's physical, emotional, or substance, please ask for help.

Thank you for taking part in Camden's story.

http://dss.mo.gov/cd/can.htm
http://www.samhsa.gov/find-help/national-helpline

ACKNOWLEDGMENTS

Where would I be without God and the many blessings He's bestowed upon me? All glory belongs to Him, always.

My guys…Chase's sweet laugh, Dustin's insane imagination, Derrick's constant belief in me. You guys are my superheroes.

Mady Valle-G, the sister God gave me about twenty years too late. Thank you for being so enthusiastic about all of stories and for the many wine nights that work as some pretty great ideas for books.

Jill Sava, there aren't enough words to accurately describe what you mean to me. You don't just work tirelessly to help me and so many other authors; you're also an incredible friend I treasure.

Lee Casey, you were the first to read Camden and the first to love him. Your suggestions sparked what I hope are great ideas and transformed this story into so much more than I ever imagined.

Mary Johnson, you, my friend, are the type of friend every girl needs in her life. True, kind, and funny, I don't know what I'd do without you.

Tammy Matson Norris…the Thelma to my Louise, you always manage to brighten my day. One day, we'll meet in person for a crazy girls' weekend that'll leave our husbands wondering if we should ever meet again. Or in jail. Either way, it'll be a great time!

Alison Evans-Maxwell, I love and appreciate your enthusiasm, friendship, and suggestions. But mainly your friendship. You're one in a trillion.

Makenzie Smith, authors make the best critique partners because we think so differently than anyone else. I value your input and admire your work as an author. Thank you for going into so much detail while beta reading and putting forth the extra effort that helped make Camden something I'm so incredibly proud of.

My parents, grandma, and sister, your unwavering support in me leaves me speechless.

Stacy Kestwick, Logan Keys, and Neeny Boucher, three amazingly, talented authors and woman. I'm grateful to know you, and I appreciate everything you did to help me with this story.

Carmen Reyes and Tesrin Afzal, what can I say? You girls really came through for me, and I can't thank you enough for taking time to read Camden's story and letting me know your thoughts.

Maria de la Cruz, one of the first people I met after my debut, and I'm still in shock you've stuck it out with me this long. Thank you for the awesomeness you've sent me. You know I'm dying for a canvas of *Pieces of Camden*, too, right??? Now, it's your turn to let the world see your amazing talents. P.S. I want more Emmett!!!

LJ Anderson at Mayhem Cover Creations, I should probably dedicate this book to you for being so patient with me. I had a particular cover idea when it came to this book that then changed to a different idea. Thank you for bringing my idea to life. As usual, you outdid yourself.

Jovana Shirley at Unforeseen Editing, wow, just wow! Jovana, you're incredible. Truly. Working with you is a dream. I've said this before, and I'll say it again. I am never, ever, ever using another editor. Ever.

Jennifer Van Wyk, your attention to detail when proofing Camden made such a huge difference. Your feedback was spot-on and very much appreciated.

My wonderful Sadistic Sweethearts, some of you have been with me from the beginning and others I've met along the way. The friends I've made in this group will last a lifetime. I'm grateful for each and every one of you. Your constant support keeps me moving.

Bloggers and reviewers, you guys rock! I can't thank you enough for your support and encouragement. Your work is endless, in reading, reviewing, and promoting, and I hope each one of you knows how valuable you are to fellow authors. With my whole heart, thank you.

If I've missed anyone, please know it wasn't intentional. Ask anyone who knows me, I'm a scatterbrain—so much so that Yanelys, Olivia, and Camden's eye and hair color changed sporadically throughout this story.

ABOUT THE AUTHOR

Yessi Smith lives in South Florida with her husband and two sons. She is also owned by a neurotic Border Collie and "ferocious" Rottweiler.

She has a Bachelor's degree in Business Management and a Master's in Human Resource Management and has held several jobs, from picking up dog poop to upper management positions. And now she hopes to leave the business world behind so she can live full time in a world that does not exist until she places her fingers on a keyboard and brings them to fruition.

Other work by Yessi include:

Life's A Cappella

Love, Always

New Forever

Life Interrupted

CONNECT WITH YESSI

Facebook: www.facebook.com/yessismithauthor

Twitter: http://twitter.com/_YessiSmith_

Instagram: www.instagram.com/_yessismith_

Amazon: www.amazon.com/Yessi-Smith/e/B00GUJ6MQG

Goodreads: www.goodreads.com/author/show/7365697.
Yessi_Smith

Website: http://yessismith.com

Or you can email her at authoryessismith@gmail.com. She loves hearing from her readers!

www.ingramcontent.com/pod-product-compliance
Lightning Source LLC
Chambersburg PA
CBHW061142170626
46809CB00003B/954